searching for hope

redwood coast rescue
book six

Tonya Burrows

part one

hope

Hope in reality is the worst of all evils because it prolongs the torments of man.

- Friedrich Nietzsche

chapter
one

THE MAN WAS EVERYWHERE.

There was no escaping him.

When Ellie Summers signed up for a yoga class at the local gym, he was there, lifting weights, his biceps straining against his t-shirt, sweat plastering his dark blond hair to his forehead. Every time she looked over at him, he was glancing her way. She tried to ignore it, focus on her breathing, but it was difficult with the constant feeling of his eyes on her.

When she offered to babysit a friend's seven-year-old daughter, there he was at the park, pushing his eight-year-old niece on the swing. He was so cute with both of the girls, laughing and joking, making them giggle with his funny faces and tickle attacks. Ellie's heart ached to watch him. There was something terribly endearing about a grown man who wasn't afraid to be silly with children. It stirred something inside her, a gut wrenching feeling of longing that she instantly quashed down.

When she went to the flower shop to get a bouquet to liven up her small, dated rental house, he was there buying flowers for his mom.

The man bought flowers for his mom every week.

He made it so hard to hate him.

But she did.

She hated Callum Holden.

Hated everything he stood for.

And no amount of muscle-flexing, flower-buying, child-doting charm could change that fact.

When Ellie went to the bookstore to escape into the worlds of romance novels, she found him there, perusing through detective thrillers. He even had the audacity to suggest she'd like a particular mystery series. She thanked him curtly and walked away without another word, leaving Cal standing there with a kicked-puppy expression on his handsome face.

She would *not* feel bad for hurting his feelings.

When she took a cooking class in the next town over to expand her culinary skills, Cal was there, too, with his younger brother, fumbling with a whisk and creating a mess of flour and egg. He apologized for his clumsiness with an easy smile, and she gritted her teeth, hating his casual charm.

She would *not* be charmed by him again.

He was an aggravating constant in her life, an open wound that wouldn't heal. Steam Valley, California was a small town, but come on. He had to be following her. There was no way they just kept accidentally bumping into each other.

"Maybe I should get a restraining order," she'd mused out loud after running into him yet again at the coffee shop.

Alexis just rolled her eyes and blew across the top of her steaming coffee. "I think you two should just kiss and make up already. It's been over a year."

Ellie scowled at her sister. "How can you suggest that after what he did?"

"Because if anyone holds it against him, it should be me. But I don't. He was just doing his job, Elle, and he's a good guy. I like him. More than that, I like him for you. Maybe you should give him another chance."

"No." Ellie's response was crisp, her tone final. "He chose his path, and I chose mine. They don't cross. Not anymore."

"They seem to be crossing a lot."

"Whose side are you on?"

"Yours. Always yours." Alexis held up both hands in surrender and her engagement ring sparked in the light. "But you need to at least make peace with Cal. This town is not like Chicago. You can't expect to never see him again, especially since you two have the same circle of friends. Avoiding him just isn't feasible."

"I can try."

Alexis sighed. "You're stubborn as an ox, you know that?"

But that night at the grocery store, Cal again appeared behind her in line, holding a basket filled with healthy greens and a dozen organic eggs. She wanted to hate him for that too —for his presumptuous perfection. But instead, she found herself inexplicably moved by his quiet patience as an elderly woman fumbled with her change in front of them.

Why did he have to be so... *good?*

And why had someone so good decided on a profession where he defended the worst of the worst?

Every day, Callum Holden wore his smile and charm as easily as his suits, heading into courtrooms to stand beside criminals and fight for their freedom. Murderers, rapists, drug dealers—he defended them all with a passion that seemed to burn brighter with each increasingly vile client.

"Everyone deserves a fair trial," he'd told her.

Everyone... including the man who had tried to kill her sister. Alexis had survived, thankfully, but that didn't change the fact that Jaxon Thorne had intended to murder her. He'd slit her throat and left her for dead, and only the quick response from her former SEAL fiancé and the men of Redwood Coast Rescue had saved her life.

And yet Cal thought that monster deserved a good defense, taking him on as a client without even a second thought for how Ellie would feel about it. Or how it would kill their budding relationship.

He'd cared more about defending a murderer than her or her sister.

And for that, she would never forgive him.

Every time Ellie saw him, she was reminded of the courtroom, of Cal standing beside Jaxon with that same easy smile, arguing for leniency for a man who made monsters look like angels.

Every time she saw him, she was reminded of the lies, the twisted truths he spun so easily, in his attempt to paint Jaxon as a victim. She could still hear his smooth voice, arguing that Jaxon had been under the influence of drugs and untreated PTSD and wasn't in his right mind when he'd committed his crimes.

Which, okay, maybe that was true, but none of it justified what the man had done to Alexis.

When she tried to explain her fury to Cal over coffee one chilly afternoon, he'd simply looked at her with those piercing blue eyes of his, the faintest hint of regret marring his handsome features.

"I'm sorry," he'd said quietly. "But if I don't defend him, who will?"

She'd stared into his eyes, stunned. The warmth she once felt toward him faded into a cold and bitter fury. She remembered leaving him there, alone at the table, his hand outstretched in a meaningless gesture of peace.

And then there were the times when he wasn't even there—the times she found herself sitting in the coffee shop across from his law firm, watching through the big glass window as he paced back and forth in his office, talking on his phone or going through case files. She hated how she would still find herself drawn to the sight of him, how a part of her ached at the sight of his troubled brow. She hated that her heart would still flutter when his eyes met hers through the glass – a split second before he looked away, quick as lightning. But most of all, she hated how she'd catch herself wishing things were different. That they had taken a different direction, that he had made a different choice.

One evening, as the sunset painted the California sky in hues of orange and purple, Ellie took her puppy for a walk in the park. Puzzle was a ball of energy, a floppy one-year-old Golden Retriever with a sunshine temperament and a sock fetish.

As Puzzle bounded through the park, Ellie watched him with a mix of affection and worry. He was prone to being a tad too friendly with strangers and a little too curious about every-thing. His boisterous enthusiasm for life reminded her of someone she used to know. Someone who had brought that kind of unbridled joy into her life at one of her darkest moments.

Dammit.

She shook her head, trying to rid Cal from her thoughts.

Suddenly, Puzzle bolted across the park, his leash flying out of her hand.

"Oh, no. Puppy! Wait! Come back!"

But Puzzle was off like a shot, his yapping echoing around the park. She chased after him, but the pup was fast, and she wasn't exactly in top shape. He zoomed past a group of picnickers, causing screams and laughs as he snatched a sand-wich with a wag of his tail.

"Puzzle!" She yelled again, running after him. He darted between trees and raced across the open fields, oblivious to his owner's panicked calls. Finally, he slowed near the edge of the river and sniffed something on the ground.

Ellie sighed in relief as she jogged over. But just as she was about to reach him, Puzzle picked up speed again to chase after a passing squirrel. "Puzzle! No! Bad dog!"

And then, from her periphery, she saw a man launch at her runaway puppy. A strong pair of arms wrapped around Puzzle's middle, lifting him off the ground before he could terrorize another group of picnickers or, even worse, dive into the river.

Ellie came to a stop, her breath rasping in her chest as she watched the man wrestle with her squirming puppy and finally get him under control.

When the man turned around, her heart dropped into her stomach. There, holding Puzzle against his chest as if he weighed nothing at all, was Cal. His hair was mussed from the chase and his white dress shirt had a muddy paw print on it, but he was grinning at her as if he had just won the lottery.

"Evening, Ellie." His voice was rich and warm like honey and seemed to vibrate through her whole body. Puzzle tried to lick his face and he laughed. "New friend?"

She grabbed the dog's leash. "He doesn't have any manners yet."

He chuckled, a deep, low sound that seemed to echo around them. "Let me guess, he was Zak's idea?"

She flushed. She still couldn't believe she'd let Zak Hendricks—the leader of Redwood Coast Rescue's tactical K9 team—talk her into fostering the puppy. She'd been feeling isolated and alone, her friends mostly all married or engaged, and Alexis blissfully nesting with her fiancé Shane. Fostering the future search and rescue dog seemed like a good way to fight off the loneliness. At least it gave her a warm body to come home to that wouldn't break her heart.

"I'm just fostering him." Ellie offered him a tight smile and extended her hand to take Puzzle from him. But Cal didn't release the pup immediately. Instead, he rubbed his hand vigorously on the dog's belly, making Puzzle squirm with delight.

The sight tugged at her heart. Despite everything that had happened between them, she couldn't deny that Cal looked ridiculously adorable with Puzzle in his arms. Her normally hyperactive dog was snuggling against his chest as if he belonged there.

"He likes you."

Cal shrugged, his eyes twinkling with amusement. "What can I say? I'm a likable guy."

She scoffed. "I don't like you."

His smile faltered for a moment, but he recovered quickly with another grin. "Well, you obviously have poor taste because dogs are great judges of character." As if to prove his point, Puzzle gave him a big, slobbery kiss. He laughed and dodged another lick. "You do realize that if Zak gave him to you, he's yours. There's no fostering at the Rescue."

Yes, she was aware. Zak had the uncanny ability to pair people with their perfect dog, but she still wasn't convinced Puzzle was the right dog for her. "Thanks for catching him."

"My pleasure." As he handed the puppy back to her, their fingers brushed and a spark of something ignited between them. It happened every time their skin touched, a chemistry that was impossible to deny. But Ellie quickly pulled away, holding Puzzle close to her chest.

An uncomfortable silence fell over them, broken only by Puzzle's excited panting and the distant laughter from the picnickers by the river.

"Well," she said finally and set Puzzle down, making sure to keep a firm grip on his leash this time. "Good night."

"Ellie..." Cal caught her hand before she could turn away. "Can we talk?"

She stared at his hand on hers, the heat of his touch seeping into her skin. She missed this – the contact, the connection – and that thought scared her. It was a dangerous thing to miss someone who could hurt you so much.

She looked up at him, her heart thundering in her chest. "There's nothing more to say."

"But there is. So much more," he insisted, and a twisted part of her took pleasure in seeing him beg.

Pulling her hand away from his grasp, she stepped back, creating a physical distance to match the emotional one between them. She was all too aware of the curious onlookers, their stares on her back as they speculated about the high-profile lawyer and the woman with the runaway puppy. There was nothing more this town loved than a bit of juicy gossip and she wasn't about to give them a scene to whisper about over beers at The Mad Dog.

"I need to get Puzzle home now." She keep her voice and face neutral. Puzzle wagged his tail and gave her a look of pure puppy love, oblivious to the tension crackling in the air. "Thank you again for catching him."

Cal looked as if he wanted to say more, but in the end, he didn't. He let out a slow sigh before nodding. His eyes held a mixture of regret and something else— hope? Longing? Ellie couldn't decipher it, but she knew better than to try.

She turned away, clutching Puzzle's leash so tightly that her nails dug into her palm.

"You'll forgive me one day," he called. "You might even love me again."

She stopped in her tracks but didn't turn around. The words, so softly spoken, were charged with a raw desperation. He was right about one thing—she might forgive him someday.

But love him again?

Ha.

Fat chance.

She looked down at Puzzle, who was now tugging at his leash, eager to continue their walk as if that was an option after his little run across the park. "I can't tell who is more delusionally optimistic. You or the puppy."

As she walked away, she heard Cal's soft laugh. "Me. Definitely me."

chapter
two

CAL *WASN'T* STALKING HER. At least not according to the laws of the state of California, which stated that the stalking victim must fear for their safety. He'd die before hurting Ellie, and despite all the pain between them, she knew that.

Okay. Yeah. Even in his head, sounded kind of stalker-like. Fuck.

He'd waited patiently for nearly a year, hoping she'd give him a second chance, but she was still stubbornly determined to avoid him. So maybe he'd arranged to run into her occasionally, but that was not stalking. That was... strategic coincidences. Yes, he liked the sound of that much better.

As he watched Ellie's retreating figure disappear into the distance, loss settled heavily in his chest. The sight of her walking away was always like watching a piece of his own soul fade into nothingness.

"You're being creepy," a familiar voice called from behind him. "I told you not to be creepy."

He turned to see Connelly Davis sitting at one of the nearby picnic tables with his ever-present laptop, his dark hair wind-mussed, the stubble on his jaw about three days past a five o'clock shadow. Obviously, Connelly was deep into a book. He always started to look a bit homeless by the time he finished one, though it wasn't quite as bad now that he was a married man. Veronica reminded him to interact with real humans, not just fictional ones, and she kept him from going full hobo.

"You're one to give relationship advice, Conn. Didn't you pine after Veronica for decades before finally doing something about it? And, dude, you slept on her front porch for weeks until she let you in."

"It was one week." Connelly glanced up from his laptop and looked at him flat-eyed, unamused. "And I'm not giving you relationship advice. I'm giving you don't-be-a-stalker advice."

"Strategic coincidences," Cal corrected. He walked over and slipped onto the bench across the table from him.

"Jesus, you're such a lawyer." Connelly snorted and returned to his writing. "That's the worst euphemism for stalking I've ever heard."

Over the past year, Cal had come to respect the horror writer's opinion on most things, but in this case, Connelly was wrong. "I was helping her with her dog. Explain to me how that's creepy, O Mighty King of Horror."

"Helping with the dog isn't creepy," Connelly said, not looking up from his screen. "Hanging around hoping she'll change her mind about you and give you another shot? Or that look you get when you're watching her, the one like you're about to break into a Shakespearean sonnet or something—"

"I do not have a look."

Connelly ignored him. "*That* is borderline stalker territory."

Cal scowled. "I'm not maliciously harassing her or making threats to her safety. Hence, I'm not stalking her."

"Uh-huh." Connelly finally glanced up, his expression neutral. "Look, Cal, man to man... let it go. She doesn't want anything to do with you. It may not be stalking according to the law, but Vee has become pretty good friends with both Alexis and Ellie, and I've overheard them talking. You *are* creeping her out."

"Shit. That was never my intention." Cal dropped his head into his hands and groaned. "I just... I don't know what to do. I've never felt like this about anyone. She's..."

"She's what?" Connelly prompted when he trailed off.

"She's... she's everything. She's brilliant and funny. She's independent and stubborn as hell. She's so goddamn beautiful but doesn't know it. She's passionate about her work and has more compassion in her little finger than most people have altogether. I've never met anyone like her."

"All right," Connelly said after a pause. "I'm going to give you some advice then. Straight-up relationship advice this time."

He lifted his head from his hands. "I'm listening."

Connelly leaned forward on the table. "If you care about her as much as you say you do, then respect her decision. Maybe she'll come around again, but it won't happen because you've engineered some situation to run into her. It'll happen because she decides she wants to see you."

All the air left him in a hard exhale. He'd been trying so hard to prove to Ellie that their relationship was worth another shot, but all he had accomplished was driving her further away.

"Whatever happened with your little side project?" Connelly asked suddenly.

He winced. One night over beers at The Mad Dog, he'd told Connelly about the plan to win Ellie back by finding out what happened to her long-missing older sister, Hope. It had been a stupid long shot, but he'd been desperate enough—and cocky enough—to think he could solve a mystery that had stumped investigators for twenty years. "In 2004, Hope Summers left her home in Chicago, climbed into a black 1977 Trans Am with California plates and a Mt Humboldt sticker on the back window—and vanished off the face of the Earth. For all the information I have, she could've been abducted by aliens."

"Well, that's probably for the better," Connelly said with a decisive nod. "You wanted to unearth a two-decade-old tragedy and parade it in front of the woman you claim to love? Man, that's not a gesture of love. That's a horror story."

Cal rubbed his face with both hands, guilt gnawing at his gut. He had considered the possibility that reviving the old wounds might cause Ellie more pain than peace but had dismissed it, assuming she'd want answers more. "When you put it like that... Yeah, it does sound rather creepy."

"And desperate." Connelly folded his arms over his chest. "And manipulative. You really suck at romantic gestures, Holden."

"Okay, okay, I get it." Cal spread his hands in surrender. "It was a bad idea. All of it was a bad idea."

Connelly sighed, and his expression softened. "Look, I get what it's like being in love with someone who doesn't return the feelings. It sucks. But using manipulative tactics isn't going to change her mind. It will only end up hurting her."

He opened his mouth to respond, but Connelly's phone sounded, and he shut his mouth as Conn dug the thing out of his pocket and checked the screen.

"Shit." Connelly grabbed his laptop and stuffed it into his battered leather case. "Call out. I gotta go."

"Where?" In addition to being a former pararescue jumper and best-selling author, Connelly also served as a medic for

Redwood Coast Rescue's K9 search and rescue team. His wife Veronica was their pilot.

"Up on the mountain." He jerked his chin toward the mountain looming against the blue summer sky to the northeast of town.

Cal stood. "I'll help."

"We can always use more volunteers, but don't you have lawyer shit to do?"

"That's the great thing about self-employment, my man. I set my own hours."

"I hear that." Connelly studied him for a moment. "You're not just volunteering because Ellie will be there?"

Genuine surprise coursed through Cal. "Wait, Ellie will be there?"

"Probably. Her dog's training for SAR."

Cal swallowed, realizing he'd walked right into a situation he had just sworn to avoid. But backing out now would seem petty and cowardly. "I... didn't know that," he admitted, striving for nonchalance. "But I swear I'm not volunteering because of Ellie. I'm volunteering because you guys always need extra help, and I have the time."

Connelly held his gaze for a moment longer before nodding approvingly. "Good answer." He stood up and started to walk away, then turned back and shoved a hand against Cal's chest. "One more piece of relationship advice, Holden. If Ellie ever does give you another shot, don't fuck it up again. You won't get a third chance."

The rescue went about as smoothly as it could. One of the dogs easily found the injured hiker in a canyon right off the main trail, and within hours, the guy was patched up by Connelly and airlifted to the nearest hospital by Veronica.

Ellie had indeed been there with Puzzle, his fuzzy golden tail wagging furiously in excitement at all the commotion. She scrambled over the rough terrain, not caring about the dirt or sweat coating her face, and patiently gave the puppy instructions and encouragement when he went awry. She always threw herself wholeheartedly into whatever she did.

It was just another reason Cal loved her.

But he kept his distance, sticking to Connelly's advice about giving her space. Instead, he focused on helping where he could—lugging equipment up the trail and handing out water bottles to the searchers. And if he were honest with himself, he found he genuinely enjoyed being part of the rescue effort.

The sun was setting by the time they made it back to Redwood Coast Rescue's headquarters. Ellie was there, too, sitting on a bench with her curly blonde hair pulled up into a ponytail, her face now cleaned of dirt. There was a lightness about her now that he hadn't seen before. She laughed and joked with the team like she'd always been a member. Knowing he wasn't part of her happiness hurt. But at the same time, if this was what she wanted—to be free of him—then he would respect it.

Cal's heart flipped when she looked up, and their eyes met. There was a momentary flash of surprise in her gaze before it turned cold. She quickly looked away, moving her attention back to Alexis, who was saying something while gesturing with her hands.

"Hey." Zak Hendricks clapped a hand on Cal's shoulder, pulling him out of his thoughts. "Great work today."

"Yeah, thanks," Cal said, trying to keep his voice steady. "Glad I could help."

"You're a good man, Holden."

That brought a bitter smile to his face as his gaze drifted back to Ellie. "I wish she believed that."

Zak followed his gaze and smirked. "She's a tough one, our Ellie. Got a heart as big as the ocean but walls thicker than a bank vault."

"You wouldn't know how to break into a bank vault, would you?"

"Sorry, man. Not my area of expertise."

Ellie's eyes met his. She quickly looked away, but not before he saw a flicker of something else in her gaze—uncertainty? Sympathy?

His heart clenched in his chest. He wanted to go to her, to ask her if there was any chance they could try again, to tell her how much he missed being with her.

But instead, he turned to Zak. "I'm gonna head home. I have a long day in court tomorrow."

"Hey, if you ever want to change careers, there's room for you on the team. We just have to find you a dog."

"Nah. I'll stick to the lawyering and leave the rescuing to you guys. Besides, who would bail your asses out of legal hot water if I quit?"

Zak rubbed a hand over his short hair and looked toward his men. "We do seem to find ourselves in legal trouble a lot, don't we?"

"Redwood Coast Rescue is single-handedly paying my student loan bills."

Zak's deep laugh followed him to his car. As he opened his door, Puzzle came bounding over, tail wagging and tongue lolling out. He dropped a slobber-covered ball at Cal's feet and then proceeded to sit down, looking up expectantly.

"Hey, buddy." He stooped down to pick up the ball, only to find it wasn't a ball at all. It was a rolled-up sock. Puzzle fiercely claimed it back, growling, engaging him in a game of tug-of-war.

"Puzzle, drop it!"

At Ellie's voice, Cal dropped the sock and rose to his feet, his heart jumping around like a damn kangaroo in his chest. She was walking toward him, her cheeks flushed, blue eyes wary behind her glasses. The puppy seized the opportunity and ran off with his victory sock, all ungainly legs and paws, tail waving like a flag.

"Ellie." Cal managed, swallowing the lump in his throat.

She stopped a few feet away, wrapping her arms around herself as if to ward off the chill of the night. "Hi, Cal," she said softly.

She was so stiff and formal with him—so different from the way she interacted with everyone else. He just wanted her to laugh with him like she did with the others and maybe, just maybe, to look at him with the same warmth that used to make his heart race.

"Hey." He shoved his hands into his pockets to hide the fact they were suddenly shaking.

"I didn't know you were volunteering with us now." Her gaze flicked over the worn Redwood Coast Rescue jacket that Zak had loaned him. Her voice didn't betray a trace of emotion.

"Yeah, I... erm..." He rubbed at the back of his neck. Why was he so flustered? "Well, I thought it was about time I contributed more than just legal advice."

"That's... that's good."

There was an awkward silence as he scrambled for something more to say.

"I should go," she said suddenly, taking a step back. She called for Puzzle, who came romping over. The sock was gone.

She rolled her eyes and clipped on his leash. "I really hope you didn't eat that."

"Whose sock was it?"

"No idea. He's like a sock detector. If there's one nearby, he always finds it."

She turned away, and his chest tightened in protest. He fucking hated watching her walk away from him.

"Ellie," he called before he could stop himself. "I've missed you."

His words hung heavily in the air between them, the sound of the team's laughter behind them seeming miles away.

She turned around, her eyes wide in surprise, lips slightly parted as if to say something. "I…"

Cal's heart pounded as he waited for her to continue, each passing second stretching into an eternity.

"It's late, Cal. I should go home."

Ignoring the sharp stab of disappointment, he nodded and attempted a smile. "Right. Yeah, of course."

Ellie nodded, too, but there wasn't even an attempt at a smile on her face. Her eyes still seemed surprised—confused even—as they held his gaze for one more heartbreaking second before she turned around and walked back toward the group with Puzzle following at her heels.

Cal stood there watching until the group's laughter and chatter swallowed her up. He watched as Ellie threw her arms around Alexis, and even from this distance, he saw her face light up with laughter at something her sister said. It was a sight that brought back memories so fond that they were almost painful to relive. Memories of when he was the one Ellie threw her arms around.

Cal drove home in silence, the hum of the engine doing little to drown out the loud thoughts screaming in his head. By the time he pulled into his driveway, the stars were out in full force, glowing in a sky devoid of town's lights. He savored the tranquil silence as he climbed the stairs of his porch. Unlocking the door, he stepped inside and was greeted by a dark, lonely living room.

Maybe Zak was right.

Maybe he did need a dog.

As he kicked off his shoes, he found himself replaying every word, every glance, with the masochistic urge of a desperate man.

He sighed and tossed his borrowed Redwood Coast Rescue jacket aside before collapsing onto his couch. He let his head fall back against the cushion, utterly drained. He should go shower and go to bed, but he couldn't find the energy to move. His eyes drifted shut...

And his phone rang.

A slow sigh escaped him as he opened his eyes and rubbed his face with both hands. He checked the time. Four a.m. Shit. He'd slept right there on the couch for three whole hours.

"Goddammit." He rubbed at the crick in his neck. That three hours was going to have to be enough. A call this late meant one of his clients had gotten into trouble, which meant a trip to either the sheriff's office or the prison.

He leaned over the edge of the couch and fumbled around on the floor until he found his phone in the pocket of the jacket. The screen flashed "Unknown caller." He hesitated for a moment before answering. Usually, his late-night calls came from the jail.

"Hello," he said, forcing his voice to sound neutral.

"Is this Callum Holden, the lawyer?" A girl's voice, barely more than a whisper.

"It is. How can I help you?"

She was silent for a moment. "You've been asking around about Hope?"

He bolted upright so fast his head swam. "Who is this?"

No answer.

"Is this about Hope Summers?"

There was a long pause on the other end of the line. When

she finally spoke again, he had to strain to hear her. "She's missing."

"I know. She's been missing for twenty years."

"No, I…" Her voice trailed off. When she came back, she sounded scared. "I-I shouldn't have called."

The line went dead.

He redialed, and it rang and rang and rang.

No answer.

He hung up and dialed the sheriff. It took two calls, but Ash Rawlings finally picked up.

"Holden," Ash growled. He sounded out of breath and more pissed off than usual. "This better be important."

Cal winced. It didn't take much imagination to figure out what the sheriff and his wife had been doing. "Sorry to interrupt."

Ash's grumble of irritation rumbled over the line. "Well, you did. So what's so important you had to call me in the middle of the night on my one day off?"

"I just got a call from an unknown number… a woman. Or girl. She sounded young and scared. She asked about Hope Summers."

The other end of the line went silent. The only sign that Ash hadn't hung up was the faint sound of his breathing.

"What did she say?" Ash asked with reluctant interest.

"She said that Hope was missing."

"That's not news, Holden."

"I know, but there was something about the way she said it. It sounded… recent."

"Did she say anything else?"

"She hung up before I could ask."

"Did you get a name? A number?"

"I have a number. I called back, and it rang, but nobody picked up. Something's not right about this. I could hear it in her voice. She seemed scared, Ash. Really scared."

Ash grunted. "You've got to be kidding me. It's probably just some kid playing a prank."

Every instinct he had screamed otherwise. "I really don't think so. Could you trace the call?"

There was another moment of silence, then a resigned sigh. "Yeah. I'll see what I can do. In. The. Morning."

"And keep me posted."

"Yeah, yeah," Ash said dismissively and hung up, but Cal knew he'd do it. Despite their constant bickering and Ash's tough exterior, he was a good cop and a better man. He wouldn't brush this off.

Knowing sleep would be impossible, he ran through a shower, changed his clothes, and headed into his office. To his surprise, Ash called back less than two hours later. Apparently, the sheriff hadn't been able to sleep, either.

"It's a payphone."

He sat back in his office chair. "I didn't realize payphones still exist."

"Me either, but there are still two working ones in the county. One's at the truck stop outside of town. It works, but it's more of a novelty than anything else."

"And the other?"

"At the old general store on Redwood Road."

Cal frowned. The general store used to be the last stop for campers and hikers heading up the mountain, but it had been closed for years. "And it's still working?"

"It matches the number you gave me," Ash replied, his voice heavy with exhaustion. "And the bill for it is paid every month, so yeah. It's still working. That's where your mystery girl called from."

"Thanks."

"Holden, don't go doing something stupid, or I'll—"

Cal ended the call before the sheriff could finish his threat. If there was a chance, however slim, that this could lead him to

Hope or any information about her disappearance, he had to follow it. While his quest had started as a way to win Ellie back, sometime over the last few months, it had become personal. He wanted to find out what happened to Hope for himself. He needed to know what happened to her.

He grabbed his coat from the back of his chair and headed out into the chilly dawn.

chapter
three

THE DRIVE UP Redwood Road was a familiar one. He drove on autopilot as the road went from paved and well-maintained to gravel to a barely there pitted path flanked by towering ancient trees. Morning fog wound around the trunks like fingers and thickened the farther up the mountain he went.

As he pulled up to the old general store, it struck him how desolate it was. The windows were grimy with a layer of dust that had accumulated over years of neglect, and the red paint was peeling off in large patches, revealing the weathered wooden slats underneath. The payphone was right where Ash had said it would be— attached to a wooden pillar by the entrance.

Cal approached the phone, his hands shoved deep into his pockets to ward off the damp cold of the fog. It looked like it hadn't been used in years, and yet someone had called him from it just hours ago. He picked up the receiver, half expecting it to be dead. There was a dial tone. Faint and crackly but present all the same.

He hung up and took a moment to look around. Something caught his eye, something out of place in the dreary, neglected setting—a small security camera was tucked up under the eaves of the store, shiny and new.

Who the hell would put a security camera here?

He squinted, not entirely sure he wasn't imagining things. But no, it was there, a speck of modernity among the weathered wood. The uneasy feeling that had been nagging him since the anonymous call now bloomed into full-blown concern. He pulled out his phone, glad to see he had a signal, and dialed Ash.

"This is getting weird."

Ash grumbled. "Now what?"

"There's a security camera here next to the payphone. Brand new, and it looks top of the line."

"Why the fuck would there be—"

"Like I said, getting weird."

"You shouldn't have fucking gone out there by your fucking self. Don't touch anything. I'm on my way."

Despite the creeping unease, Cal had to chuckle at Ash's predictable response. The sheriff was a gruff, no-nonsense man, but underneath all that tough exterior was a soft heart that cared deeply about his town and the people in it.

As he waited for Ash to arrive, he wandered around the perimeter of the old store. Dew-damp leaves crunched under his boots, and the sharp, earthy scent of damp wood filled the air. The sun was just starting to peek over the treetops, casting long shadows on the ground.

His gaze landed on something nestled in a patch of daisies near the side door of the store. It shimmered slightly against the green leaves and white petals. Curiosity piqued, he stepped closer and bent down to examine it— a small hair clip shaped like outstretched wings. Tiny faux gemstones caught the weak rays of sunlight, making it gleam. He went back to his car and found the stack of police evidence bags he kept in his glove box for just such an occasion. He picked up the barrette with the bag and then sealed it inside. He turned it over in his hand, examining the details. It was old but well-kept, the silver still shiny, and the gemstones still securely in place. This wasn't a piece of junk someone would lose and not care about.

And it looked familiar.

He'd definitely seen this somewhere before and searched through his memory for the when and where.

Hope.

He sucked in a sharp breath in surprise.

There was a picture of Hope Summers taken a few months before her disappearance. It was the one used on all the missing posters, and she wore a similar hair clip, the wings sparkling against her curly brown hair. Ellie once told him that giving the barrette to Hope was one of her earliest memories. She'd only been six at the time and had so looked up to her big sister, carefully choosing the hair clip from a department store for Hope's eighteenth birthday. Hope wore it every day from then on.

Could it really be the same one?

Ash's Tahoe skidded to a stop beside his car. The sheriff jumped out, his face a storm cloud.

"Holden," he barked, striding over. "What did I say about touching anything?"

"I didn't touch it." Cal held up the bagged hair clip. "I bagged it."

A frown furrowed his brow as Ash took the bag and examined it. "Jesus. This looks like..."

Cal nodded. "The hair clip from Hope Summers' missing poster."

Ash looked up, his eyes grave. "You sure about that?"

"I'm certain, but you could ask Ellie to be sure. She bought it for Hope."

Silence fell between them as they both stared at the small piece of jewelry.

"Jesus," Ash finally muttered. "Okay, I'll get it to the state lab for testing. Maybe we'll find some DNA." He put the evidence bag in his car and then came back. "Where's the camera?"

Cal pointed to the left side of the store. Together, they crossed the dew-soaked ground, their breath misting in the chilly morning air.

The lines deepened around Ash's mouth as he studied the camera. "Nobody owns this piece of shit store anymore. The last owner died some fifteen years ago, and his children wanted nothing to do with it. They've been trying to sell it ever since." He nodded to the faded FOR SALE sign in the grimy window, then pulled a pair of latex gloves out of his jeans pocket and snapped them on. He pulled himself up on the window ledge to get a better look at the camera. "No reason for this to be here. Wireless. Someone is transmitting the footage directly to a remote server somewhere."

"Can they see us?" Cal asked.

"Probably."

"Can we get the footage?"

Ash shook his head. "Not without a warrant."

"What?"

"C'mon, Cal. You know this." He dropped back down to the ground, pulling off his gloves. "There's no evidence of a crime."

"Someone called me about a twenty-year-old missing person case. That camera might be our only lead."

Ash held out his arms. "But where's the crime here? Point me toward it, and I'll apply for the warrant."

"Fuck," Cal muttered and ran a hand over his head. Ash was right. No judge in their right mind would give them a warrant with what they had now.

Ash sighed and dropped his arms back to his sides. "Okay,

listen. I'll try to get in touch with the realtor and see if the previous owner's kids will permit us to take it down."

Cal scowled up at the camera. "By then, whoever installed it will have it removed or wiped."

"You know better than anyone my hands are tied by the law." Ash went back to his Tahoe but paused with his hand on the door and glanced back. A small smile curved the corner of his hard mouth. "But, you know, if a private citizen were to wander up here and the camera disappeared, I doubt whoever put it there will report it."

"Why, Sheriff Rawlings..." Cal grinned at him. "Are you telling me to steal it?"

"I said no such thing." Dante, Ash's big black German Shepherd, poked his head out the window with a sloppy grin. Ash grunted a soft laugh and nudged him back before sliding into the car. "Whatever you do, Holden, I don't want to know about it."

Cal watched the Tahoe until it disappeared in a cloud of dirt on the unpaved road, then turned back to the store. "Didn't plan to start my day with petty larceny, but... okay."

He returned to his car and rummaged through the trunk until he found the old toolbox that his uncle, a mechanic, had given him when he graduated high school.

"This is for your car," Uncle Rob had said firmly. "You keep this in the trunk. Never know when you'll need to fix something."

He could count on one finger the number of times he'd actually used the toolbox, but he'd dutifully kept it in his trunk all these years to make his uncle happy.

The box was well-stocked. He found a pair of wire cutters and a screwdriver and grinned. This probably wasn't what his uncle had in mind.

He made his way back to the old store and climbed up on

the window ledge. With a bit of effort and a couple of scraped knuckles, he managed to pry the camera from its perch. Jumping down, he studied the thing, turning it over in his hand. It was compact, sleek, and looked expensive. Whoever had installed it wasn't using some cheap surveillance tech. They meant business.

Was there also some kind of encryption on the video?

He had no idea, but he knew exactly who to ask.

"Can you hack it?"

In Redwood Coast Rescue's command center, Sawyer Murphy sat back from his computer, his blind eyes staring straight ahead as he ran his hands over the camera. "Yeah, but..."

Cal groaned. "Oh, c'mon, don't give me a but."

"But," Sawyer said again, stressing the word, and hit a button on the side of the camera. A compartment on the back popped open, and he pulled out a small chip. "I don't need to hack it because it has local storage."

Cal blinked, then grinned at the sudden wave of relief. "And here I was thinking you'd have to do some Hollywood-level hacking to get into it."

"I never get to do Hollywood-level hacking," Sawyer said somewhat glumly and turned the chip over in his hand, tracing its contours with his fingers. "It's most likely a redundancy in case the live feed gets interrupted or there's a problem with the server."

"Do you think my mystery caller is on there?"

"How long ago did you get the call?"

"Early. Before dawn."

"These cameras can hold up to a few days' worth of

footage locally, so unless someone already erased it, she should be." Sawyer shrugged and slid the chip into a card reader connected to his computer. "Let's find out."

A series of clicks later, Sawyer was sifting through files, his nimble fingers flying over the Braille keyboard. The room filled with the rapid-fire babble of his screen reader and the occasional snore from Zelda, his seeing-eye dog, who lay curled up on his feet under the desk.

"Uh oh," Sawyer finally said, breaking the silence.

"Uh oh?" Cal echoed, alarm prickling at the back of his neck. "What 'uh oh'?"

"There's a lot of encrypted data in these files. Whoever installed this camera really didn't want anyone peeking at the footage." Sawyer frowned, resting his fingers on the keyboard. The reader's fast-paced voice fell silent as he stopped his exploration.

"Can you get in?"

Sawyer hit one last key and let out a low chuckle, leaning back in his chair and folding his hands behind his head. His grin was feral in the dim light of the command center. "Already have. They'd be so pissed to know a blind man cracked it in less than five minutes."

As video clips flashed onto the screen, Cal gave Sawyer's shoulders a grateful squeeze. "You are a fucking genius, Murph."

Sawyer waved him off. "Tell me something I don't know. Now..." He pushed back from his desk, and Zelda raised her head, her eyes filled with longing. Sawyer stood and motioned for Cal to take the chair. "You're on your own for this part. Look at this footage and find your mystery girl while I take my girl out for a potty break."

Zelda scrambled out from under the desk, her feet tippy-tapping with excitement.

Sawyer grabbed her harness, and they slipped out the

door, leaving Cal alone with a flickering monitor and files upon files of surveillance footage. He settled into the vacated chair and took a deep breath, his hands hovering over the keyboard apprehensively. He wasn't a tech wizard like Sawyer, but he was confident he could handle at least this much.

A list of video files, each labeled with a date and time stamp, spread out before him. He clicked on the first one, and the screen filled with a color image of the old store. No grainy black-and-white images here. Whoever had installed the camera wanted to make sure they saw everything clearly.

He fast-forwarded through hours of nothing until, finally, a figure appeared in the long shadows of evening—a very thin woman, her face and hair obscured by a baseball cap. There was something ghostly about her as she approached the old store like she wasn't quite real. Like she didn't fully belong to this world. She paused and looked back in the direction she'd come from and then disappeared from view. She never went near the pay phone. He froze the video and stared at the shadowed figure, tilting his head slightly in an attempt to make out any distinguishable features. She was not just slender but gaunt, her body cloaked in ill-fitting clothes from the early 2000s that kids today would call "vintage." But that was all he could see. It was too dark, and she'd done a good job keeping her face turned away. She'd known the camera was there and hadn't wanted whoever was at the other end to see her.

Was this woman his mystery caller?

But he would've sworn from his caller's voice that she was young. This woman carried herself with a sense of purpose and grace that only came from age.

And, besides, the timestamp was wrong. He'd received the call around four in the morning. This woman appeared more than a day before that, so unless she came back...

He clicked on the next file and sat back as the screen filled with the familiar image of the old store. This file was time-stamped just hours before he received the call. He fast-forwarded through it, the on-screen time ticking away in the corner.

Nothing.

The woman didn't come back.

He blinked and pressed his fingers to his tired eyes. What if there was nothing here? What if whoever installed the camera had already deleted the footage of his mystery caller?

He clicked on another file.

And there she was.

She appeared at the edge of the frame, flitting nervously around the old store like a hummingbird. She paused near the payphone, glancing around uneasily before picking up the receiver. She wore a robe with a rope belt similar to what he used to wear as an altar boy during Sunday mass, but her belt was gold, and the robe was made of a gauzy, see-through material. He watched her pull a card out of the folds of her robe and study it. The cardstock was creased and battered, but he could clearly see his own name printed on it.

So that was how she'd gotten his number. She'd found one of his old business cards. They wouldn't be difficult to come by. When he first went into private practice, he'd thrown his cards at people around town like confetti and had left a stack at every local establishment that would allow it.

She picked up the receiver, dialed his number, and put the receiver to her ear.

His heart stopped as she turned fully toward the camera.

Hope.

But that wasn't possible.

He blinked at the screen, unable to understand what his eyes were telling him. The girl was no older than fifteen, but she looked exactly like the pictures he'd seen of Hope—the same dark hair, the same nose, and the same eyes.

In the video, she quickly hung up the phone and spun as headlights whited out the screen.

And then she was gone.

He rewound the footage and watched it again and again until Sawyer returned.

"You found something," Sawyer said before he could even open his mouth to tell him.

Cal turned in his chair to stare at the guy. "How the hell did you know that?"

"I can feel it. Your energy changed, charged the room."

"Is that another of your superpowers?"

"Yep. It's called the power of observation."

Cal opened his mouth but closed it without asking exactly how a blind man could observe anything.

"I don't need eyes," Sawyer added as if he'd asked. "I have four other senses. Five, if you believe in all that woo-woo sixth sense shit."

"Do you believe in all that woo-woo?"

He just grinned and put a hand on Zelda's harness, letting her guide him across the room toward Cal. "So, what did you find?"

"This is one thing you'd have to see to believe." Cal returned his attention to the frozen image of the girl on screen. "Do you have a printer?"

"Not in here, but you can send it to the printer in Anna's office."

He did just that and then pushed out of the chair. "Thanks."

Anna wasn't in her office, but her husband was. Zak lounged back in the desk chair with the lights off. His boots were propped up on the edge of the desk, and his eyes were closed until the printer started humming. He sat up just as Cal opened the door.

"Oh. Sorry, man. I didn't think anyone was in here."

"It's okay. I was just trying to catch a few Z's. Poppy has been having nightmares, and she's keeping us all awake." Zak yawned wide enough that his jaw cracked, then swiveled in the chair to grab the printout. He started to hand it over but stopped short, his brow furrowing as he studied the picture. "This is your mystery caller?"

Of course he already knew about that. It was impossible to keep anything a secret in this town.

"I think so."

"That looks like—"

"Yeah."

"But—"

"Yeah," Cal said again and took the print from him.

"Jesus." Zak ran a hand over his face in disbelief. "What are you going to tell Alexis and Ellie?"

"I don't know that there's anything to tell yet. It could be a coincidence."

"Your face says otherwise."

"Yeah, well, sometimes, faces can be misleading and right now, all I have is a face in a picture that looks like a younger version of Hope. I'm not going to tell them anything that might give them... uh, well, hope."

"You think that's Hope's daughter." It was a statement, not a question.

His gaze fell back to the image of the girl. He hadn't wanted to voice that thought out loud until he had more information.

"Zak, I need you to keep this quiet for now," he said finally instead of answering.

Zak leaned back in the chair and studied him. "Why did she call *you*? Why wouldn't she call Alexis or Ellie or, hell, Ash?"

"I don't know," Cal admitted again, frustration crawling up his spine to curl around his shoulders. "All I know is that she got my number from one of my old business cards."

"Are you sure it's not a setup of some kind? Have you pissed off anyone lately?"

"Oh, I specialize in pissing people off. But none have threatened me if that's what you're asking."

"Alexis and Ellie offered that reward money for information about their sister. Maybe it's someone after that?" Even as Zak asked the question, he shook his head. "But that doesn't make sense either. If the money's the goal, why call you?"

"I don't know," Cal said for the third time, letting out an exasperated sigh. All these questions were the same ones circling in his mind like relentless vultures. But he had no answers, only speculation and a gut feeling that told him this was far from a coincidence. This was something big. "Maybe she thinks she needs a lawyer."

Zak studied him for a moment longer. "Does Ash know about this?"

"He does, but he can't do anything until I have proof a crime was committed. And, right now, I don't even know if one was."

Zak nodded to the printout. "Girl could be a runaway."

"I got that sense, but from where? There's no report of a fourteen or fifteen-year-old girl matching her description missing from anywhere in the county. If there were, Ash would've been able to do something to help."

Zak lifted a shoulder. "Mountain people. I bet a lot of kids up there have no formal records—no birth certificates or social security cards. She could be one of them."

If that were the case, she'd be nearly impossible to find, but Cal had never met a challenge he couldn't conquer. This was another puzzle to be solved—a complex and urgent one, but a puzzle, nonetheless.

"Could be," Cal murmured, turning the printout this way and that, as if that might help him make sense of the girl's story. "Guess I'll need to start knocking on some doors up in the hills."

Zak grunted. "Be careful. They're not exactly welcoming to outsiders. First time I went up there asking questions, I got shot at."

"Wasn't it Shane that shot at you?"

"The bastard. I've mostly forgiven him." Zak sat up again, the chair creaking under him as he straightened. "You coming to the wedding this weekend?"

Shit, he'd nearly forgotten Shane and Alexis were getting married this weekend and, for a moment, he considered begging off. After all, he was the last person Ellie wanted to see, and she'd be there, standing at her sister's side as maid of honor. No doubt in a dress that would hug her curves and drive him mad all night with the urge to peel her out of it. He could easily make up an excuse—work was always a convenient one since his job required he be on call twenty-four/seven. But he'd already sent in his RSVP. And maybe it made him a masochist, but he really wanted to see Ellie in that dress.

"Wouldn't miss it," he said finally, tucking the photograph into his jacket pocket. But he was already thinking beyond the wedding, his wheels turning with ways he might gain the trust of the mountain people. He was a lawyer, after all. Convincing people was part of his job description.

He made a move toward the door. Just as his hand

touched the knob, Zak's voice stopped him in his tracks. "One more thing…"

He turned back. "Yeah?"

Zak's eyes bore into him, serious and intent. "Before you go stirring up a hornet's nest, being a white knight and all… Remember, you're not just risking your neck. There are other people who'd be affected if something happened to you." He cracked a smile. "And for some reason, we like you around here, Holden. So stay safe, and if you need anything, you let us know."

chapter
four

THE WEDDING LOOKED like something out of a fairy tale. The towering redwoods created a natural cathedral, and sunbeams filtered through the leaves above, casting a magical glow throughout the entire scene.

Ellie stood to the side of the rustic arbor, watching with teary eyes as her sister moved toward a future she once doubted Alexis would have. A year and a half ago, she'd flown to this remote stretch of California in a panic after Alexis was abducted from in front of her motel, terrified her last remaining sister was gone forever. But now, Lexi was getting married in this beautiful forest, with wildflowers spilling along the edges of the aisle.

What Alexis had survived was beyond comprehension, and yet, in all that darkness, she had found light in Shane. He wasn't the kind of man Ellie had pictured for her sister. He was intimidating—his face, body, and soul all badly scarred from a mission gone wrong when he was a Navy SEAL—but the love shining in his eyes as he watched Alexis approach was tangible. He was more relaxed now than when Ellie first met him, more at ease with himself and others. He'd done a lot of work on himself over the past year to make sure he could be what Alexis needed, and Ellie loved him for it.

Shane's gaze never left his bride as she approached in a satin sheath gown with her hair spilling in soft golden waves over her shoulders. He looked awe-struck, and who could blame him? Alexis was always beautiful, but today she glowed. When he slipped the ring on her finger and declared his vows, his words weren't the overly romanticized phrases that Ellie had heard in past weddings she'd attended. Instead, they were raw and truthful, baring his soul to the woman he loved and promised to protect.

As the couple sealed their marriage with a kiss, Ellie dabbed away her tears and let her gaze drift over the small crowd. Zak, Anna, and their two daughters, Bella and Poppy, took up one row of chairs on the groom's side. Donovan, Sasha, and their ten-month-old son, Hudson, were in another row with Ash and Rose. Behind them sat the intense Pierce St. James with Sawyer Murphy and Sawyer's dog, Zelda, who was decked out in a lace tutu for the occasion.

Shane's teammates.

His family-by-choice.

Alexis and Ellie's parents sat on the bride's side, along with a handful of friends from Chicago. It was surreal seeing those friends again. Chicago felt like a lifetime ago now. The Summers girls had traded tall buildings and loud city noises for towering redwoods and gentle whispers of the coastal wind. A different life, a different world. But it was here that Ellie found a sense of belonging she had never felt in Chicago.

It was here that felt like home.

And he was here.

Cal.

She hadn't seen him since last week in the park, and she hated that she missed him. She should have been relieved she was no longer running into him everywhere. Instead, she found herself searching for him at the grocery store... the coffee shop... the park... the gym... The whole time, she was annoyed that she couldn't be annoyed at him for crossing her path and irritated that she ached in his absence.

He stood at the back of the gathering with Connelly and Veronica Davis, tall and handsome in a charcoal gray suit with a big grin on his face. He always looked a little bit rumpled in his suits, his hair always tousled, reminding her of a boy who had been playing too hard at recess.

As if sensing her gaze, he turned. His eyes were filled with a soft warmth that made her stupid, traitorous heart flutter.

Their gazes locked, and there was a moment, just a moment when Ellie could've sworn everyone else had faded away. Cal was smiling at her, a small, crooked smile that looked like it belonged only to her.

Someone cleared their throat softly, breaking the spell, and Ellie's cheeks flushed as she quickly looked away from Cal. Rylan Cross, Shane's best man, was standing there with his prosthetic arm extended, waiting for her. Alexis and Shane had already made their way back down the aisle to the cheers of the guests.

Rylan smirked at her as she accepted his arm. "Daydreaming about a certain lawyer?"

Ellie shot him a scowl and pushed her slipping glasses up her nose. "I wasn't daydreaming."

"Uh-huh."

"And even if I were, it wouldn't ever be about Cal."

"Of course not," he said with mock gravity. "You obviously hate him."

"Shut up, Rylan."

He chuckled and gave her arm a friendly squeeze. As they walked down the aisle, she resisted the urge to look for Cal again.

She had wanted him to come for Alexis's sake. After all, he

was part of the close-knit community that had rallied around her sister during her darkest days. But now that he was here, Ellie wished he wasn't.

She didn't like this. She wasn't the kind of woman who became enamored with a man just because he was attractive and charming. She'd always prided herself on that. Dating was an afterthought. She was busy with her career and perfectly happy being single.

So why couldn't she keep her eyes off him?

Ellie did her best to mingle with the guests post-ceremony while Alexis and Shane had their first dance. She laughed at eight-year-old Poppy's jokes and chatted with Bella about her college plans. She discussed Puzzle's training progress with Zak and Anna and entertained Hudson with a game of peek-a-boo to give Donovan and Sasha time to hit up the buffet. Her gaze, however, kept wandering to Cal, who was engaged in an animated conversation with Connelly over by the bar. He caught her eye once more, raising his glass in her direction before returning to the conversation with a chuckle. But then Ash approached him, and his smile faded.

Ash, tight-lipped and stern as usual, led Cal away from the festivities toward a quieter part of the garden. They were out of earshot, but their postures screamed tension. She watched as Cal took a step back as if in surprise. A few years ago, she wouldn't have given it another thought, but now that she knew the uneasy history these men shared, she anticipated an explosion. For while Cal was defense and Ash was offense, both were good at their jobs, and they were two of the most stubborn men she'd ever met.

Ash punctuated his words with sharp hand movements, jabbing a finger into Cal's chest every time he made a point. Cal stood tall and resolute under the onslaught, his face hard as granite. He waved away whatever Ash was saying with an impatient flick of his hand.

Ellie excused herself quietly from Sasha and Donovan and made her way through the crowd toward the pair. She didn't intrude into their conversation but parked herself within hearing distance under the pretense of admiring one of the flower beds.

"...need to stay out of this," Ash was saying, arms crossed over his chest.

Cal, visibly annoyed but keeping his calm, replied, "I don't think you understand, Ash. I can't walk away. It's not that simple."

"Of course, it's not simple. Nothing ever is with you. But this doesn't concern you."

"I have every right to be involved," Cal said, his voice icy and calm. "She called me for help."

Ash sighed and took a step back, dragging a hand over his face. "I didn't come here to fight with you. I came here to warn you."

"Warn me?" Cal's laugh held no humor. "About what?"

Ash glanced around before leaning in closer. "Just... stay away from Hope's case. There's more going on here than you realize."

Hope?

Ellie's heart surged into her throat. They couldn't be talking about her sister, could they? But why would they be after all these years?

"Just because you wear a badge doesn't mean you have a monopoly on justice," Cal shot back.

"All I'm saying is that there are certain things you don't understand, certain angles to this that you can't see," Ash said, obviously striving for calm.

Cal scoffed, rolling his eyes. "And let me guess, you can't tell me what those angles are?"

"That's right. Because it's an ongoing investigation, and I don't need you snooping around and messing things up."

"I'm not some amateur bumbling my way through," Cal replied, his voice rising with anger now. "I know my way around a sensitive case."

"Do you?" Ash asked, raising an eyebrow. "Because sometimes it seems like you're more interested in playing Ellie's hero than in actually finding Hope."

Cal looked as if he'd been slapped. "Don't you dare question my intentions. I want closure for Ellie, yes. But I'm invested now, too. If she's still alive, we need to do everything in our power to get her back to her family."

Hope was alive?

Ellie clamped a hand over her mouth to hide her squeak of shock.

The two men stared each other down, tension crackling between them like a live wire. But before either of them could say anything else, they were interrupted by the sound of clapping and cheering from the party. They both turned and spotted her loitering by the raised flower bed. Ash's expression closed down. Cal's eyes narrowed slightly, but when he met her gaze, his features softened.

"We're not done talking about this," Cal said without breaking eye contact with her.

Ash, with a scowl and a reluctant nod, turned and made his way back to the party, leaving Ellie alone with Cal.

She didn't say anything at first, just stood there under the starlight, blinking against the sudden brightness of the patio lights. Her heart was pounding so hard she felt lightheaded with it. She had barely managed to stammer out a "hi" before Cal closed the distance between them.

"How much did you hear?" he asked, not bothering to pretend she hadn't been eavesdropping.

"Enough. Why were you talking about my sister?"

Cal sighed deeply and looked back toward the party. "It's... a long story. One not really appropriate for a wedding."

"Is she alive?"

"I don't know."

Frustration surged through her. She was tired of waiting for answers—and tired of old wounds being ripped open without warning. "Hope disappeared twenty years ago. How can there possibly be anything relevant now?"

Cal sighed again, running a hand through his sandy hair, messing up the neatly combed strands. "Someone called me about her a few days ago."

She inhaled sharply. "What? Who?"

"I don't know who. She was young and sounded scared. She asked for my help, said Hope was missing."

"A prank call."

"No," Cal said quietly.

He seemed so sure. She stared at him, waiting for him to elaborate. How could he be so sure?

When he finally spoke again, it was in a tone so soft she barely heard him over the murmur of the party. "I thought it was a prank at first, too, but... Ash and I tracked down where the call came from and obtained security footage. And, Ellie, this girl looks like Hope. Like a teenage version of Hope." He took a piece of paper from his pocket, unfolded it, and held it out.

Ellie slowly took it, and the world tilted on its axis. Her mind spun with questions and doubts and a fierce, gnawing longing. Finding Hope had always been Alexis's dream, but until that moment, she hadn't realized it was so important to her, too. The girl in the image looked so much like Hope that it was like stepping into a time machine. The same high cheekbones, the same wild curls...

"But... how? How is it even possible? It has to be a weird coincidence. If Hope is still alive, she'd be forty years old now, not a teenager."

"It's her daughter."

Her gaze snapped to his in disbelief. "What?"

"We found a hair clip near the phone she called me from. Ash had it tested, and the preliminary report came back nearly one hundred percent definitive—the girl is Hope's biological daughter."

"A daughter?" She understood the words he was saying at a basic level but couldn't seem to actually comprehend them. "Hope has... had... a daughter?"

Cal nodded solemnly, and the reality of it hit her like a punch to the gut. She had to sit down and took a few wobbly steps toward a nearby bench. Cal was right there beside her, his arm sliding around her waist to support her.

"Easy," he murmured.

She couldn't stop staring at the photo. Hope had a daughter. A daughter who was a virtual replica. A daughter who had reached out for help...

God. Her sister had left behind more than just memories and heartache. She'd left a part of herself in this world.

"Who is she?" Ellie demanded. "Where is she? Why hasn't she come forward before now?"

"We don't know yet. There's no record of her."

"But if the girl is Hope's daughter and she told you Hope is missing now... that means... Hope was... is... alive somewhere. But how could she be alive? She hasn't been seen in twenty years! She never touched her bank account after she disappeared, never used her credit card. This is impossible. This is —" Alexis called her name from the reception, and she jumped to her feet. "Oh my God. I need to tell Alexis. I need to—"

"Ellie." Cal wrapped both of her hands in his, stopping her. "Take a breath. We all have a lot of questions, and there aren't any answers right now. And you don't need to tell Alexis. This is her day. Let her have it without Hope clouding it."

He was right.

Of course, he was right.

God, she was shaking.

She looked down at their entwined hands, then back up into Cal's earnest brown eyes. His grip was warm and firm, steadying. She wanted to lean into his touch, to draw from his strength and grounding presence, and because of that, she pulled away. She pretended she didn't see the flash of hurt in his eyes.

Alexis called her name again. She sounded closer.

Ellie drew a fortifying breath and although it pained her to lose the connection to Hope, as tenuous as it was, she handed the photo back to Cal. "I should go."

Cal nodded, but his hand lingered, brushing hers before he let her go. "Of course."

As she walked back toward the reception, the laughter and music seemed distant and surreal. She found her sister at the top of the terrace steps looking out over the garden, her dress shimmering in the fairy lights draped around the winery's patio.

She really was stunning.

Ellie had always felt plain in comparison, with her unruly curly hair and oversized glasses, but she could never hold her sister's beauty against her. She loved Alexis too much. And now wasn't the time to wallow in her insecurities. This was Lexi's day, and she would do whatever she could to keep it happy and upbeat, despite the storm of emotions raging inside her.

"Hey," Ellie said as she joined her sister on the steps.

"Where have you been?" Alexis asked, a line of concern forming between her brows.

Instead of responding, Ellie pulled her into a tight hug, breathing in the floral perfume that always reminded her of love and comfort and home. She forced a smile as they pulled apart.

Alexis's concern only deepened, and she opened her mouth to say something but stopped short when she spotted Cal in the garden below. A small, knowing smile tugged at her lips. "Oh. I see."

"Lexi, don't start."

"I'm telling you, give him another chance."

Ellie scowled. "You know my feelings."

"I know, and I'm sorry, but in this case, your feelings are stupid. He's a good man."

"He defends criminals for a living. I could never date a man like that."

"And I never thought I could date a man like Shane, but look how it turned out."

"That's different."

"How?"

Realizing she didn't have a good answer, Ellie pushed out a breath. "Okay, maybe it's not different, but I could never date someone who would willingly defend the man who hurt you, Lexi."

Alexis sighed. "That's his job, Elle. It doesn't mean he agrees with his client's actions." She paused and looked toward her husband, who was deep in conversation with Zak and Donovan on the other side of the dance floor. "Besides, he defended Shane, too. And, if local rumor is to be believed, Donovan."

Ellie opened her mouth to retort but closed it again because she didn't have a counterpoint. Shane had once lived off the grid on the mountain, and because he looked the way he did, he'd been branded a criminal, wrongly accused of crimes he didn't commit. Cal had fought for him, proved his innocence, and got him released. She didn't know all the details of Donovan's story since that happened before she arrived in town, but she imagined it was similar.

Cal *was* a good man.

But then he'd gone and defended the man who actually committed the crimes that Shane had been accused of. The man who sliced open Alexis's throat and left her for dead.

She just couldn't forgive him for it, even if Alexis could.

She glanced toward Cal again, watching as he laughed at something Sawyer said while he bent down to slip Zelda a treat from the charcuterie board. There was an ease about him that made people trust him, a warmth that reached out and embraced those around him. Yet underneath all that charm lay a formidable tenacity.

Was it any wonder he was the one to find Hope finally?

"...want you to fall in love," Alexis was saying, and Ellie snapped back to the conversation.

"You're just saying that because you have little cartoon hearts circling your head." She took her sister's hand and squeezed it. "And I will find love. Someday. But not with Callum Holden."

"God, you're stubborn."

"Learned from the best."

"Mom?"

That made them both laugh because, yes, all three sisters had received an oversized dose of the stubborn gene from Amy Summers.

"Okay, c'mon," Alexis said after a moment and tugged her toward the winery. "We need to find the bathroom so you can help me fix my makeup. It's all streaky from crying during the ceremony."

Her makeup was perfect, but Ellie didn't say so and followed her sister inside.

chapter
five

"I CAN'T BELIEVE you're married."

Seated at the vanity in the winery's restroom, Alexis sparkled. There was no other word for it. "I know. It's crazy, right? I swore marriage wasn't for me, and now..." She finished touching up her mascara and sighed. "I'm so happy, Elle."

Ellie wrapped her arms around her shoulders and gave her a light squeeze. "You deserve it, sis. It was perfect. Like a fairytale."

Whatever reservations Ellie once had about Shane Trevisano were long gone. She couldn't have asked for a better man for Alexis. Her heart ached with happiness for her sister. And maybe her heart also ached with deep yearning, but she wasn't about to explore that because it would inevitably lead her back to Callum Holden, and she did not want to think about him anymore tonight. "But I have to say I'm surprised you talked Shane into a traditional wedding."

"I didn't! It was what he wanted—the pomp and circumstance and me walking down the aisle in a gown to him in his dress whites. I was afraid it would be too much for him and would've been perfectly happy just going to the courthouse and calling it done." Alexis's smile dimmed a fraction. "I wish

Hope could've been here. She would've loved the ceremony of it all."

Hope.

She seemed to be on everyone's minds lately.

Ellie considered mentioning the girl, but Cal was right. This wasn't the time or place for it. Not on Lexi's wedding day. It could wait until she got back from her honeymoon.

"I wish I could remember more about her." Ellie had only been six when Hope disappeared, but she recalled the way Hope's laughter used to ring through the house. She also remembered the intense shouting matches between Hope and their mother.

Alexis turned away from the mirror. "She loved you. Loved us both so much. I don't remember much about her anymore, but I know that for a fact."

"Did Mom ever tell you—" She broke off as the door opened and, as if on cue, their mother came into the room.

Amy Summers looked like a woman half her age thanks to a strict diet, rigid exercise routine, and plastic surgery—which she adamantly denied having done. She prided herself on her looks and loved it when she was mistaken for their older sister rather than their mother. The dress she'd chosen for her daughter's wedding was too short, too bold, and too revealing with its plunge neckline, but Ellie wasn't about to say that out loud. It would only cause problems, and she wanted the rest of the day to go smoothly for her sister's sake.

Not that Amy would intentionally ruin it. She wasn't cruel or abusive or anything like that. She had been a good mother, and they both loved her, but their relationship had grown complicated as they matured into adults. They realized Amy was a little too self-absorbed to be the quintessential mother figure they longed for. Her love was deep for her girls, but she tended to put her needs before theirs, and it led to instances when both Alexis and Ellie felt more like the parent than the child.

Amy sashayed into the room, her crimson dress swishing around her thighs and her platinum hair styled to perfection. "Did I ever tell you what?"

Ellie looked at her sister for help. They both knew better than to mention Hope's name. Their mother always closed down whenever her eldest daughter came up in conversation, but Ellie was also tired of tiptoeing around the topic.

Alexis nodded and mouthed, "Ask her."

Ellie drew a breath, faced their mother, and broke the unspoken family rule. "We were talking about Hope."

Amy's expression froze into a brittle mask. Ellie could almost see the memories flicker in her mother's eyes before they hardened into a cold, distant gaze.

"Hope," Amy echoed as if it was a foreign word. She smoothed down her dress. "I don't see why you'd be talking about her on a day like today."

"We just... we miss her, Mom."

Amy's lips thinned into a line, and she looked at her youngest daughter curiously as if trying to decipher an unsolvable puzzle. Then her gaze slid toward Alexis.

"I wish she could've been here," Alexis added.

The silence stretched on until it was almost unbearable. Then Amy shrugged with practiced nonchalance.

"It's been over twenty years, girls." Her voice was soft but firm, offering no room for argument. "She made her choices, and they didn't include us, so let's not spoil such a beautiful day by talking about her."

"Why do you make it sound like she wanted to leave?" Ellie asked.

Amy Summers sighed and leaned over Alexis to check her makeup in the mirror. "I don't want to talk about it." She pulled a tube of lipstick from her clutch and layered it on even though she didn't need more. "It's not an appropriate conversation for a wedding."

"Well, I'm the bride," Alexis said. "And I get to decide what's appropriate. I want to know, too. What really happened when she disappeared?"

"And why did you never look for her?" Ellie pressed. "You never really seemed to care."

"I cared," Amy said and snapped the clutch shut. "I've always cared. She's my daughter."

"Then why don't you show it?"

"Because I'm tired." Amy set her purse down on the vanity with a clatter. "I was tired of her drama then, and now I'm tired of her ghost hanging over this family. She left on her own accord. She wasn't forced into that car or tricked. She wanted to leave. She chose to leave us."

"Did she really?" Ellie shot back. "Or did you choose to let her go?"

The accusation hung in the air between them like a lethal blade ready to sever fragile ties.

Amy, for her part, didn't balk at Ellie's words, but her blue eyes bore into her daughter's. "Both."

"Please, Mom," Alexis said softly. "Just tell us what happened. Don't you think it's time we know?"

She sighed and dropped to the chaise beside the vanity. "Oh, I'm sorry, girls. I know I should've talked to you both about this a long time ago. It's just... difficult for me. Hope was always different. From the moment she was old enough to walk and talk, she was all emotion, energy, and mischief. You were too young to understand the turmoil she caused in our family. She was damaged. I don't know if she was just that way from birth, or if I damaged her, or maybe both. I was so young when I had her. Only seventeen, still a child myself, and I made so many mistakes until I met your father. But by then, it was already too late to fix what was broken in Hope. But I tried, girls. So did he. He even adopted her, gave her his name so we could be a complete family. I swear, we tried everything. Discipline, affection, therapy... but nothing seemed to reach her. She didn't want my help, and she certainly didn't want your father's. She was barely a teenager when she started the drugs and the partying, and then came the much older men... I had to choose between helping her or keeping you two safe. It's a choice no mother should ever have to make, but I made it. And when she walked out that day and didn't come home... God help me, I was relieved. I was relieved not because I wanted her gone but because it meant you girls were safe from her chaos."

"But why didn't we search for her?" Ellie asked.

Amy looked down at her hands. "We did," she said quietly. "Your father and I exhausted every resource we had, but it was like chasing a ghost. She didn't want to be found, and life was so much easier without her. Eventually, I realized that maybe I didn't want to find her."

"Did you love her, Mom?" Alexis whispered.

Amy's eyes welled up with tears, and for a moment, there was silence. "More than you'll ever know," she said at last. "She was my firstborn. My baby girl. She was beautiful and full of life. But her life... she was a hurricane damaging everything in her path."

Ellie's heart ached at the pain in her mother's voice. For years, she'd thought that their mother had been negligent, more concerned about a semblance of peace than finding Hope. But hearing Amy's confession tore away that illusion, revealing the heartbreaking truth of a mother caught in an impossible situation. And now she realized she'd been too harsh on their mother. Amy had a lot of faults, but she loved all of her daughters in her own way.

Alexis took a deep breath, breaking the silence that had settled between them. "Mom..." she started tentatively. "Did

Hope ever give any indication about where she might go? Any friends or boyfriends who might have an idea?"

"Girls, please don't go digging this up again." When they both just stared at her in response, Amy sighed heavily, her shoulders drooping as if the weight of those years was pressing down on her. "No, she never gave any indication. She didn't tell me things. We didn't have that kind of relationship, and she didn't trust easily. She kept her secrets close. And those people she did associate with... well, they weren't the sort to help us find her."

"Do you think she's still alive out there somewhere?" Ellie asked.

"No."

The answer was said with such finality that it made Ellie blink with surprise. "Why not?"

"Because I would feel it. A mother knows." Her face crumpled, and she wrapped her arms around herself as if physically trying to hold her grief inside. "I would know if my baby was still in this world. Hope..." She swallowed hard, choking back a sob. "My Hope is gone. She's been gone for a long time."

Alexis reached out and took their mother's hand, offering a comforting squeeze while Ellie folded her arms over her chest, holding back her tears. She opened her mouth to tell Alexis and her mother about the girl Cal had found—the teenager who was apparently Hope's daughter—but Alexis gave a small shake of her head.

"No more," she mouthed.

She was probably right. She'd tell Alexis soon, but telling Mom that Hope had been alive long enough to birth a child seemed cruel. But if Cal found the girl, it would all come out eventually.

Maybe she should tell him to drop it and stop looking?

She mentally scoffed at the thought. He wouldn't stop, even if she asked. Giving up wasn't in his DNA.

An insistent tap came from the door, and Shane opened it before they could respond, his sharp gaze scanning the room before settling on Alexis. The man seemingly had a sixth sense when it came to his new wife's discomfort. "Everything okay?"

"We're fine," Alexis assured him with a small, sad smile. "Just digging up old family skeletons."

His gaze softened. "Hope?"

"Yeah." Alexis sighed and absently fiddled with the ring he'd given her. "Hope."

He came into the room fully then, moving to stand behind Alexis and settle his scarred hands on her shoulders. There was so much love in the way he looked at her. He didn't have to fill the silence with empty words; he simply needed to be there, providing rock-steady support.

For a moment, Ellie wondered if Cal could provide the same support for her. Cal was so different from Shane—funny where Shane was serious, bright with optimism, whereas Shane was a stark realist, unburdened by trauma, while Shane had more baggage than an airplane. Cal was like her puppy—sweet but chaotic. She'd never be able to rely on him for the kind of sturdy support Shane provided Alexis. It was ridiculous even to compare the two of them.

Amy smiled at him. "I don't think I ever thanked you, Shane."

"For what?"

"For saving my daughter. For loving her."

He shook his head. "I should be thanking you for raising a stubborn, fierce, brilliant woman," he said with an admiring look at his bride. "Without her, I'd—" His voice caught. "*She* saved *me*."

"We saved each other." Alexis closed her eyes, leaning back into Shane's steady presence.

Ellie hated herself for the sudden pang of envy. She had always been the kind of woman who prided herself on her independence. But at that moment, watching the quiet strength of their union, she couldn't help but wish she had someone in her life to lean on like that.

Cal.

No. Dammit.

Why was she so hung up on Callum Holden anyway?

Okay, she knew the answers to that question. His roguish smile. His light-hearted charm. His sexy arm muscles—she never could resist a guy with nice arms—and oh so squeezable butt. The way he made her feel all jittery inside when he was near, like she couldn't stand still...

But he wasn't what she wanted in her life.

Right?

Right.

But even as she firmed up her resolve, her heart betrayed her, drumming that traitorous name against her ribcage.

Cal. Cal. Cal.

She curled her hands into fists and told her heart to shut up. Cal was not to be thought about or dwelled on. He'd only been a fling—a charming, confusing fling that wasn't good for her. Nothing more. Certainly nothing her stupid heart needed to be concerned about.

Amy cleared her throat, pulling Ellie from her thoughts. "All right, girls. Enough of the past. What's done is done. We should get back to the party before people think we've vanished."

Shane offered his arm to Alexis, and with a glance at her mother, she placed her hand in his.

As they returned to the reception, Ellie kept a close eye on her sister. Alexis had this amazing ability to bounce back from anything. Even now, she was pulling herself together, ready to dazzle their guests with her charisma and charm.

God, Ellie admired her.

Alexis had been through so much over the years—the disappearance of Hope, the Shadow Stalker case, her kidnapping, and a near-death experience. Somehow, she always came back stronger and brighter.

Ellie wished she was that resilient. She felt flayed open, raw, and exposed. She wanted to crawl into bed, bury her face in Puzzle's fur, and cry until her tears ran out for the sister she barely remembered but missed with her entire heart.

She felt rather than saw him approach. Cal was like that, emanating a warmth that she recognized every time. She turned to find him right there, watching her with those earnest eyes. As always, he was a chaotic blend of concern and cheerfulness, his hair even more ruffled now than it had been earlier. She adored that he always looked just a little bit rumpled.

"You okay?" he asked, his gaze searching her face.

Ellie looked away. She wanted to ask him about the girl who looked like Hope. She wanted to voice her feelings, but they were so jumbled up inside her like a ball of yarn, and she didn't know how to begin unraveling them.

So, instead, she forced a smile and nodded. "Yeah, I'm okay."

For a moment, he looked like he wanted to say something —comfort her, maybe—but he seemed to think better of it and simply offered her the glass of champagne he held. "You look like you need a drink."

She accepted the glass, their fingers fleetingly brushing. The contact sent a shock through her system, but she ignored it and avoided his gaze.

"Thanks." At least her voice was steadier than she felt.

"Did you tell Alexis?" he asked and snagged another glass from a passing server.

"No." She took a long drink. The bubbles fizzed against

her tongue, the golden liquid not quite managing to wash away the bitter taste of old sorrow. "I'm not ruining this day for her."

He smiled as he watched Shane and Alexis together. "They look happy."

"They are." As she watched them, she realized Cal's gaze was back on her. It was disconcerting— partly because she wasn't used to being the center of anyone's attention, but mostly because she knew there was nothing she could hide from him. He had a way of seeing right through her, dissecting her thoughts and emotions in an instant. It was both terrifying and exhilarating at the same time.

"Want to dance?" he asked, extending his hand toward her.

She looked at his offered hand and then back up at his face. For a moment, she hesitated. She wanted to, but at the same time, dancing with Cal felt dangerous. "I'm not really in the mood."

"Come on, Ellie. You love to dance."

"Not with—" She bit off the automatic response, realizing it was cruel to say out loud.

There was a flash of disappointment in his eyes, but he quickly masked it with a nod of understanding. Why was he so understanding? It made it really hard to maintain her defenses and keep him at a distance.

"Not with me," he finished.

"No," she whispered around the lump in her throat. "Not with you."

"I get that." He took her glass from her, placing it on a nearby table. "But I refuse to be the reason you don't have a good time tonight." He closed a hand around hers and tugged her toward the dance floor.

"Cal..." Despite her protest, she didn't pull away. She could've. His grip on her hand was loose, giving her plenty of opportunity to escape, but she allowed him to lead her to the dance floor. The music shifted to a slower ballad as they reached it. Of course. The universe really had a wicked sense of humor.

Or...

She glanced toward the DJ booth and saw Alexis standing there with a big grin on her face.

Not the universe. Her sister.

She should stop this before it went any further. She should—

Her thoughts ground to a halt when Cal pulled her into his arms. God, he felt good, and she couldn't seem to find the willpower to step away.

"Relax," he murmured in her ear, his breath tickling her skin. "I'm not going to bite. Unless you ask."

She gave a soft laugh despite herself. "That's not what I'm afraid of."

His arms tightened around her. "Then what?"

She didn't answer. How could she? How could she explain that she was afraid of how he made her feel—afraid of the way her heart throbbed when he looked at her, afraid of how easily she could fall into his arms and forget everything else. Callum Holden was too much. Too beautiful, too kind, too dangerous. He was a whirlwind, and he'd crash through her barriers and then leave her shattered and breathless in his wake. The closer she got to him, the more she risked losing herself.

He moved with an easy grace that Ellie couldn't quite match, but he made her feel as though she was floating. His hand was firm and comforting on the small of her back, and his warmth radiated into her as if he were her own personal sun. For a moment, just a moment, Ellie closed her eyes and let herself imagine what it would be like to truly let go. To let Cal hold her, to feel his arms around her not in a dance, but in life. To listen to his heartbeat against her ear each night as they fell asleep. To know the feel of his fingers tracing lazy patterns on her skin on a Sunday morning. To feel the imprint of his lips on hers, not stolen in a quick, heated moment but given freely and with abandon.

A soft sigh escaped her lips. She hadn't realized how tense she was until she felt him gently rub circles on her back. His touch was soothing, grounding. A reminder that this was real, that he was real.

What was she afraid of?

"I'm afraid to let you in," she whispered against his chest. "But I still want to."

He stilled. She didn't need to see his face to feel his surprise. "What did you say?"

She shook her head, instantly regretting her boldness. The words had slipped out before she could catch them. "Nothing."

Cal tightened his hold on her, and she opened her eyes to look at him. His gaze was intense, focused solely on her. She could see the concern there, the question he wanted to ask.

He never got the chance. The song ended, and the DJ announced that it was time for the newlyweds to cut the cake. The soft bubble around them burst, the noise of the other wedding guests flooding back in. She drew away from him, but he tightened his hold for an instant as if unwilling to let her go.

"I... need to go, Cal."

Emotions battled over his expression, but then his cheerful smile returned, only slightly strained around the edges.

"All right," he said, stepping back and giving her the space she desperately needed.

She turned and fled, all but pushing people out of the way as she made a beeline for the restroom. The door closed behind her with a soft click, and she breathed a sigh of relief.

Her heart fluttered like a frightened bird behind her ribs.

She leaned on the bathroom sink and stared at her reflection in the mirror. Her cheeks were flushed, eyes wide with shock. She looked like a woman who had just been kissed for the first time.

But she hadn't been kissed. She had danced with Callum Holden, and she had loved every second of it.

And that terrified her more than anything else.

chapter
six

THE REST of the evening was a blur. The cake cutting, the toasts, the laughs and smiles— Ellie participated in all of it, but her thoughts were elsewhere. She kept stealing glances at Cal, who was mingling and laughing with guests, always so charming.

It was infuriating.

And exhausting.

By the time the boisterous crowd sent the newlyweds off on their honeymoon, she was completely drained and just a bit tipsy from too much champagne. Maybe she shouldn't have grabbed a glass every time Cal got close.

As soon as her duty as maid of honor ended, she escaped onto a terrace below the hotel overlooking the ocean and drew in several deep breaths of the cool air. She was finally alone, with only the rolling waves below to keep her company...

Or so she thought until a warm voice broke the silence. "It's peaceful here, isn't it?"

She whirled around. Cal was standing there with his hands in the pockets of his trousers. He looked so handsome and a little bit dangerous, like a rogue duke from one of the historical romance novels she so loved.

"Sorry, didn't mean to startle you," he said, offering an apologetic smile that made her heart flutter.

God, she wished she could harden her heart against this man. "Why did you follow me?"

If he was embarrassed at being caught, he didn't show it. "I wanted to make sure you got home safely."

"I'm not going home." She motioned vaguely back toward the winery's on-site hotel. "I have a room here."

Ugh, had that sounded like an invitation? Her face burned, and she turned back toward the ocean, letting the salted breeze cool the embarrassment from her skin.

His silence filled the air, a gentle weight that stirred the edges of her awareness. She didn't need to look at him to know his gaze was on her.

"Ellie..." There was an emotion she couldn't quite place in his voice. Or maybe she just didn't want to name it.

She turned back to him. "Yes?"

There was a moment's pause before he spoke again, his words nearly carried by the wind. "I did hear what you said earlier. About wanting to let me in."

Dammit. Of course he'd heard her.

"I didn't mean anything by it," she said, attempting to keep her face neutral. "It was... was just the champagne talking."

Cal didn't look convinced. His brows furrowed, and his gaze held a deep intensity that made her swallow hard. He stepped forward, closing the distance between them until his heat seeped into her skin. The scent of him, something crisp like autumn leaves and balsam wood, invaded her senses.

"I don't believe you," he said softly.

Then he did something she never expected. He reached out and brushed a single finger down her cheek, tracing the line of her jawbone with a sweetness that made all of her nerve endings tingle to life. Her lips parted, and her eyes drifted closed as his fingers slid around the back of her neck.

He drew her closer.

"I don't want you to be afraid of me, Ellie. I'm not here to hurt you. That's the last thing I want to do."

His thumb brushed her lower lip, and she released a shuddering breath. It was as if the world had stopped spinning, time pausing in this moment between them. A terrifying thrill coursed through her, igniting every nerve, every cell of her body, with a dangerous need.

"I know," she whispered, opening her eyes to look at him. "I'm not afraid of you. I'm afraid of how much I want..." She let the sentence trail off. It hung between them, heavy with unspoken truth.

She didn't know who moved first. Maybe they moved at the same time. Their lips met in a ferocious, long-denied kiss. Their bodies collided as if they couldn't get close enough to each other. The night air was forgotten, the crashing waves below a distant hum. All that mattered was his touch and his taste and the heat that had been searing between them for far too long. His hands slid down her waist and grasped her hips, pulling her even closer. She moaned into the kiss, her body molding against his like she'd never left.

His fingers tangled in her hair, dislodging curls from her updo as he tilted her head back to deepen the kiss. Each sensation seemed magnified— his tongue sliding against hers, his breath mingling with her own. He tasted of champagne and sweet things she couldn't name.

Then his hands crept lower, sliding down the curve of her hips, his grip firm and possessive. Her heart pounded a rhythm that echoed with each touch, her entire being consumed by this man who had been so tirelessly patient.

"Cal," she gasped, breaking away from him to catch her breath. Her glasses had fogged up in the heat of their embrace, and she removed them to wipe them clean on the hem of her dress. Through blurry vision, she watched him watching her and could feel his smile more than see it.

"Ellie," he murmured back, his voice hoarse with desire. His gaze never left hers as he reached out and gently took her glasses from her hand. He carefully finished cleaning the lenses with the pocket square from his suit, then slid the glasses back on her, his fingers lingering at her temples. His touch sent an electric current through her, igniting a fire that was far too hot to extinguish now.

Blinking up at him to adjust her focus, she was met with a soft gaze full of hope and desire.

"Thank you," she said.

"Always." He dipped to capture her lips once more, and she didn't protest as his hands went back to exploring her body, roaming over the smooth silk of her dress and the soft curves beneath.

Ellie responded eagerly, reaching up to bury her fingers in his hair. She tugged him even closer, their bodies flush against each other.

"I've wanted you for so long," he confessed when they finally came up for air again. "Every time I see you, every time I'm near you... it's becoming harder for me to breathe without touching you, without knowing how your skin feels against mine."

She should pull away and put an end to this now. But she had wanted him for so long that she had forgotten what it felt like not to want him. She felt fuzzy from the champagne and needy from denying herself, and all she could do was cling to him tighter, her lips seeking his.

"Then touch me," she said against his mouth, her hands trailing down his chest. She felt his intake of breath as her fingers fumbled with the buttons of his shirt. "Cal... I need you to touch me."

His only response was a low growl in his throat as he slipped off his jacket and tossed it onto one of the nearby chairs. He eagerly helped her unbutton his shirt, pulling it free from his pants and tossing it away carelessly.

Now, their bodies were separated by a thin veil of silk and cotton.

She could still put a stop to this. She could still pull away. She didn't.

She ran her fingers across his chest. Taut muscles rippled beneath her touch. She was always surprised at how muscular he was under those rumpled suits.

Cal's hand brushed the side of her face, and she looked at him. His brown eyes held a look she hadn't seen before— a promise of something more than just physical attraction. He leaned down, pressing his lips to hers with an intensity that took her breath away. "We should go up to your room."

"No." She didn't want to give herself time to second-guess this.

"No?" A ripple of surprise laced his question, and his lips quirked in that adorably appealing way.

Ellie shook her head, all her previous hesitations and insecurities slowly fading away. "No." Her fingers tightened around the fabric of his trousers, pulling him closer to her. "I want you here... now... tonight."

And maybe once she had him, she could stop obsessing about him and move on with her life.

Not going to happen, a little voice of reason whispered at the back of her mind. *You told yourself that last time. And the time before that. And the one before that.*

She told the voice to shut up. She didn't want reason now. She was tired and lonely and wanted Cal.

"Ellie." Her name left him like a breathed prayer.

Oh, no. He wasn't going to be all chivalrous and turn her down, was he? "Please, Cal."

One hand curled around her waist, and he decisively backed her against the far wall of the terrace under a waterfall of vines. The small, relieved gasp that escaped her lips was swallowed by his mouth descending on hers in a kiss that was all heat and fire and desperate need. The world spun with dizzying speed as he devoured her with a possessiveness that left no room for doubt.

Thank God.

He unzipped her dress, his fingers steady and unhurried despite the rapid rise and fall of his chest. The silk fabric pooled at her feet, leaving her bare to him. His gaze devoured her, a soft sound of appreciation leaving his throat.

"You are utterly breathtaking, Ellie," he murmured, brushing his thumb over the hardened peak of her nipple, sending a jolt of desire coursing through her.

That was the thing about Cal that made it so hard to resist him—he didn't just touch her; he worshipped her. His fingers traced over every inch of her like he was memorizing the feel of her under his hands. His mouth left a trail of heated kisses down her neck, across her collarbone, and down to the swell of her breasts. His tongue flicked over her nipple, and she gasped, tightening her hands in his hair, holding him to her. He kissed his way across to her other breast, mirroring his actions until she was writhing beneath him.

"Cal," she whimpered, tugging at his hair. She needed him closer, needed all of him.

His lips moved lower, trailing kisses down her stomach. Her breath hitched as he carefully lifted one of her legs over his shoulder, pressing a kiss to the inside of her thigh.

Oh, God, this was a bad idea.

Sleeping with him wouldn't get him out of her system. It would only make her want him more.

And, still, she didn't care.

A soft chuckle rumbled from his chest as she pressed her hips toward him.

"Patience." His breath was warm against the sensitive skin of her inner thigh.

She didn't want patience. She wanted Callum. She wanted him inside her, filling her with warmth and pleasure. A soft moan escaped her, and she bit her lower lip to keep more sounds from slipping out. His grin widened, a devilish gleam in his eyes before he moved lower and merely brushed his lips against her clit.

She nearly screamed at the touch, her hips bucking off the wall in response. Cal's hands on her hips kept her steady as he continued his exploration, his mouth working miracles that made her see stars.

"Cal!" She cried out his name, clawing at his shoulders. Her climax was powerful and sudden, washing over her in an overwhelming wave of pleasure. Through it all, he continued his relentless assault on her senses until she was left a trembling mess against the wall.

His lips traveled back up her body, peppering kisses across her stomach and breasts until he finally met her mouth with his. She could taste herself on his lips, and it only served to reignite the spark of her desire.

"Your turn," she murmured against his mouth and trailed her fingers to the fastenings of his trousers. With one swift movement, she pushed them down along with his underwear, and they pooled at his feet.

The feel of him against her, hard and pulsing with need, sent another wave of desire coursing through her. She wrapped a hand around him, and a low groan rumbled from the back of Cal's throat.

"Ellie," he rasped, his voice strained with need.

She liked it when he sounded like that—like he would break apart without her hands and mouth on him.

She wrapped her hands around the thick base of him again and teased her tongue over his tip. His hands fisted in her hair as she sucked him into her mouth. He tasted of salt and masculine heat, a heady mix that made her pulse thrum with a new, heightened sense of hunger. She traced every vein with the tip of her tongue, loving the way he trembled and the increasingly desperate noises coming from him.

"Jesus…" His head fell back against the wall, eyes screwed shut.

The steel in his grip softened as she increased her pace, relinquishing control as he succumbed to the pleasure.

The groans falling from his lips turned into ragged breaths, each one punctuated by her name.

"Ellie… Ellie…" His voice was hoarse, the usually composed attorney being reduced to broken pleas.

She made a tiny, pleased sound against him, a vibration that elicited a choked cry from Cal. His control snapped, and with one final decisive pull, he fell over the edge, his release pulsing against her tongue. She savored the taste of him, pulling back only when she felt his hands gently tugging on her hair.

They stared at each other.

His gaze was hot. Hungry. He was already lengthening and hardening again in her hand. He hadn't had enough yet. Truthfully, neither had she. She was uncomfortably wet between her legs, the hollow place inside her throbbing to be filled.

"Ellie," he breathed again, but it was a different kind of plea. "Are you still on birth control?"

She nodded. He exhaled with relief and lifted her off her feet, their bare skin sliding against each other as he pinned her to the cold wall behind them. Her legs wrapped around his waist as he quickly stepped out of the trousers still gathered at his ankles.

With one hand supporting her back, he used the other to guide himself into her. She gasped as he entered her, stretching and filling the emptiness that had been aching for him. She could barely believe this was happening, that she was here with him again, succumbing to the potent chemistry between them.

But, oh, she'd missed this.

She'd missed him.

Even if she didn't dare admit it out loud.

The feeling of him, the scent of him, the sight of him consumed her. She clung to him as he began to move, ever so slowly at first, his eyes locked with hers, watching every shift of emotion on her face. They'd only been together for a short time, but he'd studied every inch of her body. He knew where to kiss, where to touch. He knew how to drive her wild and how to make her climax so hard she had an out-of-body experience.

His thrusts were measured, bringing her right to the edge of pleasure before he slowed down again. He was torturing her in the best way possible, and all she could do was moan his name. She felt deliriously high, the pleasure building into a tsunami that threatened to sweep her into oblivion. Her nails dug into his shoulders as each thrust pushed her closer and closer to that delicious edge.

"Yes... Cal... yes," she said in a breathless whisper, too overwhelmed to articulate anything more.

A wicked grin played on his lips as he increased the pace, driving into her hard and fast. She threw her head back against the wall, biting her lip to stifle a scream of pleasure.

The terrace echoed with the sound of their bodies slapping together, Ellie's panting breaths, and Cal's low groans. If anyone wandered by, they'd know exactly what was happening in the shadows against the stone wall.

And she didn't care one bit.

Sweat trickled down her back, her body hot and flushed under his touch. The coil of tension inside her tightened further, her climax looming closer with each thrust.

He held her up against the wall with one arm, allowing his other hand the freedom to explore. It dipped between their bodies, and his thumb found her clit, circling it with a precision that sent another wave of pleasure coursing through her.

"Let go, Ellie," he growled against her ear. "Come for me."

That was all it took. With a hoarse scream of his name, she came undone around him, shattering into pieces as the most intense orgasm she'd ever experienced ripped through her.

"Ellie... Oh, fuck, I've missed you." His free hand splayed wide on her lower back to pull her closer to him. "I've missed you so goddamn much. I think about you every night. I dream about this..."

His thrusts became more erratic as he neared his own climax. He held her tighter, his arms like iron bars, and he buried his face in the crook of her neck.

She gasped, tilting her head to give him better access as he nipped at her sensitive skin.

"Cal... I..." It was all she managed before his lips were on hers again, his tongue demanding entrance, which she willingly granted. His taste was intoxicating, a potent mix of him and her that sent her senses reeling. His thrusts quickened, the force of them pushing her higher against the wall.

His rhythm faltered, his movements becoming more urgent as he neared the edge. His breaths were hot and ragged against her skin, his body knotted with tension.

"Your turn now to come for me." She caught his lower lip between her teeth and tugged.

It was all he needed.

His grip tightened on her hips, his body stiffening against hers as he let out a guttural groan. She felt him throb inside her as he drove into her one last time. A primal growl escaped him as he came, a sound that sent shivers down her spine and pulsated deep within her. They clung to each other as he emptied himself, his breath ragged against her neck, and she unraveled again in a soft aftershock that left her shaking.

Slowly, he pulled out and gently lowered her onto wobbly legs. Her body hummed with pleasure as he rested his forehead against hers.

"Ellie, I..." He started but seemed at a loss for words.

And reality slammed back.

She'd fucked Callum Holden.

Again.

When the last time, she'd promised herself it wasn't going to keep happening.

Dammit. Dammit. Dammit!

A rush of emotions flooded her body—remorse, ecstasy, and an underlying sense of dread. Had she crossed a line she could never step back over? Her heart squeezed as she disentangled herself from Cal, her eyes darting away from his intense gaze.

"I can't do this again," she whispered, her voice barely audible over the roaring in her ears. "I can't..."

And there was his kicked-puppy expression again—there and gone in a flash. She hated seeing it, hated that she was always the one to put it on his handsome face.

"I understand," he murmured. But his eyes told a different story. His gaze was heavy with unspoken emotions. It was enough to make her question whether she should keep this promise to herself.

What was the worst that could happen if she gave in?

They could fall in love.

Then, fall out of love.

And fall into hate.

Then their friends would be put in the awkward position of choosing sides, and she didn't want that, mostly because she wasn't sure they'd pick her. She wasn't charming like Cal, and she wasn't useful to the Rescue like he was.

Yeah, they'd definitely choose him over her if it came down to it. So she couldn't let it come down to it.

She turned away from him and nearly tripped over her dress and discarded shoes. She bent to snatch them up. She felt him watching as she hastily pulled her clothes back on, but she didn't dare look at him.

"Ellie..." His voice was a hoarse plea. It was the same tone with which he had been whispering her name earlier in a haze of pleasure, but now, it sent a pang of regret coursing through her.

"Please, don't." She zipped up her dress as best she could, keeping her back turned to him. She hurried to the stairs that would take her back up to the hotel.

"I love you," he called after her, his voice catching on the words.

The admission was a punch to her gut. She froze with her hand on the railing of the stairs. She didn't dare look back, afraid of what she might see written on his face or, worse, what he might see on hers. Some things were better left unsaid, and some truths were too painful to bear.

"I have to go," she muttered, her throat tight with unshed tears, and all but ran up the stairs, leaving him alone on the terrace.

Ellie didn't usually consider herself a coward, but tonight, walking away without a backward glance was cowardly. She loved him and hated him in equal measures— just as much as she loved and loathed herself for succumbing to him again.

As her feet moved mechanically through the hotel to her room, she thought about the last time they'd been together. A moment of weakness six months ago, when Jaxon Thorne was proven not guilty of all of the crimes he'd been accused of. Cal had gotten him off for everything except the final attack on

Alexis, playing a flawless defense in the courtroom, and Ellie's world had shattered. She'd come to hate him for it then, as much as she'd loved him before.

But, even so, he'd offered her comfort that night—the warmth of his arms around her when she was falling apart, and the tenderness in his touch had made her feel cherished when she felt humiliated and exposed. A momentary lapse that saw them intertwined in a flurry of passion and regret.

The thought of their last encounter sent Ellie into a spiraling whirlwind of raw pain, leaving her breathless. She had to remind herself to breathe. And then remind herself again.

Her fingers fumbled with the key card to her hotel room. She pushed it into the slot, missed, and tried again with shaky hands before the door finally clicked open.

She collapsed onto her bed, still dressed. The smell of him on her skin, the taste of him on her lips, the throb between her legs—it was somehow both a comfort and a torment. She squeezed her eyes shut, fighting back tears as she remembered the way his eyes softened whenever he looked at her, the way he'd whispered "I love you" with such raw sincerity.

She pressed her palms to her eyes.

It wouldn't happen again.

It couldn't.

Because every time she found herself in his arms, she only craved him more.

chapter
seven

IT WOULDN'T HAPPEN AGAIN.

Every time, he thought if he just fucked her hard enough, he'd imprint on her as indelibly as she had him. If he just made her come enough times, she'd drop her defenses and admit that she needed him as much as he needed her. But it always ended like this—with her leaving and him standing in the cold, empty silence of his self-inflicted heartbreak.

Cal let out a self-deprecating chuckle as he slowly buttoned his shirt. His gaze lingered on the staircase Ellie had fled up just a few minutes ago, the faint echo of her hurried footsteps still ringing in his ears.

She was right. They couldn't keep doing this.

He loved Ellie Summers with an intensity that sometimes scared him. But the woman was stubborn—more stubborn than anyone he'd ever met. She had built a fortress around herself, and no matter how much he tried, he couldn't breach those walls.

It was time to stop trying.

Time to move on with his life.

Maybe he could try dating again. He'd attempted it after

she dumped him, but none of the women lived up to Ellie's sparkle, and he'd always gone home alone.

He had to cut all ties this time—a clean break. Ash had warned him off Hope's case anyway, so he had nothing left to hold onto. He had to let her go.

But even as he thought of it, everything in him resisted the idea. He pulled out his phone and stared at Ellie's number—his thumb hovering over the call button. But what would he say? His fingers moved before he could stop them, typing out a message:

I'm sorry.

Then he pocketed his phone and headed home.

The following week flew by.

Cal was in court almost every day, and between trials, he poured himself into three new cases that came in. One was a DUI, one was a bar fight gone wrong, and the last was a repeat client, a twenty-year-old kid who never had a chance to be anything but a criminal and was now looking at a potential life sentence thanks to the three strikes law. Taking on three new clients when he was already slammed meant a lot of long hours, but at least it kept his mind occupied.

But he couldn't escape Ellie completely.

Every stray moment between his hectic schedule, he fought the urge to call her. He'd see a flash of blonde curls or blue eyes behind glasses, and his heart would stop, only to start again with a painful lurch when it wasn't her. He'd catch a whiff of her perfume on a passerby, and for a second, he was back in her arms. It was torture, but it was better than the nothingness that threatened to consume him otherwise.

Every day, it felt like she was slipping further from his grasp. She never answered his text, and it never even showed that she'd read it. Had she blocked his number?

It felt final this time. He could feel Ellie moving away from him—physically, emotionally... and, worst of all, irrevocably.

So on Friday, when he finally won a hard-fought, drawn-out court battle and turned to shake hands with his client's father, he was shocked to see her sitting at the back of the courtroom.

Was he imagining her?

Other people came forward to congratulate him on the win, momentarily blocking his view. He shook hands and exchanged pleasantries, but his eyes were constantly drawn to the back of the room.

When the crowd thinned, she was still there.

It was actually her this time, not a figment of his ever-hopeful imagination. There was no mistaking those bright red glasses—her favorite pair in her seemingly endless collection—and that explosion of blond curls that she could never fully tame.

She stared at him, her expression unreadable. His heart pounded in his ears as he excused himself from the crowd and headed toward her.

As he approached, Ellie looked at him with a kind of clinical detachment, as if she were studying something under a microscope. Her impassive gaze was colder than any he'd received from her in the past, and she held up a hand as he opened his mouth to say... something. He had no idea what. He wasn't going to apologize for what happened between them last weekend.

"I'm not here to talk about what happened at the wedding," she said flatly.

"Okay." He drew the word out. "Then why are you here?"

Instead of answering, her gaze shifted toward his client as the bailiff led him out in handcuffs. "What did he do, kill someone?"

The kid had non-fatally shot someone in a panic as he tried to rob a convenience store for drug money. He'd used the drugs to self-medicate untreated schizophrenia. It was precisely what the insanity defense was made for, but going that route was always dangerous. A plea of insanity worked in a defendant's favor only around twenty percent of the time, so he'd had to get creative with his defense.

But he couldn't tell her all that, so he simply said, "No, he didn't kill anyone."

A furrow formed between her brows. "Didn't you win?"

He watched until the kid and the guard disappeared out the side door. "I did."

"Then why is he still in handcuffs?"

"Because he's still in custody and will remain so for several years, but now, instead of going to prison, he's going to get medical help."

She studied him for a moment, then nodded, her gaze drifting away from him. "That's good," she murmured.

"Yes, it is." His voice was soft, intentionally gentle. "He needed help, not punishment."

She flinched. He'd once said the exact words to her about Jaxon Thorne, who was also now serving out his sentence in a prison psychiatric hospital due to severe untreated PTSD and drug addiction.

The courtroom slowly emptied around them, the hum of conversation dying down as people filed out.

Cal waited a moment longer before asking again, "Why are you here, Ellie?"

She picked up a thick file from the bench beside her and handed it to him. "This is everything I have about Hope—all the research I've done, every lead I've followed over the years."

He slowly took the file and thumbed through it. There was a lot of information here, far more than he ever managed to extract from the few police reports he'd found concerning her disappearance. He supposed he shouldn't be surprised. Ellie researched every case she and Alexis covered on their podcast, and she was nothing if not thorough.

"Okay," he said, closing the file and handing it back to her. "But that doesn't answer my question."

She refused to take it back and curled her hands into fists in her lap. "You've managed to find out more about her in a matter of months than I've found in years. You found—" Her voice broke, and she cleared her throat before trying again. "You found her daughter."

"More like she found me."

"She reached out to you because you're... you. People trust you. I don't inspire that level of trust, so..." She wouldn't meet his eyes, focusing instead on the far wall over his shoulder. "I need your help to find her again."

He grinned. "That hurt, didn't it?"

"What?"

"Admitting you need my help."

Her eyes snapped to his, sparking with indignation. "You are such an ass sometimes."

Something in him unclenched at the insult, a sliver of hope piercing through the fog of heartbreak. Yeah, okay, she'd called him an ass, but her voice no longer held the cold detachment she had been addressing him with earlier.

"I'll take that as a compliment," Cal replied, his grin persisting.

Ellie frowned, but there was a hint of something else in her expression. It wasn't quite amusement, but it wasn't far off—

a spark of the Ellie he knew and loved buried beneath the frost.

"You would," she said, and her posture relaxed ever so slightly. "You know, it's insufferable how you manage to turn everything around."

He shrugged. "It's a lawyer thing."

That earned him an eye roll. "Of course. It's always a lawyer thing."

He studied her for a moment longer, soaking in her presence. She was here, asking for his help. This was his chance—not necessarily to make everything right between them, but at least to prove that he could be there for her.

"So, will you help or not?" she asked after a moment of silence.

"Of course I'll help. I'll always help you, Ellie."

She looked down at her hands, twisting them anxiously in front of her.

He reached out to take her hands, and still the nervous gesture, but she pulled away.

"Alright then," she said in a rush and took a step back from him, putting more distance between them. "As long as we're clear that this is strictly professional."

Cal nodded. The rejection of his touch stung, but he made sure to keep his face neutral. "Absolutely, strictly professional."

She studied him for a long moment, her blue eyes guarded behind those red glasses. There was fear there, and pain, and an undercurrent of longing that made his heart jump.

"Thank you," she said quietly.

Someone called his name from the front of the courtroom. He didn't look to see who it was but lifted his hand in acknowledgment. "I have a few more things to do today, but I can meet you at my place at about six. We can order take-out for dinner."

"No," she said too quickly, and color infused her cheeks. She pushed her slipping glasses up her nose. "I'd rather meet in public."

Right. Because the last time she came over to his place to talk about something, they'd ended up in bed together. She probably didn't want to risk it happening again.

"Okay, then. The Mad Dog at six?"

She was already backing away. "Yep, it's a date. I mean, not a date. It's definitely not a date. This is professional. We already said it was strictly professional, nothing else. I meant... six is good. The Mad Dog is good. I'll, uh..." She trailed off, and the color in her cheeks deepened.

God, he loved the way she babbled when she was nervous. It was adorable. "See you then, Ellie."

She made a distressed squeaking sound and turned around, her blond curls bouncing around her face as she rushed from the courtroom. He watched her for a moment before giving in to the grin tugging at the corners of his mouth. This was going to be so much more interesting than the evening he'd initially planned.

"Cal."

The sharp bark of his name had him wincing. Ash was striding toward him with his usual scowl etched on his face.

"Hi, Ash. How are you? I'm great, thanks for asking. The weather is particularly nice today, isn't it?"

Ash's scowl only deepened. "What was Ellie doing here?"

Cal shrugged nonchalantly, attempting to keep his booming heart from broadcasting in neon letters on his forehead. "Just chatting."

"About what?" Ash asked, crossing his thick arms over his chest.

"Personal stuff." He looked away from Ash's piercing gaze to watch the last of the courtroom clear out.

"Personal stuff," Ash repeated as if tasting the words and

scowled even deeper at their flavor. "You told her about the girl. About Hope."

Cal turned back to Ash, meeting his gaze head-on. "You're right, I did." He wasn't going to lie to the Ash, a man he respected despite their differing views on most matters. "She deserved to know."

The sheriff shook his head, rubbing his temples in frustration. "This is a criminal investigation, Cal."

"I thought you said there was nothing criminal to investigate."

"Yeah, I was wrong. And—" He bit off whatever he'd been about to say. "Just stay away from this." He nodded toward the door Ellie had exited through. "And keep her away."

"Did you forget who we're talking about?" Cal shoved his hands into his pockets and leaned back on his heels. "She's not going to back off. You should know that about her by now."

"Listen, Cal. This has the potential to get ugly fast. I don't want either of you tangled up in this mess." The sheriff held his gaze for a moment, then sighed, pinching the bridge of his nose. "But you're gonna do whatever you want anyway." It wasn't a question.

Cal grinned. "I'm glad we understand each other."

"We never understand each other," Ash muttered as he walked away. At the door to the courtroom, he paused and looked back. "Keep her safe. If anything happens to her, I'm holding you responsible."

chapter
eight

THE MAD DOG Pub was packed, as usual. Business had picked up a lot since that whole mess with Rose Rawlings and the white supremacists who tried to take her bar. The uptick had probably started with morbid curiosity as people wanted to visit the only place in town that had experienced a drive-by shooting. But then everyone started to realize what Cal had known all along—the beer was good, and the food was better.

Rose always had a smile for everyone who walked in, even when the place was packed, and today was no different. When the bell over the door chimed, she glanced over from the taps behind the bar, where she was filling several tall glasses with ale.

"Hey, Cal. Your usual table is open."

"Thanks. Ellie's meeting me."

Rose's smile widened. "Oh, really? Have you two finally kissed and made up?"

I wish. "Strictly professional, I'm afraid."

She clucked her tongue. "That's too bad. Well, I'll send her over when she gets here. Want your usual?"

"That'd be great. I'm starving."

"You're always starving, Holden."

That was true, but mainly because he often forgot to eat while at work. He crossed the room and slid into the booth that had become "his" over the last few years. He'd spent as many hours working in this booth as he did in his office. It was where he met friends for drinks and sometimes clients. It was where he and Ellie had their first date.

He liked the comfortable familiarity of it.

Rose came by a moment later with his stout. He nursed the dark beer while he opened his briefcase and flipped through the file he'd compiled on Hope's disappearance. It was sadly thin. After a year of investigating, he thought he'd have more to show for it.

The only new information he'd found in months was the girl. Her picture lay right on top, and he picked it up, studied it. Now that he knew she was Ellie's niece, he could see the resemblance. Same face shape. Same cute button nose. And they both had curly hair, though the girl's curls were dark and much looser than Ellie's tight blond ringlets.

He set the picture down just as Ellie slid into the seat across from him. As always when he saw her, his heart did a little boogie in his chest. "Hi. You made it."

"Hey." She looked at him over the rim of her glasses, and he was momentarily struck by how damn pretty her blue eyes were. They constantly changed shades. Sometimes, they were dark like a lake at sunrise, and other times, they were light and clear like the midday sky. Today, they were a stormy mix of the two, emotion swirling in their depths.

She nervously twirled a lock of hair around her finger. "You're looking at me like I'm a puzzle you're trying to solve."

You are.

He shrugged, suppressing the feelings that always fluttered in his stomach when she was near. It was a battle he constantly lost.

After a moment, when he did respond verbally, she broke

eye contact and unzipped her bag, pulling out the thick binder she'd had with her earlier. "I did some more research…"

He grinned at that. Of course she had. Research was her life. "Find anything new?"

"Maybe. Look at this." She shifted the binder to open it and pointed at a printed photo. It was of the girl—maybe five years younger—in the same white robe, but it was a group photo this time. There were about twenty people, all wearing the same flowing garments, their faces varying degrees of serene and stoic. They stood before an old but well-kept house nestled among towering redwood trees. "I found it in a Reddit thread about escaping cults. The user who posted it didn't respond when I asked about the picture."

Before Cal could comment, Rose appeared at their booth with another mug of beer for him, a glass of white wine for Ellie, and a plate of nachos piled high.

"You're mostly through that one, Cal," she said, nodding at his half-empty pint. "Thought you might want a top-up."

"Thanks," he replied, sliding his original glass toward her.

But her attention had already moved on to the picture on the table between them. Something in her eyes had Cal sitting up straighter. He held up the photo. "Do you recognize these people?"

Rose hesitated a beat. "Not the people specifically, but they're all from the commune."

Both Cal and Ellie stared at her.

"What commune?" Cal asked.

"The one on the mountain. My parents and I lived there for a while when I was a kid, but I guess they started getting weird vibes, so we left."

Ellie frowned. "What kind of weird vibes?"

"I don't know. I was only five or six when we left, but I do remember those robes." She hitched a chin toward the kitchen. "My dad's here today working the kitchen. I can ask if he's willing to come out and talk about it if you want."

"We'd appreciate that," Cal said. As Rose started to turn away, his conscience got the better of him, and he added, "You should know your husband warned us away from this."

She glanced back and lifted an eyebrow. "Did he?"

"Thought you should know before you got involved. I don't want to cause any problems between you."

Rose scoffed and waved a dismissive hand. "Aw, don't worry about us. Fighting is our love language. If Mr. Grumpy has a problem with me talking to you, he'll get over it. Eventually."

Ellie gave a soft chuckle, toying with the glass Rose had just placed before her. "I wish I could be more like her," she said more to herself than anyone else. "Not caring what others think."

Cal turned his gaze to Ellie, her glasses reflecting the pub's dim light. He reached out to touch her hand, still wrapped around the glass. She looked surprised but didn't pull away, which he took as a sign she was softening toward him again.

Progress.

"You're perfect just as you are."

She avoided his eyes, focusing on the melting ice cubes in her drink. "This is strictly professional," she reminded and drew her hand away from his.

Fuck.

He smothered a flare of annoyance with a long drink of his beer. With her, it was always one step forward, two steps back.

A few minutes passed in awkward silence before a man appeared at their table. Pete Galasso. He looked every bit the aging hippie he was. He wore a tie-dye T-shirt under his apron and had his long gray hair pulled back into a ponytail under a hair net. His eyes were kind, albeit wary beneath bushy brows. He pulled the hairnet off and took a seat next to Cal.

"Hey, Pete," Cal said.

Pete nodded a polite hello even though apprehension filled his eyes. "So my Wildflower says you're looking into the commune on the mountain? What do you want to know?"

"We think my sister Hope may have joined them at some point, probably around twenty years ago." Ellie pulled up a picture of Hope on her phone and showed it to him. He studied it carefully before shaking his head.

"Sorry, we left around that time. I don't recognize her."

Disappointment flickered over Ellie's face before she hid it. "She's been missing for all these years, and the commune is the first real lead we have. Whatever you can tell us about them will be helpful."

"I'll tell you what I remember. There were..." He trailed off and gave a self-deprecating laugh. "A lot of drugs involved in those days."

"Do you mind if I record our conversation?"

"No, not at all."

She took her phone back, opened a recording app, and set it in the middle of the table.

Pete glanced at the device, then blinked and leaned back in his seat. "Well, where do I start?"

"Let's start with the basics. What was the commune called?" Ellie asked, adjusting her glasses as she looked at Pete.

God, she was sexy when she went into podcaster mode.

And that was not an appropriate thought right now.

"When we were there," Pete began, "they called themselves The Free People. We thought it was perfect—my wife, Harmony, and I were young and idealistic with a baby girl that we didn't want to raise in a greedy capitalist society. We were looking for community and spiritual enlightenment. The People taught that shunning the trappings of modern society allowed you to live closer to nature as God intended. And it was so peaceful at first. Communal living, self-sustainability.

They even had their own schooling system." He frowned. "But a few years in, things began to change."

"What kind of changes?" Cal asked.

"It was subtle at first. New rules and obedience to those rules became paramount. Our contact with family and friends outside the commune became severely limited, which had never been a problem before. Nobody cared if you wanted to go into town, but suddenly, leaving the commune became almost taboo. We had these communal confession sessions that I thought were so freeing, but then they started to feel like interrogations, public shaming. People were expected to confess their darkest secrets, and then the council would use it against them later as a means of control."

Ellie frowned. "How did they use the confessions to control people?"

Pete sighed, running a hand over his ponytail. "Well, for example, if you confessed that you missed your family on the outside, it would be seen as you being attached to the materialistic world. You'd be shamed for it and then made to do some atonement work."

"Atonement work?" Cal did not like the sounds of that.

Pete winced. "Physical labor mostly, breaking rocks or digging holes. They put up an eight-foot fence around the commune that way. Sometimes, depending on the severity of the infraction, the atonement could last for days on end with little food or water."

Ellie gave a small gasp. "That... that's inhumane."

Pete nodded sadly. "Yes. Yes, it was. And that was when I started seeing the writing on the wall. Our peaceful commune was starting to give Jonestown vibes, and I didn't want to be involved anymore, but it took Harmony a bit longer to come around." His gaze drifted over to his daughter as she laughed with their patrons at the bar. "It wasn't until Shepherd, the leader, started showing an inordinate amount of attention to our girl that Harmony finally saw it, too. We left that night. Moved back to town, eventually opened this pub..." He waved a hand to encompass the room. "And tried to forget about them."

Cal followed his gaze to Rose, and his stomach churned. "Any idea if Hope could have been brought in for... the same reason you mentioned?" He had to force the question out.

Pete's gaze was grave as he looked at Ellie. "It's possible. Shepherd had a thing for pretty young women."

Tears welled in Ellie's eyes, but she blinked them back. She put up a brave front, but Cal could see her trembling hands. He resisted the urge to reach out and wrap his hand over hers. She wouldn't accept the gesture. Not from him.

So, instead, he refocused on Pete. "Do you know if anyone tried to leave after things started to get bad? Is there anyone else we can talk to who might have seen Hope?"

Pete frowned. "There were more defectors, from what I heard, but they were few and far between. Shepherd had a way of making people fear the outside world—he called it the corrupting influence of capitalism and industrialization. His favorite saying was, "The more time spent outside the walls, the more corrupt the soul.' It was bullshit meant to keep people inside."

His voice grew faint and distant like he was lost in the memories. "You know, it sounds weird, but the hardest part wasn't leaving. It was adjusting back to normal life. By then, we'd lived in a constant state of fear for so long that small things—like going grocery shopping or watching TV—felt strange, almost unnatural."

He shook his head and seemed to come back to the present. "I know it don't make sense how folks get pulled into something like that, but they prey on the vulnerable, ya know? We were just searching for something, a place where we could belong and be free. But it turned out to be anything but. if your sister got involved and hasn't been seen since... I'm sorry to say you might never get her back. Their hold is that great."

Ellie was quiet for a moment, staring at the table with a hard set to her jaw. She was fighting back tears, trying to keep her emotions in check. She slid her file across the table and pulled out the print of the girl from the country store. She set it in front of Pete. "Can you tell me the significance of the robe and belt?"

Again, he studied the photo closely, his brows drawn together in concentration. "I'm sorry. The robes weren't really a thing when we were there. Shepherd wore a white one occasionally, but it was mostly for special occasions like weddings."

"Thank you, Pete," Ellie said. Her voice was soft and strained. "You've been incredibly helpful. I... we appreciate it."

"Wish I could do more," Pete replied solemnly as he slid out of the booth, his face lined with years of worry and regret.

"You've done enough. We know more than we did, and that helps."

Ellie gathered her things and got up from the table. Cal resisted the urge to tell her it would be okay. The truth was he didn't know that—they were dealing with potential cult activity, and there were far too many unknowns.

Which made him think of another question. "Hey, Pete?"

The older man paused. "Yeah?"

"You said the commune was called The Free People when you were there. Did they change their name?"

His eyes flickered to Ellie with something like shame before he nodded. "After I left, heard they started calling themselves Hope's Embrace."

chapter
nine

"THAT CAN'T BE A COINCIDENCE." Ellie felt like she'd downed five espresso shots and then chased them with a Red Bull. She couldn't relax enough to get into her car and drive home, so she did laps around it in the parking lot instead.

They finally, finally, after all these years, had a solid lead.

Cal leaned against the hood and crossed his arms in front of him, watching her pace. "Hope disappears, and at the same time, the cult starts to change? No, it's not a coincidence."

Ellie nodded and pressed a hand to her chest to keep her heart from trying to hammer out of her ribcage. "What if... what if Hope is still there? Still with them?"

"Except the girl said she's missing."

The girl.

God.

Hope's daughter.

Ellie slammed to a halt at the reminder and swung around to face him. "She was raised there, wasn't she? If Hope has been there all this time, then she's never known life outside of the commune. She's never known her family. Did Hope tell her about us? Did the cult convince her we abandoned her?

We never would've left her there if we'd known! We didn't know..."

Cal pushed off the car to stand in front of her. She didn't realize how hard she was suddenly shaking until his hands landed on her shoulders, grounding her.

"Ellie." His voice was gentle. "We don't know anything for sure yet. We have leads, and we need to follow them before we start assuming."

He was right. As always, he was the voice of reason when her thoughts were zooming by at breakneck speed, and her heart threatened to overtake her head. "We know she's my niece."

"Okay. We do know that for sure."

She sucked in a deep breath and released it, feeling it carry away some of her frenzied energy. "We need to be smart about this, not just... run in screaming."

A smile tugged at the corner of his mouth. "Exactly. We need more information and a plan."

Okay. Right. Information she could do. It was kind of her whole life, after all. Now that they had a name for the commune, she'd dig up everything she could find on it.

She took a step back, out of Cal's reach, and pulled out her phone, quickly typing into a search engine.

And there they were.

Just like that.

"They have a website," she said incredulously. "It looks like they're still active. They even have a contact number and an address."

Cal leaned over to look as she scrolled through their homepage. "Wait. Go back." He pointed. "What's that?"

She scrolled back to the advertisement that had caught his eye and frowned at it. "It looks like some kind of couples retreat," she said.

"For the low, low price of four thousand dollars." His

eyebrows winged up. "And here I thought they were against capitalism."

"Apparently not against profiting from it." She scanned the details of the retreat. It was a five-day immersive experience in 'building trust and communication,' whatever that meant. She shook her head and moved to scroll past it, but an idea struck. "What if...?"

Cal shook his head. "If it's the same crazy idea I just had, it's not a good one."

A shiver of anticipation rippled through her. She loved Cal's crazy ideas; they were usually incredibly effective, so if his mind had gone to the same place, maybe it would work. "We could sign up for the retreat. It starts on Monday."

"Dammit, Ellie. Don't make me be the voice of reason here. It's too risky."

"But it's an opportunity for us to get inside. If my sister and niece are there, I owe it to them to do everything in my power to get them out. And the girl reached out to you. She wanted you to help her."

He crossed his arms over his chest. "If we do this, we can't stay strictly professional."

Right. Shit. She hadn't thought of that.

"We can... pretend to be a couple for a few days." Her cheeks flushed hot, and she looked back down at the screen, scrolling through the pictures of couples with weirdly ecstatic expressions. Her heart sank. "No, you're right. That's stupid. Nobody will believe us."

He scowled and closed the distance between them. "Why the hell not? We were a couple once."

"Barely." He was too close, and he smelled too good. She swallowed hard as memories washed over her and tried to back away, only to find herself trapped by the side of her car. Yes, they had been a couple. But that was a lifetime ago, and despite the occasional lapse in judgment, like after the wedding, she wasn't about to jump back into that part of their past. "But that was different. We were real then."

Cal's scowl softened as his hands skimmed from her shoulders down her arms. His gaze lowered to her lips before returning to hers. "What I feel for you is still real, Ellie. You may deny it, but it is."

The words hit her like a punch, knocking all the air out of her lungs. She squeezed her eyes closed. As if shutting out the sight of his serious expression would make the feelings he stirred inside her less potent. "This is not the time to—"

"To what? To remind you that I love you?" His voice was a soft caress. "There's always time for that."

"No." She took a determined step back from him, straightening her spine. "This is about Hope. Not us."

"It doesn't have to be one or the other." There was a vulnerability in his gaze that she'd rarely seen in him. It unnerved her, making her feel raw and exposed.

Ugh. Why had she suggested they pretend to be a couple? Since moving to California, Cal had always been a constant in her life in one way or another, but she'd always been able to push him away when things got too deep, too real. But if they were stuck together for a week in a potentially dangerous situation, she'd have no defenses against him.

What a stupid idea.

"Cal," she warned, but her voice sounded weak even to herself. "Just forget I mentioned it. I'll find someone else to—"

"Oh, hell no. If you think you're going up there with anyone else, you're mistaken." He closed the distance between them. "You can't fake it convincingly with anyone else. You're not that good of a liar, sweetheart. You wear all of your emotion on this beautiful face." He cupped her cheeks in his hands, his thumb stroking lightly over her lips, sending shivers up her spine. "We can be a couple having trouble, which we technically are."

She rolled her eyes, trying to push down the warmth that was spreading through her at his touch. "No, we're not."

"But we could be if you weren't so damn stubborn."

"Cal..." She couldn't think clearly when he touched her and took a step to the side, breaking their contact. He let her go, dropping his hands to his sides, but he didn't back away. His gaze remained steady on hers, an intensity in his eyes that she didn't care to interpret.

She cleared her throat and looked back down at her phone again to avoid his gaze. "Okay," she said reluctantly. She could do this. She had to do this if she had any chance of finding Hope and her niece.

Cal nodded and let out a breath as if he'd been holding it in. "So we agree? We book the retreat as a couple and use that time to snoop around while we're there."

Ellie shot him a sharp look. "I just want a look inside the commune. We're not spies, Cal."

He grinned, and she hated how much she loved that mischievous glint in his eyes. "Speak for yourself, Summers. I always fancied myself as Bond. James Bond."

Despite herself, Ellie laughed. And just like that, the tension between them eased. Only Cal could make her laugh in the face of danger—albeit danger they were willingly walking into. "Be that as it may, if it starts to get dangerous, we leave."

"Agreed. I'll handle the registration," he said, taking her phone to enter their details into the online form. "We'll be... Calvin and..."

"Elena," she suggested. "It's what people always think Ellie is short for. I don't know why it has to be short for anything. It's just my name."

He sent her a quick grin and typed it in. "Elena. Perfect.

Calvin and Elena Smith—no, that's too obvious." He deleted the surname and considered it for a moment. "Miller. It's common enough but not so common that it sounds fake. Cal and Ellie Miller from... Eureka."

Ellie watched him, her heart thumping in her chest. Part of her was thrilled at their plan, and another part was terrified of what it might mean for them. "But what if they check our IDs?"

"I doubt a place like this is big on government identification. They're doing this retreat because they want money and probably converts. They're not going to care who we are or where we're from. Yeah, see?" He showed her the phone. "They want us to bring the payment in cash. Cults don't like digital trails."

As Cal handed back her phone, his fingers brushed against hers. The tiny touch sent an electric shock through her that had nothing to do with static electricity.

She pulled her hand back quickly, tucking a loose curl behind her ear. "Right," she murmured, trying to focus on the task at hand, not the sparks that Cal seemed to ignite in her with his every touch. "What about our story?"

He leaned against the side of her car and crossed his ankles as he pulled a pack of gum from his pocket. He offered her one. She declined, and he unwrapped his piece in thoughtful silence. With it came the bright scent of citrus that she always associated with him.

"We met a couple of years ago," he said finally, folding the stick of gum into his mouth.

"Well, yeah. We did."

"Exactly. We stick as close to the truth as possible." He pointed at her. "It was love at first sight, and we were married within a year."

She snorted. "I wouldn't marry anyone after only a year."

"I swept you off your feet." He gave that crooked smile

that had beguiled more women than just her. "You couldn't resist my dashing good looks and charm."

"I have so far."

He ignored that and continued like she hadn't spoken. "I recited poetry to you under the stars, and we danced to a single guitar playing soft music. You realized I was the one for you."

"That's cheesy."

"You like cheesy."

She rolled her eyes but couldn't help a small laugh. He was right. She was a sucker for cheesy romantic gestures. "Right, and I suppose you convinced me to move to Eureka for a fresh start."

"Exactly. And now the honeymoon is over, and we're having trouble. We stumbled on their website and felt a spiritual calling to attend the retreat. They eat that stuff up."

It was a reasonable story, close enough to the truth that they shouldn't trip up over the lie. "What about our jobs?"

"I'm a lawyer, and you're..." He trailed off and rubbed a hand over his face. "Aw, fuck. We can't tell them you produce true crime podcasts. They won't like that." He snapped his fingers at a sudden thought. "But they will if we leave out the true crime part. We'll tell them you're a podcast producer specializing in spiritual and self-help topics. That's close to the truth and might earn us some brownie points with them."

She made a face. "They're going to try to recruit me, aren't they?"

"Oh, definitely. They're going to try to recruit us both, Elena."

Her heart stuttered at the new name, making her feel like a different person already. The invisible strings drawing her closer to Cal tightened around her heart. She forced a laugh through her tightening throat, chiding herself silently. This was just another ruse. Another thing they had to play at.

But even as she told herself this, she couldn't help but

wonder if it would feel real — and what it would do to her already shaky feelings for him.

"Just remember this is just a cover, *Calvin*." She congratulated herself at his slight wince when she stressed the name. "Once we're out of there, everything goes back to normal between us."

Cal just smiled at her, his eyes sparkling with the irresistible, mischievous light that made her heart race. "Nothing about us is ever going to be normal, sweetheart."

She swallowed hard as she met his eyes, suddenly overwhelmed by the intensity of his gaze. She felt a jolt of something unfamiliar in her stomach— fear? Excitement? She couldn't tell.

"I have to get back to the office and rearrange things for the week." He pushed away from the car. "And you need to find someone to puppy sit."

Oh, crap.

Puzzle.

She hadn't even considered what she'd do with him while they enacted this crazy plan, but now the thought of leaving him for so long had her stomach twisting into knots.

She must have looked shell-shocked because Cal leaned in and brushed his lips against her cheek. "We'll be okay. It's only a week. Go deal with your pup. I'll call you this weekend."

chapter
ten

"I **HAVE** to go out of town for a week. It's... for a work thing." It wasn't entirely a lie—Ellie was planning to pitch the idea of a podcast on cults, so the trip could be considered research—but the way Anna was watching her made it feel like one. She told herself to stop fidgeting. "And, uh, I was hoping Puzzle could stay at the rescue while I'm gone." She looked down at her puppy. Puzzle leaned against her leg and stared back with big brown eyes that reminded her of Cal's.

"Of course he can stay," Anna said. "He's always welcome, and Clue is here while Alexis and Shane are on their honeymoon so they can room together."

Puzzle's tail swished on the floor at the sound of Clue's name. He loved playing with her, but his excitement still didn't assuage Ellie's guilt for leaving him. "Thank you so much."

Anna frowned as she accepted his leash. "But I thought you were taking time off, too, this week."

"I was." She ruffled Puzzle's soft fur with her free hand, avoiding Anna's probing gaze. "But something came up. It's... complicated."

"Complicated," Anna echoed doubtfully. "You mean Cal complicated?"

Dammit, why did she have to be so fair-skinned? She couldn't hide the slight flush that spread across her cheeks. "No, not... It's not like that."

Anna's frown deepened, her grip tightening on Puzzle's leash. "El, you don't have to hide anything from me. You know that, right?"

"Yeah, I know..." Ellie stammered out, shifting uncomfortably under Anna's knowing gaze. She knew she could trust Anna with everything, but this—this was different. She wasn't even sure if she understood what was going on between her and Cal fully. How, then, could she explain it to someone else?

"Look," she said finally, "I'll be fine. We—I mean, Cal and I—we're working on something together. Something important." She hesitated, then added, "It's about Hope."

Anna's eyes widened in surprise. "Hope?"

"It may be nothing, but we're going to look into it."

"You and Cal." Anna's brows disappeared under the fringe of her bangs. "Together."

"We're not together. It's strictly professional. I'll be back in a week."

Anna gave a slight nod, but her face was still etched with concern. The usually bustling kennel was quiet, the dogs either out on walks or curled in their beds asleep. Anna walked over to the holding pen, unlatching the door and allowing Puzzle to gallop in with a happy bark.

"I have everything he needs for the week packed in his bag," Ellie said as she handed over a duffle bag filled with dog food, toys, and his favorite blanket. She crouched down to level with Puzzle, scratching behind his ears. "You be good for Anna, okay? Mama will be back soon." Puzzle wagged his tail violently in response.

As she straightened up, she noticed Pierce entering the

room out of the corner of her eye. He nodded in greeting before passing them by to fetch his dog, Raszta, from a nearby kennel.

She watched as Pierce signed a series of commands to the dog. Raszta responded instantly, dropping into a sit and giving the former soldier his undivided attention.

For a moment, she felt a pang of envy. The connection between them was palpable, formed out of trust and respect and something more— companionship. It was the same bond she longed to share with Puzzle.

"You sure you're okay?" Anna asked, breaking her from her thoughts.

She nodded and forced a smile. "Yeah, I'm fine. I'm just going to miss this little troublemaker." She gestured to Puzzle, who was sniffing around his new surroundings.

Anna didn't seem entirely convinced. "Whatever you two are doing, please be careful."

"We will," she promised and glanced back one last time at Puzzle, who was now happily playing with a squeaky toy. The guilt almost overwhelmed her. She had no idea what was waiting for her on this 'retreat' with Cal. She only hoped she was making the right decision by going.

Back home, Ellie packed her bag with an unnerving sense of uncertainty. Maybe it was the way Cal looked at her earlier, or maybe it was just the unease of getting involved in something beyond her control that made her hands tremble ever so slightly as she folded her shirts—either way, she couldn't shake the feeling of apprehension.

She chastised herself for her nerves, knowing that if she wanted any answers about Hope, she needed to be strong. She made sure to pack her recording equipment for her podcast as well— this could potentially be the story of a lifetime.

As she zipped up her suitcase, her phone buzzed with a text from Cal.

6 am tomorrow. I'll pick you up.

She shoved the phone into her pocket, feeling slightly sick. She had never been good at masking her feelings – they were written all over her face and, more often than not, acted upon impulsively.

How the hell was she going to convince people that she and Cal were a couple?

The next morning, as promised, Cal was waiting outside. Instead of his flashy sports car, he had a dust-covered SUV. There was something eerily peaceful about it all—the stillness of the morning, the barely audible rustle of the trees in the chilly breeze, and the soft purr of the engine. It felt like the calm before an inevitable storm.

As Ellie approached, Cal stepped out of the vehicle and walked over to her. The wind had tousled his hair, and his eyes held that familiar mischievous twinkle. He all but buzzed with excitement, like a kid on his way to Disney.

He was enjoying this.

How the hell was he enjoying this when her stomach was in so many knots that she felt like she'd swallowed a ball of yarn?

"Morning." He reached for her suitcase, then pulled open the passenger door for her. "Ready?"

His voice was casual, as if they were headed out on a simple road trip. Nothing more.

No. She wasn't ready in the least.

"As I'll ever be. Where's your car?" she asked as she slid into the seat. Her heart pounded with anticipation and anxiety. She wished she could match his carefree demeanor, but the effort was beyond her reach. She was too nervous.

"Traded with Pierce for the week," Cal replied. "Figured we'd run into rugged terrain."

"I just saw him last night when I dropped Puzzle off at the rescue. He didn't mention..." She trailed off and flushed. Of course Pierce didn't mention it. He couldn't talk due to an injury he'd sustained in the Army and communicated primarily through sign language. While she'd learned a little bit over the past year, it wasn't enough to hold a conversation. "When did you find the time to learn sign language?"

Was the man made of energy?

"When I realized it would be useful in my line of work. Defendants come in all shapes, sizes, and communication methods. And I like Pierce. He's an interesting guy, and I wanted to be able to talk to him." He gently shut her door, circled the back to stow her suitcase, and then climbed behind the wheel.

"You continue to surprise me, Callum," she murmured.

For once, Cal didn't respond with a smirk or a cocky retort. Instead, he flicked a glance at her. "It's important to stay versatile."

Ellie looked at him sidelong as he shifted into reverse and backed out of her driveway. He wore an expression of seriousness that she seldom saw in him. Could it be that he was as nervous as she was about their little excursion?

She wanted to ask him, but some part of her was afraid of what his answer might be.

"Oh," he said suddenly. "Check in the glove box."

Ellie hesitated before opening it and sucked in a sharp breath when she saw the ring box sitting there.

She slowly picked up the box. It was expensive-looking, a velvety black case that could only mean one thing. She glanced at Cal, who still wore that unfamiliar serious expression.

"I— what is this?" Her voice was strangled. Her heart banged around in her chest like a wild thing trying to escape.

"Just open it," Cal responded, his voice firm but gentle.

With trembling fingers, she did. A beautiful princess-cut diamond sparkled at her from its satin bed. She gasped, caught between awe and panic. She couldn't form words.

"We're playing a married couple," he reminded.

Nope.

No way.

She shut the ring box and stuffed it back into the glove compartment. "Okay, I think we should set some ground rules for this... this undercover mission."

Cal blinked at her in surprise. "Ground rules?"

"Like... while we're at the retreat. We're just pretending to be a couple, so no..." She looked down at her hands in her lap. "No physical stuff. No kissing. Definitely no sex."

He frowned. "If I can't touch you, people will get suspicious."

"Not necessarily. Lots of couples don't like PDAs. Besides, we're playing the part of a couple in marital trouble. This is the last-ditch effort for Cal and Ellie Miller to save their marriage."

His scowl only deepened, and it looked weird on him. His face was made for grinning. "But we want them to think their program is healing us, so, at some point, we'll need to at least—"

"We can hug," she decided. "Nothing else."

"Okay," he said slowly and focused on the road. She crossed her arms over her chest and tried not to look at the glove box.

chapter
eleven

THE CAR ROLLED TO A STOP, the gravel beneath its tires crunching like bones in the quiet. Cal killed the engine, and for a moment, they just sat there, the weight of their mission pressing down on them like the thick silence of the surrounding woods.

"Here we are," Cal murmured, his gaze lingering on Ellie, her silhouette haloed by the morning sun streaming through the car window. He noted the way her curly blond hair framed her face, the freckles on her cheeks more pronounced from the reflection of light. Her blue eyes, usually so full of joy, were now steely with a stubborn resolve that reminded him why he'd fallen for her. The woman who loved facts and danced through life was ready to dance into danger.

Jesus, this was a stupid idea.

He turned to face her. "Elle, we don't have to— there are other ways to—"

"Let's do this." She pushed her glasses up the bridge of her nose and sucked in a deep breath before stepping out of the car.

Fuck.

Cal dropped his forehead to the steering wheel and cursed

at himself for agreeing to this. While wrapped in the familiar safety of the town, it seemed like a great idea. They were both intelligent, logical people, so he'd thought there was no chance of them falling for the cult's line of bullshit. He thought they'd simply spend the few days of the retreat poking around and then go back to Ash with some solid proof that something nefarious was happening up here. But he'd spent the last few days reading everything he could find on cults, and now he wasn't so sure. Intelligent, logical people got sucked into them all the time. In fact, most cults wanted intelligent, well-educated people.

Heaving a sigh, Cal climbed out of the car, squinting against the bright morning light. There was a peaceful serenity to this place that unnerved him. All was quiet except for a gurgling brook somewhere nearby and the rustle of leaves overhead. A half dozen buildings painted a cheerful yellow, rose from the middle of an emerald sea of grass. Farther away, he could see what appeared to be a large garden, a neat array of brightly colored flowers forming a kaleidoscope against the backdrop of the towering Redwood trees surrounding them.

A breeze lifted his hair, and for a fleeting second, he allowed himself to be awed by the undisturbed beauty of the mountainside.

But every paradise had its snake.

As they approached the commune, a group emerged from the main building. All of them wore light blue robes, and their smiles were as bright as the sun. They opened their arms to embrace Ellie first and then Cal, like a long-lost family. There was an ease to their gait, a tranquility in their eyes that made Cal's inner Golden Retriever want to trust them.

No. Down, boy.

"Welcome!" they chimed in unison, a chorus so perfectly pitched it sent a shiver down his spine.

"Hello," Ellie responded with a stilted smile. Nobody here

would see the tension in it, but only because they'd never been blinded by her real smile, the one that made her eyes twinkle, her cheeks rosy, and warmed his soul—the one that he'd fallen for, the one he yearned to see every day.

The cult members surrounded them with a buzz of conversation, the air thick with the scent of lavender and something else, something Cal couldn't quite place. Something that spoke of earth and growth but also carried a note of something... else. Something ugly. Something hidden just beneath the surface, like the subtle hint of decay beneath a bed of roses.

A woman stepped forward from the group. Her long golden hair cascaded down to her waist, reflecting the morning sun like a halo. She was in her mid-twenties and radiated tranquility as if she were part of the landscape itself. "My name is Serenity. I'm here to ensure your journey within our community is enlightening, so do not hesitate to seek my guidance." She spoke with a gentle smile. "You must be Calvin and Elena Miller."

Cal glanced at Ellie. Her posture, rigid with tension, contrasted sharply against Serenity's calm demeanor. He reached out, his fingers brushing lightly against Ellie's in a silent reassurance. She gripped his hand and seemed to relax a tiny bit.

"Yes, I'm Ellie, and this is my"— there was a slight hitch in her voice— "husband, Cal. I hope we're not late."

"Oh, no. You're right on time. Come," Serenity beckoned, turning to lead them toward the cluster of yellow buildings. "Let me show you around."

As they followed their ethereal guide down a wooded path. They passed more people in robes along the way—some were green, but most were brown.

"What is the significance of the robes?" Cal asked.

Ellie's grip tightened on his. Her hand was cold, and he

could feel her pulse thrumming like a trapped bird beneath his touch. She needed reassurance, comfort. He gave her hand a gentle squeeze in return, rubbing his thumb soothingly over the back of her knuckles.

Serenity smiled back at them. If she was startled by the question, she didn't show even a flicker of it. "It's the path we all follow to enlightenment. The lighter the color, the closer you are to Mother God."

"So you think God is female?"

"I know she is. Women are creators of life." Serenity swept a hand toward a field of wildflowers spilling down the mountain from the edge of the compound. "A man couldn't create this kind of beauty. He couldn't even dream it."

A man stepped into their path then. Tall and broad-shouldered, he carried himself with a military bearing and assessed them with an unmistakable wariness. He was the only one they'd seen so far not wearing a robe. Instead, he wore tactical pants and a tight black shirt that showed off his heavily muscled arms.

"Vigil," he grunted by way of introduction, extending a firm hand toward Cal. "Head of security."

Cal shook the offered hand, clamping down on the urge to grimace at the vice-like grip. If this guy thought he could be bullied, he was dumber than he looked.

"Calvin," he answered with an easy smile. "Friends call me Cal."

Vigil didn't seem to like that he wasn't intimidated. His lips thinned into a hard line, his dark brown eyes flitting to Ellie, then back to Cal. "A pleasure," he said, voice just this side of polite. "If you have any cell phones or other recording devices, you need to leave them with me."

"Our phones?" Ellie's eyebrows shot up, and her hand twitched toward the pocket of her jeans, where her phone was tucked away.

They'd expected this. Had planned for it, bringing along phones that matched their cover stories. No way they were going to hand over their real phones for someone to snoop through.

Stay the course, Elle.

Cal squeezed her hand again, but his gaze never left Vigil's. Something about the man had all of his internal alarm bells clanging.

"No problem," he replied smoothly, reaching into his pocket to retrieve his phone.

Ellie still didn't move.

He nudged her. "Sweetheart? I know you're glued to that thing, but that's part of our problem, isn't it? We already decided no phones this week."

"But I didn't know we had to actually give them up! What if—"

"Honey..." He made sure to inject a bit of exasperation into his tone. "We discussed this. Give the man your phone. You can live without it for a few days."

Reluctantly, Ellie withdrew her phone from her pocket and handed it over.

Vigil inspected each phone once over before putting them inside a metal box that he carried. "Thank you for your cooperation," he said flatly, sliding the box shut with a clunk. His gaze lingered on Ellie a moment longer before he turned and disappeared into one of the yellow buildings.

"We do things a little differently here." Serenity's voice was soft, her blue eyes full of what seemed to be genuine sympathy. "We believe in connection and presence, not virtual distractions. Our community is based on transparency, trust, and understanding. We believe that by disconnecting from the technology of the world, you grow as a person and as a couple. And that's why you're here, isn't it?"

"Yes," Ellie admitted grumpily and glanced at Cal. "I guess

so. This was his idea." Her words had a slight accusatory tone that was hard to miss.

Okay, so she was going for a good cop, bad cop approach and painting herself as the skeptic. He could play the part of the eager potential convert.

"I've done some reading about this place. About how it helps people communicate again. To feel again." He rubbed Ellie's back soothingly even as he met Serenity's gaze like they shared a secret. "We're here to find a way forward. To reconnect with each other."

Serenity nodded, a smile playing on her lips. "That is precisely what we aim to achieve. We hope you will find the experience transformative."

As they moved further into the compound, Cal's eyes swept the area, taking in every detail—the layout, the people. He noticed one building in the center of the compound that wasn't dusty yellow like all the others but painted a bright white with gold trim. It reminded him of a smaller version of the ornate Mormon temples he'd seen while visiting a law school friend in Salt Lake City last year. "What's that over there? Looks fancy."

Serenity's gaze followed his pointing finger. "That's our sacred space. It's off-limits except to a select few."

In the communal garden, they passed another woman in a blue robe. With round cheeks and loose, gray-streaked hair falling over her shoulders, she gave off cozy grandma vibes—not really what Cal pictured when he thought of a cult member. She was tending to a cluster of herbs, and the scent of rosemary and thyme drifted on the breeze, mingling with the rich aroma of freshly turned earth.

"This is Remedy," Serenity introduced. "Our healer."

At his side, Ellie sneezed.

"Sorry," she apologized. "Must be allergies."

With a gesture that was at once gracious and soothing,

Remedy lifted her stained hands from their work and approached them. "Perhaps a cup of nettle tea might help? It has wonderful anti-allergic properties."

"Oh. Um... I've never had nettle tea."

"You're in luck. I happen to have some brewing now." She wiped her hands on her apron and crossed to a kettle hanging over the small fire pit. She poured steaming liquid into two small, handmade cups and handed one to Cal and one to Ellie. "Just one sip, and I promise you'll feel better."

Ellie looked at the cup for a moment, then up at Cal. Part of him wanted to knock it out of her hands. After all, they had no idea what was really in the cup. But the commune wanted to impress them, right? By offering these retreats, they were hoping for converts, so it was unlikely they'd put anything harmful in there. He finally lifted a shoulder, silently telling her it was her choice.

Ellie nervously twisted the cup in her hands. "Did you know that during World War I, when traditional sources of cotton were scarce, nettles were cultivated and used as a substitute for making uniforms and other textile goods?"

Remedy chuckle. "I did not know that."

Yep, Ellie was definitely nervous. She only spouted off random facts like that when she was flustered.

Cal gave her a reassuring smile as he took a tentative sip of his own tea. It wasn't terrible, a little bitter, but not unbearable.

She watched him, then took a hesitant sip from her own cup, and her face brightened with surprise. "That's... actually really good. Kinda sweet and... earthy."

"Nettle tea is much maligned," Remedy said, a hint of amusement creeping into her voice. "But it's rather like us, don't you think? A bit weird and prickly on the outside, but warm and comforting once you get to know us."

Cal had to admit the woman was good—disarmingly so.

"Oh. Um..." Ellie seemed flustered. "I'm so sorry if I'm coming off as suspicious. I just..."

Remedy offered her a kind smile. "It's only natural. Change can be quite unsettling. But your presence here is healing already. Now, I have to return to work. The garden won't weed itself. It was very nice to meet you both." She bowed slightly to Serenity before drifting back to her garden, her bare feet silent on the grassy path.

Cal lifted his cup to his mouth again but didn't drink it. His attention snagged on the newcomer striding confidently toward them. The man exuded precision, from the crisp lines of his white tunic shirt under his blue robe to his measured gait.

"Cal, was it? I'm Merit." He extended a hand, the handshake firm and assessing. "I understand you're a man of the law. Must be fascinating work."

Cal recognized the type—men who calculated every move, every word, to maintain control. "Every day is different."

"Merit tends the community's monetary resources," Serenity explained. "He's here for your retreat fee."

"Oh, of course." Cal dug the envelope out of his pocket and tried not to wince as he passed it to the man. Defending criminals in rural California wasn't exactly a lucrative line of work, and he'd had to dip deep into his savings for the fee. Ellie had offered to pay, but he knew her financial situation was a bit more precarious than his since she and Alexis's new podcast network had yet to launch fully. "So, you're the money man?"

"Ah, it's a bit more than that. I manage all of our resources and ensure we thrive without outside dependencies." As Merit tucked the envelope into his robe, his eyes flickered with what might have been pride—or a well-disguised arrogance. "We're self-sufficient, a closed ecosystem of sorts. Our members contribute what they can, be it skills or finances, and in return, they share in the abundance we create."

"Sounds like an ideal arrangement," Cal said, choosing the words carefully to sound intrigued but not too eager.

"It is," Merit agreed, tilting his head slightly. "But enough about us—tell me, what brings a man with your background to our sanctuary?"

"Curiosity," he answered truthfully—or, at least, partially truthfully. He just didn't add that his curiosity was investigative, not spiritual. "I've always been interested in different ways of life."

"Ah, a seeker then!" Merit's eyes gleamed with approval, or maybe that was anticipatory dollar signs. "Well, you'll find no shortage of new experiences here."

Serenity gently cut into the conversation. "We should let them settle in before tonight's ceremony." She gave Merit a pointed glance, earning a small, contrite nod from the man.

"Of course," Merit said. "Please excuse my curiosity. It's refreshing to have new faces around."

With that, Merit turned on his heel and departed, leaving Ellie and Cal alone with Serenity once again.

"Everyone's so nice here," Ellie said. to anyone who didn't know her, they'd take the statement at face value, but he read the subtext was clear: everyone was too nice in her opinion, and she was silently freaking out.

As they continued their tour, they got a glimpse of the commune's daily life—members tending to gardens, practicing yoga under leafy canopies, or meditating near a burbling brook. Each person exuded an air of contentment that was palpable.

"Look at them," Ellie whispered, nodding toward a group of members tending to a lush vegetable garden. "They seem truly content."

He leaned down close to her ear so as not to be overheard. "Seem is the operative word there."

"Over there is our dining hall," Serenity pointed toward a massive thatched-roof structure with open sides. "And beyond it, you'll find our guest accommodations. Let me show you to your new home."

New home.

Like Serenity was already fully expecting them to convert.

Jesus.

She led them through a maze of tiny, cookie-cutter cottages nestled among the towering redwoods. The scent of pine filled the air, along with the distant murmur of a waterfall. It looked more like one of those fashionable eco-resorts popping up all down the coast rather than a cult's hideout, and the tranquility of it almost made Cal forget they weren't here for a romantic getaway.

"We hope you find everything to your liking," Serenity said and opened the door to one of the cabins.

Ellie stepped inside and froze. "Where are our suitcases?"

For the first time, a frown creased Serenity's brow. "You agreed to leave all earthly possessions behind when you signed up for the retreat."

Ellie whirled on him, wide-eyed. "You agreed to that?"

Cal didn't remember that in the fine print of the contract. And he'd read all of it. Twice. But he had to play his part.

"I, uh, didn't really read it."

Ellie scoffed. "I can't believe you. What will we wear?"

"You'll find fresh clothes inside, all made by us," Serenity said helpfully and crossed to the closet.

The dresses she pulled out were simple and plainly stitched in soft neutral shades. Ellie was more of a jeans and T-shirt kind of woman. Other than the dress at Alexis's wedding, he couldn't remember another time she'd worn one.

The clothes Serenity pulled out of the dresser for him

weren't much better—long tunics without a belt and cotton pants.

"Rest. Or explore, if you like. The sun is preparing to set, and a bonfire will be lit at dusk to celebrate your arrival. It's a tradition on your first night. You'll meet the other couples here for the retreat, and we'll share stories, sing songs..."

"Sounds cozy," Cal said.

"You'll love it. I promise." Serenity smiled once last time and departed, moving with an uncanny grace that made her seem like she was floating rather than walking.

As soon as the woman was beyond earshot, he shook his head. "Nobody is that smiley. Were you getting Stepford Wife vibes from her, too?"

Ellie spun toward him, her blue eyes wide behind her glasses. "What are we doing here?"

"We're trying to fix our marriage." He hoped she read the subtext in his words—they were probably being watched and recorded, and until he could check their new "home" for listening devices, they needed to be careful.

She understood. Of course she did. Ellie was one of the smartest people he'd ever known.

She looked at the floor and exhaled a long, slow breath. "I'm sorry. I know why we're here." Her tone told him loud and clear that she understood. "I just... This place is weird. Really weird. I don't know what I expected, but they're all so..."

"Intense?"

"No, that's not quite it," Ellie said, tapping a finger against her lips. "They're sincere. And all kind of... the same? They all walk the same way. Did you notice that? Like they're floating."

"Could be the effect of the herbal tea," he suggested with a dry chuckle, but she didn't join him in laughter.

"No, Cal, I'm serious."

Of course she was. She had an eye for detail that could rival a seasoned detective.

"Alright, what's your theory?" He asked, folding his arms across his chest and leaning back against the door frame. "I know you have one."

Ellie hesitated, biting her bottom lip. "I don't know yet. But something feels off here. The tranquility they all seem to possess... It feels too perfect."

His gaze skimmed over Ellie's worried expression, her eyes shimmering in the fading light. He impulsively lifted a hand to tuck a loose curl behind her ear, his touch causing her eyes to flicker up to his.

Ellie's breath hitched, and for a moment, they were both lost in the proximity until a knock on the door jolted them apart.

A man stepped in. Unlike the others, he wore regular clothes—slacks and a polo that seemed more at home on a golf course than in a rustic commune. His sharp gaze lingered on their now widened distance with curiosity.

"Good afternoon," he said with a warm smile and held out a hand. "I'm Sincere."

Of course he was.

Cal had to cough to hide his laugh.

Ellie made bug eyes at him, then forced a smile and accepted Sincere's handshake. "I'm Ellie, and this is my husband, Calvin."

"Cal," he corrected quickly. He knew she was purposely using his cover name to annoy him. He should've picked a better one, but it had been all he could think of on short notice that was close enough to his real name to be believable.

"I know," Sincere said and shook Cal's hand next. "I handle all of the applications for the retreat. I hope you're settling in well."

"We are. Thanks."

"Excellent," Sincere said, still holding onto Cal's hand for a beat longer than necessary.

"How many other couples are here?" Ellie asked, and Sincere finally dropped his hand.

"You're one of four couples joining us this time." He removed his glasses to clean them on the corner of his shirt, and Cal caught a glint of something shrewd in his gaze that hadn't been there before. "I hope you're ready for the bonfire celebration tonight. It's nothing like you've ever experienced before."

"We're excited," Ellie said, though her face claimed otherwise. She really was a shit liar.

Cal held out an arm toward the door. "And speaking of, we should get ready."

Sincere bowed his head slightly. "Of course. If you need anything during your stay, I'm always available."

"Thank you so much," Ellie said. "You've all been so kind to us already."

Sincere excused himself, and as he left, Ellie spun. "He's not like the rest of them. Less... robotic. More normal. Maybe he can help us." When he didn't answer right away, she bounced on her toes. "So, what do you think?"

"I think," Cal said slowly, still staring at the door Sincere had disappeared through, "that we need to be very careful who we trust here."

chapter
twelve

"YOUR FIRST TIME?"

Ellie reluctantly tore her gaze away from the mesmerizing dance of the bonfire as it crackled and roared, sending sparks soaring into the night sky with each new log thrown on. The woman who had spoken was in her mid-fifties, with long, graying hair trailing in twin braids over her shoulders. She looked right at home here, but she wasn't dressed in the flowing white robes of the other commune members. She wore a multi-layered skirt in bright colors and a tank top that dipped low enough to tell anyone looking that the woman didn't believe in bras. She didn't believe in deodorant either, and the smell of her body odor was overpowering.

Ellie attempted a smile. "Um, yeah. That obvious?"

The woman nodded and took a seat on the log beside her. "I can always tell. My husband and I come every year." She nodded toward the man with a long gray beard and hair braided much like hers. He wore a leather vest over an open blue shirt and bright beads around his neck. He was in an animated conversation with Cal and another man Ellie hadn't met yet. "That's him. My Jeff."

Ellie turned to face the woman. "Are you a member of Hope's Embrace?"

The woman snorted a laugh and whacked Ellie's arm like she'd said something hilarious. "Oh, no. Commune living isn't for us. We like capitalism a little too much to move out here, but we do make this trip once a year. It's saved our marriage." She held out a hand. "I'm Marla."

"Ellie." She accepted Marla's hand. It was thin but deceptively strong.

"Good to meet you, Ellie." Marla's gaze strayed back across the fire to Jeff and Cal. "You're here with that handsome man?"

Ellie sighed and nodded, glancing over at Cal from the corner of her eye. He was laughing at something the businessman had said; his whole body relaxed in a way that seemed impossible, given their deception. Ellie couldn't relax. She felt like everyone there could see through her, especially the security guard, Vigil, who stood outside of the group, watching them all with suspicious eyes.

"That's Cal. He's my hus—" Her voice pitched up on the lie, and she broke off mid-sentence, clearing her throat. "My husband."

Marla offered a gentle smile. "It's that bad, huh?"

"What?"

She jerked her chin in Cal's direction. "Between you two?"

Heat rushed into her cheeks, and she dipped her head to hide the flush. She hoped Marla would mistake it for embarrassment and not shame.

"It's okay," Marla said softly. "I understand. Jeff and me? We were on the edge of divorce once, too. Even signed the papers. But we decided to give it one last shot and came here. This place... it does something to you, Ellie. It saved our marriage. It can save yours, too."

Ellie glanced at Cal. His hair looked almost golden in the

glow of the firelight, and his eyes sparkled as he traded verbal spars with Nico, a young gay man from San Francisco. He was enjoying himself.

Ellie's heart ached at the sight of him, so radiant and alive. His laughter floated across the warm night air. He was so much lighter here, she thought, away from the courtroom battles and endless tension that his job as a defense attorney brought.

She watched as he leaned in to listen to Nico's partner, Tyler, who was telling a story about their recent trip to Spain.

Cal's laughter cut through the night air. The sound washed over her, igniting a pang of something—jealousy? Longing? She wanted to be the one making Cal laugh, the one catching his interest.

"Give it a chance, Ellie," Marla said. "You'd be surprised what can happen if you let go and trust the process."

She broke her gaze from Cal and turned back to Marla. The older woman's eyes held wisdom and kindness that made her feel a bit safer.

If Marla and Jeff had been coming to the retreat for years, it couldn't be that dangerous, right?

"He looks at you like you're the only woman in the world," Marla said suddenly. "Your husband," she clarified when Ellie turned to look at her. "He's got eyes for no one but you."

She glanced back at Cal, catching his eye for a fleeting moment. "Really?"

"That man is crazy in love with you. Anyone can see it. So whatever is broken between you, you need to fix it while you're here and not let him go. Love like that doesn't happen for most people." With that, Marla got up and crossed over to join the others. Ellie stared after her in stunned silence, her heart banging around like a bouncy ball.

Crazy in love?

She wanted to dismiss it as nonsense but couldn't. Because if a stranger could so easily read his feelings, maybe they were real? Whenever he said he loved her, she always brushed it off as an exaggeration. After all, Cal was known around town as a womanizer and a sweet talker, and he always dropped the L-bomb right after they had sex. Of course he was only saying it because he thought that was what she wanted to hear.

Then again, she'd made it perfectly clear it was the last thing she wanted to hear from him, and yet he continued to say it anyway.

"Ellie?" Cal's voice cut through her thoughts, pulling her back to reality.

She turned and found him standing next to her, his eyes filled with concern. "Are you okay? You looked a million miles away."

"I'm fine," she lied, attempting to sound casual as she pushed her glasses up the bridge of her nose and looked away from him. She needed to put some distance between them, needed time to process what Marla had said.

Cal didn't press. Instead, he sat on the log beside her, his body radiating heat in the cool night air. They sat in comfortable silence, watching as the flames danced and flickered, casting shadows over the faces of the couples gathered around it.

Ellie felt a twinge of regret. She was here under false pretenses. These people were truly here to rekindle relationships, seeking solace and renewal, while she was chasing a ghost. The thought left a bitter taste in her mouth.

She'd expected to find something tonight. The girl. Hope. Or... at least a clue.

Cal's arm brushed against hers, the contact sending a jolt through her body, but neither of them moved to break it. His presence was comforting in ways she didn't want to analyze right at the moment.

He was watching the fire, too, lost in his own thoughts.

It was always these quiet moments with him that got to her. He wasn't the tenacious pit bull lawyer defending criminals now. Right now, he was just Cal—warm, steady, and thoughtful Cal.

He turned toward her and smiled, and a sharp pang of longing ignited in her belly. He lifted a hand and gently tucked a stray curl behind her ear.

No. Not again. She couldn't fall for his charm again.

She shifted away, putting as much distance between them as the log allowed.

Cal opened his mouth, but whatever he'd been about to say was interrupted by a drum beat.

The sound was primitive and rhythmic, echoing through the woods and vibrating under their feet. Everyone's attention turned to the source of the sound, a tall figure slowly emerging from the darkness beyond the firelight.

Vigil, with a large drum slung over his shoulder and a stick in his hand, was walking toward them with a determined stride. Behind him followed the other members of the commune they'd met earlier—Serenity, Remedy, Sincere, Merit, and others, about fifty people in total, all of them in robes ranging in color from brown to green to light blue. Ellie scanned the faces, but she saw nobody who looked like the one picture she had of Hope. And nobody among the handful of kids and teenagers who looked like Hope's daughter. Marla and Jeff joined the commune members as they formed a circle around the bonfire.

Finally came a man who Ellie assumed must be the leader, judging by his white robe and the reverence with which the others bowed to him as he approached, but he didn't look like any cult leader she'd ever researched. He didn't have the crazy eyes of Charles Manson, the slick oiliness of Jim Jones, or the militant intensity of David Koresh. Instead, he was lean and fit and younger than she'd expected—probably in his mid-to-late forties. He had dark hair going gray at the temples, a neat goatee, and kind eyes that crinkled with laugh lines at the corners. A blurry, faded tattoo circled his bicep. He extended a hand to each of the retreat couples and welcomed them into the circle.

The leader raised his hands, and the drumming ceased. "We gather tonight under the light of the full moon to welcome new travelers to our community. Tyler and Nico, Ellie and Cal, please stand."

Ellie's heart pounded as she rose on shaky legs, clutching Cal's hand like a lifeline.

"Hello and welcome," the leader said with a benevolent smile. "My name is Hopeful. I began Hope's Embrace twenty years ago as a refuge for the lost and weary, a place where the broken-hearted could find healing and the hopeless could find home. You have come to us for different reasons, but we hope that you will find what you seek here."

He accepted the bowl Remedy handed him and dipped his fingers in the fragrant liquid inside. He then approached each of them, making a sign on their foreheads. Ellie was last. The smell of lavender and cedar and something slightly rotten filled her nostrils as he marked her with a circle. When he met her gaze, a shiver ran down her spine. His eyes, although kind, seemed to probe down to the very pit of her soul.

"In this circle, we find unity," Hopeful said and held out the bowl. Remedy appeared quick and silent to catch it when he dropped it. "We honor your courage in seeking to heal your bonds. Over the next few days, we will guide you, nurture you, listen to you." He paused, meeting Ellie's gaze again for a brief moment before continuing. "Tonight, we welcome you into our family, and we encourage you to open your hearts and minds to the experience ahead."

The ceremony continued with the newcomers being

bestowed with brown robes, a symbol of their initiation into the community. As the new couple, they were also given tokens, small, handcrafted talismans to wear around their necks.

"They will protect you and guide you during your stay here," Serenity explained as she handed them over.

"Thank you," Ellie said, looking down at the wooden pendant. It was carved into the shape of a sunrise over a mountain.

"Let this be an emblem of trust," Hopeful said, his voice echoing through the silent woods. "Trust in us to guide you. Trust in each other to learn and grow together."

Nico and Tyler were eating this ceremony up, completely enthralled with the mystique of it all. They grinned at Ellie and Cal from where they stood across the circle, their eyes gleaming in the firelight.

But she found it all too much. Too strange, too contrived. She felt exposed and frightened and suddenly missed her dog with every fiber of her being. She never felt scared or alone with Puzzle by her side. She needed to escape, to breathe in the cool night air away from the heat of the bonfire, to hide from Hopeful's penetrative gaze.

Cal's hand closed around hers in a comforting squeeze that settled her roiling nerves somewhat. She glanced up at him to find him watching her, his expression softening into something tender and warm. His thumb rubbed the back of her hand in soothing circles, his touch a lifeline in the swirling sea of strangeness.

"We're okay," he mouthed.

His words didn't comfort her as much as she wished they would have. But at least she wasn't alone in this. She didn't have her dog, but she had Cal.

The drumming resumed, the beat echoing through the forest. As one, the members of the commune began to sway in time with the rhythm, their eyes closed and faces uplifted to the moon. They were lost in a trance-like state, their bodies moving freely with no constraint or self-consciousness. It was strange and beautiful in its own way.

Ellie watched them, torn between fascination and fear. She felt like an intruder in a sacred place, and part of her wanted nothing more than to run away as far as possible. But another part of her yearned to understand what was happening around her, to uncover the secrets people were hiding. Because, to her, it was obvious they were hiding a lot.

Maybe they were even hiding her sister.

The heat from the fire was suddenly suffocating, and the smell of the oil on her forehead was making her dizzy.

It was all too much. She needed air. She needed distance.

"Breathe," Cal whispered in her ear. "You're safe. This is a show. A play with props and actors. Nothing more."

"I... I can't breathe." Her throat closed up around the words.

"Here." Cal held her by the shoulders and guided her away from the fire, toward the edge of the clearing. The air was cooler there and somewhat clearer, tainted only by a faint trace of smoke. Ellie gulped it down gratefully, her legs shaky beneath her.

Cal's hand on her back steadied her. His touch was warm and familiar - real - something she could anchor herself to in the midst of all the chaos. He stood silently beside her, his gaze focused on the figures around the bonfire. His face was set in grim lines, his eyes reflecting the flicker of flames.

For a moment, they stood there, side by side, in silence. Then Cal turned to her. "Better?"

"I-I think so."

He held her gaze for a long moment as though assessing whether or not to believe her. Finally, he nodded once, releasing a breath that sounded a lot like relief.

"Let's get back," he said quietly, his hand sliding from her back to rest at the small of her waist as he turned them back toward the fire.

As they neared the crowd again, her panic rose like mercury in a thermometer. She stopped abruptly in her tracks, causing Cal to stumble slightly.

"I-I can't." She spun and stumbled in the opposite direction. She had no idea where she was going. Her body felt heavy and clumsy, her legs barely obeying her, but all she knew was she had to get away from those people and the drums and the shadows dancing around the fire.

Cal followed without protest.

The forest around them was filled with darkness, the silence only broken by their hurried footsteps crunching on dried leaves and an owl hooting somewhere in the distance.

Suddenly, they broke free from the trees and found themselves on a small grassy hill overlooking the commune. The bonfire was a distant glow below them now. The air was cleaner here; it smelled of pine and damp earth. Ellie fell to her knees, gulping in a lungful of fresh air.

Cal joined her on the ground, his strong hands gripping her shoulders. "You're okay," he murmured, his voice filled with concern. "Just breathe."

She shook her head. She wasn't okay. She could still feel the heat of the bonfire on her skin and the weight of Hopeful's stare in her bones.

"Look at me," Cal coaxed. She lifted her gaze to his, swallowing hard against the fear lodged in her throat. "You are safe." He enunciated each word in that calm and steady tone of voice that had pulled many a person back from the brink.

"You're with me, Ellie, and I won't let anyone hurt you. Just breathe." Even in the darkness, the sincerity in his eyes was evident.

The silence of the night was only broken by the distant

sound of the drums and her ragged breathing. She swallowed hard, trying to get a grip on her runaway emotions.

"I'm sorry," she choked out finally. "I just... it was too much."

"It's okay." He rubbed reassuring circles into her back. "It was a lot of weird. Very..." He wiggled the fingers of his free hand in the air. "Woo-woo."

She exhaled a laugh and sat back in the grass, swiping at her forehead with the sleeve of her robe. "What the hell did they put on us? It stinks."

He reached up to touch his forehead, then held his fingertips to his nose. He made exaggerated gagging noises. "Smells like something Puzzle would roll in."

She laughed and lightly punched his shoulder. "You're not helping."

"Hey, you laughed. I have to be helping a little. Let's head back to our cabin," he suggested, helping her to stand up. "Leave them to their rituals."

She didn't protest when he led the way back through the trees. His arm wrapped protectively around her shoulders as they walked. They had come with the intention of pretending, but at that moment, it was real.

"I don't like this place, Cal," she said quietly after a while. "It's not right. Maybe we should leave tonight before this goes any further."

He said nothing for a handful of beats. Then, slowly, as if weighing the words, he spoke. "I saw her."

She pulled him to a stop. "Hope?"

He shook his head. "The girl."

"Her daughter," she breathed. "She was there? I didn't see her."

"She wasn't with the group. She was hanging back in the trees like she didn't want to be seen. I only saw her for a second."

"Maybe it was someone else."

"I don't think so," Cal said and rubbed his thumb between her furrowed brows. "She had the same anxious look you get—the one you're wearing right now. And she has your nose. There's no way you aren't related."

"But if she's part of all this, wouldn't she want to be involved in the ceremony?"

Cal shrugged. "Maybe she's not as comfortable with the weirdness as the others seem to be. Or maybe she doesn't trust outsiders."

"Then why would she call you for help?"

"Okay, fair point. So maybe she's afraid of Hopeful."

Ellie frowned and rubbed at her forehead again. The scent of the oil was as strong as ever. She really needed to wash it off. "Do you think she's in danger?"

He didn't respond. He didn't need to because she already knew the answer. She'd known it the moment Hopeful looked into her eyes, and that was why she'd panicked.

Yes, the girl was in danger.

They all were.

chapter
thirteen

VIGIL MET them on the path back to their cabin, his face a blank mask, giving nothing away. "You can't be out here. These woods are dangerous at night."

"We're fine." Cal stepped in front of Ellie, blocking her from Vigil's view. She was still pale, and he could feel the tremors of fear under his hand on her back. She didn't need this muscled meathead frightening her more. "Just needed some fresh air after... whatever that was."

Vigil studied them for a moment, his gaze flicking between their faces before finally landing on Cal. "You saw her, didn't you? The girl."

Ellie sucked in a sharp breath. Cal pulled her closer to his side and gave her a gentle squeeze of warning.

Going undercover with the world's worst poker player probably hadn't been the best plan.

"What girl?" he asked.

Vigil's expression was stony. "Are you here to help her?"

Well, fuck. Their cover story had lasted all of twelve hours. He'd hoped they'd at least get a couple of days before things started unraveling.

Cal kept his gaze steady, not letting Vigil see a flicker of surprise. He made a pretense of looking puzzled. "I'm sorry. I think you have the wrong idea."

Out of the corner of his eye, he saw Ellie give him a sharp look. He gave her hand a reassuring squeeze behind his back, silently telling her to trust in him.

Vigil crossed his arms over his chest, scrutinizing them. "The fuck I do," he finally said. "I know who you are. Who you both are. I'm the one who cleared you to come here." His stern demeanor melted into something more pleading. "She needs help. We all do."

Before Cal could respond, Serenity appeared on the path. "There you are. You had us all so worried."

Vigil's expression hardened back into the unreadable mask. "Go back to your cabin. We'll discuss this in the morning." He turned to Serenity, who was wringing her hands nervously. "Keep an eye on them," he ordered and disappeared into the darkness.

Once he was out of sight, Serenity turned to them with an apologetic smile. "I'm sorry if Vigil scared you. He's very protective of all of us."

"It's fine," Cal said. "We're fine."

Her smile didn't waver, but something flashed in her eyes before she could hide it. "How did you like the ceremony?"

"It was..." He glanced at Ellie, not sure how to complete that sentence.

"A lot to take in," she finished for him, her voice stronger than he expected. "I needed a moment to process it."

Serenity nodded. "The energy can be overwhelming for newcomers. Shall I guide you back to your cabin?"

"Thank you."

Serenity took them both by the hands and led them to their cabin.

The wooden cabin was large and spacious, with a small sitting area, a kitchenette, and a single king-sized bed draped in white linen. Someone had lit a fire in the fireplace in the corner, and the flames crackled merrily, casting a warm glow around the room.

Serenity gestured toward the bed. "You're probably exhausted after your journey. Rest now. Tomorrow, we begin at dawn with meditation."

"Thank you," Ellie said again.

She bowed and slipped out of the cabin as silently as she had come, leaving them alone.

Though, Cal suspected they were never completely alone within the commune's walls.

Wordlessly, he stripped off the robe, the smell of the oil now nauseating in the small, enclosed space.

Ellie sat on the edge of the bed, her arms curled protectively around herself. "What just happened?"

Cal shook his head and pressed a finger to his lips, then crossed to the bed and sat down close enough beside her that their thighs touched. He put his lips next to her ear. "I think they're listening."

Her eyes rounded behind her glasses, but she didn't panic as he half-expected her to. Instead, she leaned in until her exhale tickled his ear, sending a very inconvenient bolt of lust straight to his cock.

This is an act. Not real.

"Can we trust Vigil?" she whispered.

"We can't trust anyone." He pushed her glasses up and brushed a wayward curl behind her ear. His fingers lingered, tracing the freckles that sprinkled her porcelain skin. This was a dangerous place for them to be in so many ways.

He stood and turned away so she wouldn't see how her nearness was affecting him. "Serenity's right. We should sleep. I'll take the floor."

Ellie's voice was soft but firm in the dim, flickering light. "No, you won't."

He turned to find her staring at him, determination in her blue eyes. "We're supposed to be together, remember? We sleep in the same bed. It's plenty big enough for the both of us." She hesitated before adding, "And it'll be safer that way... in case something happens."

Their proximity would certainly not be safe for his sanity or his heart, but he couldn't deny the practicality of her words.

"Okay." He nodded toward the small bathroom. "Do you want to clean up first?"

She nodded and stood, hesitating for only a beat before picking up the plain cotton nightgown the commune had provided. She disappeared into the bathroom, closing the door firmly behind her.

While she was gone, he told his body to settle the fuck down, then studied his assigned pile of clothes. They reminded him of some of the costumes he'd seen when his cousin dragged him to a Renaissance fair—long linen tunics and loose pants.

Ellie emerged from the bathroom, and despite his mental pep talk, his body once again betrayed him. The nightgown was modest, shapeless even, reaching down to her ankles, but the way it hugged her curves as she moved made his mouth go dry. Her hair was loose around her shoulders, and he found himself yearning to bury his fingers in those curls.

"Your turn," she said, sliding under the covers.

He nodded and quickly gathered his clothes, retreating into the cramped bathroom. He turned on the cold shower, hoping to shock his cock into behaving. It worked. Mostly.

When he returned, Ellie had already snuggled under the covers, her blonde curls fanned out on the pillow. She looked impossibly small and vulnerable against the crisp white linen.

He climbed into bed beside her, his every nerve ending aware of their shared warmth in the cool room. The mattress creaked softly under his weight, and Ellie turned her head to look at him. Her glasses were off, leaving her vulnerable blue eyes wide open to him. They watched each other in the flickering light for a long, lingering moment.

"Cal?" Her voice was soft and uncertain.

"Yeah?" He forced his voice to remain steady despite the pounding of his heart that threatened to betray his feelings.

"Do you think Hope is really here?"

The question hung heavily in the air between them. He could see the hope flickering in her eyes but also the fear. The fear of what finding her sister might mean.

"If she is, we'll find her."

She nodded and rolled onto her back, staring up at the ceiling. He wanted to reach out and comfort her, but he didn't trust himself not to cross a boundary they couldn't afford to blur.

Instead, he lay on his side, watching her silhouette against the dim light.

"Goodnight, Cal," she murmured.

"Goodnight, Ellie."

Her breathing slowly evened out, indicating sleep had claimed her. But for Cal, sleep was elusive. He lay there in the darkness, his mind a whirlwind of thoughts about their current predicament and the woman beside him.

He waited a while longer before allowing himself to look at her again, studying her features in the glow of the fire. The faint frown line between her eyebrows as she slept, the gentle rise and fall of her chest beneath the blanket, her lips parted slightly as she breathed. He resisted the impulse to tuck that one rebellious curl behind her ear.

She was enchanting, even in sleep.

The longing was tangible, an ache deep in his bones. His hand twitched toward her, but he buried it under the pillow out of sight.

He closed his eyes, and time slipped away, measured only

by the soft rhythm of Ellie's breaths beside him. He was just drifting off when a noise snapped him back to alertness. His eyes shot open, scanning the dark room for any sign of danger.

It was a soft thump outside the cabin. An animal, maybe, or—

His gaze landed on Ellie, who stirred in her sleep, her brow furrowing before smoothing out again.

She was safe.

For now.

His entire body was tense, strung like a bow, ready to snap into action at the slightest hint of danger. Ellie deserved as much. She deserved a knight in shining armor— a champion. But he wasn't a hero. He wasn't a warrior. He was just a lawyer with a mountain of student loan debt who loved her.

He supposed that would have to be enough.

Deciding he was done playing possum, Cal got out of bed. His eyes finally adjusted to the darkness, and he walked around the cabin, inspecting each corner, each window. He knew the unease wouldn't let him rest again tonight.

The noise came again, followed by a soft rustling as if someone was moving stealthily in the night. His heartbeat quickened, and all of his senses screamed to high alert. His hand crept to the side of the bed where he'd left his clothes neatly folded, fingers closing around the solid weight of the small pocketknife he always carried.

He moved toward the cabin's flimsy door without making a sound. Taking a deep, grounding breath, he eased the door open, wincing as it creaked softly. A blanket of cold air washed over him as he stepped outside.

The commune was eerily silent, save for the occasional nocturnal rustling of leaves and chirping of crickets. He squinted into the shadows between cabins, trying to pick out any movement in the darkness.

Nothing.

He retreated inside, only half convinced he was just being paranoid. Despite the restless energy humming under his skin, he laid back down. He listened to the crackling fire and the distant sounds of the night. Every rustle of leaves, every creak of wood, singed his nerves, and he silently cursed their situation. They were trapped in a den of wolves, lying here vulnerable with no idea who was friend or foe. Danger lurked around every corner of this place. It was in the air, a low buzzing undercurrent like the approach of a storm. It lay heavy on his chest with each breath he took.

A shadow flickered past the thin curtains covering the cabin's only window, and he sat up.

Someone was out there.

He slipped from the bed, pressed his body against the wall next to the door, and waited, every nerve ending screaming in tensed anticipation.

The handle of the door twitched, and Cal's grip tightened around the knife.

He waited.

The handle moved again, a slow, deliberate turn.

He still didn't move, waiting until the door was pushed open a crack. And then, he pounced, grabbing the intruder by the collar and slamming him back against the door frame.

Ellie didn't stir.

"Who are you?" Cal demanded in a harsh whisper.

To his surprise, the man growled.

No, wait.

Not the man.

A dog.

He glanced down in shock at the mop of a dog. The ponytail of dreadlocks sprouting from its head was unmistakable. "Razzy?"

Raszta stopped growling and gave a tentative tail wag.

Cal stepped back and pulled the hood off his attacker's head. A familiar face scowled back at him.

Pierce St. James shook off his grip and signed, *"I knew you were doing something really fucking stupid."*

Cal glanced at Ellie as she stirred in the bed and waited until she settled again before whispering, "You followed us?"

Pierce looked at him as if he were an idiot. *"Of course I did."*

"Why?"

"Ellie looked like she was going to the gallows when she dropped Puzzle off at the rescue. Knew something was up." His gaze strayed over Cal's shoulder to where Ellie was still sleeping. *"How is she?"*

"Worried. Scared." Cal crossed his arms over his chest, scowling at the deep, genuine concern he saw in the other man's face. A sharp sting of jealousy caught him off-guard, and he immediately squashed it down. "Why are you really here?"

The former soldier shrugged. *"I was bored. Nothing much going on around the rescue."*

"You were bored, so you followed Ellie up the mountain?"

Pierce didn't respond. Whatever his real reasoning, he didn't intend to share. The man was a vault when it came to his personal feelings.

Cal shook his head. "You need to leave."

Pierce's gaze strayed to Ellie again. *"You shouldn't have dragged her here."*

"If you think anyone can drag Ellie anywhere, you don't know her," Cal hissed, pausing when she shifted in bed. He waited until she settled again before continuing. "She wanted to come and was going to whether or not I agreed to go with her. What else was I supposed to do?"

Pierce gave him a dry look that clearly said he thought Cal's decision-making skills were questionable at best.

"Look, if you're just here to criticize, then leave."

"I'll leave when I know she's safe."

Cal shifted uneasily at this, a sick feeling coiling in his gut. "She's not your responsibility."

"No, she chose you for that." Pierce's signs were sharp, pointed. *"But she's my friend, and I won't abandon her when she's in danger. Something's not right about this place. I can feel it in my gut."*

He opened his mouth to argue, then closed it. He couldn't deny that this place was wrong, a twisted version of the peaceful commune they claimed to be. A shiver ran down his spine at the thought of what could be lurking behind the faux tranquility, waiting to bare its teeth.

"You're not wrong," he finally admitted. "But she needs this closure."

Pierce exhaled a long, slow breath and glanced at Ellie again. Then he signed, *"This is about Hope?"*

"Of course it's about Hope. What did you think it was about?"

Pierce didn't respond. But he didn't need to. Cal was starting to see the whole picture.

"You thought I was trying to win her back by... what? Bringing her to a cult to be brainwashed into loving me?"

Pierce merely grunted. Not confirming, but not denying it either.

"Wow. You really don't like me, do you?" And that realization stung. He'd thought they were friends.

Again, he got no response and let the silence stretch between them. As always, Pierce was a fortress of stoicism.

Razzy, unbothered by the tension between them, gave a soft whine and nudged against Pierce's leg. Cal glanced down, his annoyance softening at the sight of the faithful dog.

Realizing he wouldn't get any more from Pierce tonight, he sighed and rubbed a hand over his face. "You can't go back down to the rescue and tell Zak we're here. Zak will tell Ash, and you know that grumpy bastard will find a way to shut this all down. Then, Ellie won't get the answers she needs. Her sister was here long enough to have a child. We know that for sure. The girl is here, and Hope could still be here somewhere, too."

"I'm not going anywhere," Pierce finally signed.

"You can't stay here. It's dangerous."

Pierce scoffed and lifted his shoulder in a nonchalant gesture that confirmed the casual disregard he had for danger. *"I lost my voice, not my balls."*

Cal glared at him, but the edge of his anger had worn off. How could he stay mad at a man who was willing to risk his own safety for someone else's? Pierce was stubborn, infuriating, and probably more than a little bit insane because none of the members of Redwood Coast Rescue were the picture of mental health. But he was also as fiercely loyal as his dog. And right now, Cal needed all the loyalty he could get.

"If you stay, they can't know you're here."

"They'll never see me," Pierce signed. *"And if you fail Ellie in any way— if you hurt her— hell, if you annoy her, then I'm stepping in and taking her home."*

Now, that was a plan he could get behind. He hated to admit it, but knowing he had backup nearby, someone ready and able to whisk Ellie away from danger eased some of the tension from his shoulders.

He extended his hand in a peace offering. "I can live with that."

Pierce studied his hand as if it were a trap, then sighed and accepted the shake.

"I'll check back in with you tomorrow night," he signed before slipping back into the darkness with the dog on his heels.

Cal turned to look at Ellie's sleeping figure bathed in the

pale moonlight filtering through the window. Her face was serene in sleep, all lines of worry smoothed away. He couldn't protect her from everything—her panic attack at the bonfire tonight proved as much. But having Pierce lurking in the shadows made him feel better about her chances of escaping this unharmed.

chapter
fourteen

THE DAY STARTED EARLY.

Very early, with a droning chant that echoed through the commune, startling Ellie awake. She was surprised she'd fallen asleep at all, but she woke feeling less than refreshed. Her eyes were gritty, and her head fuzzy. She sat up and slid on her glasses. The world came into focus—hazy pre-dawn light streaming in through the bare window, the sparse furnishings of their allotted cabin, and Cal. He was already awake and alert, dressed in the commune's provided tunic and baggy cotton pants, with the brown robe draped over his shoulders and the weird wooden pendant around his neck. He looked as fresh as if he'd just stepped out of a relaxing spa. His innate tenacity seemed to give him an inexhaustible resilience, a trait that both frustrated and fascinated her.

He noticed she was awake, and the corner of his mouth tipped up into a crooked smile. "Ready for another day in paradise?"

She groaned softly. She so wasn't. Not after the... whatever happened to her at the bonfire. Panic attack? That was the only explanation she could think of for the fear that had gripped her, the shortness of breath... just the memory had a chill raising goosebumps on her arms. She'd never had a panic attack before, but she'd also never infiltrated a cult before. The stakes were high, and the stress was higher, so what else could it have been?

"Yep," she finally replied, brushing off the memory with feigned enthusiasm. "Ready as I'll ever be."

Cal's smile faltered. He saw through her act, as he always did. It was one of the things that drove her craziest about him. He opened his mouth, but whatever he'd planned to say was drowned out by Serenity's sing-song voice at their door.

"Good morning, beloved friends! The sun greets us with its radiant smile. We have a day of shared enlightenment ahead."

Ellie rolled her eyes. "Oh my God. These people are weird."

Cal snorted with suppressed laughter and strode toward the door. "I have a feeling we've only seen the very tip of the weirdness iceberg. Get dressed. I'll distract her."

She waited until the door shut behind him, then slipped out of bed and into the shapeless dress. There wasn't a mirror in the place, so all she could do was pray her curls weren't too wild as she scooped them into a bun and followed Cal outside.

The commune was already bustling with activity. Members moved in choreographed harmony, their movements as scripted as their words, a ballet of eerie conformity. Ellie pulled her robe closer around her as she watched them, suddenly feeling exposed despite being covered head to toe.

She glanced at Cal. He was taking it all in with a bemused expression that reminded her of Puzzle when the puppy encountered something new and strange.

God, she missed that dog.

Everyone seemed to be moving toward the heart of the commune, so they followed the crowd. With their plain outfits, they blended right in as if they belonged here, which was an unnerving thought.

Cal's hand wrapped around hers, warm and comforting. "Stick close."

"Like glue," she agreed. She had no intention of navigating this place alone.

His gaze met hers, and she saw a glimmer of something more than concern there. His grip tightened as the crowd shepherded them toward the communal breakfast area. She didn't know why she'd expected a dining hall. It was more of a lawn with mats spread out, where everyone sat in neat rows.

"I feel like I'm caught in some strange version of a yoga retreat."

Cal's lips quirked into a half smile. "I've been to yoga retreats. This is weirder."

An unexpected wave of warmth washed over her. Of course he did yoga.

She noticed the systematic distribution of food and the way members were served in a certain order, which didn't seem to be according to age or gender. It seemed to go by the color of their robes, with light blue robes having their pick of food, followed by the green robes. By the time the trays reached the brown robes at the end of the table, there wasn't much left but dull oatmeal and the worst pieces of fruit. She also noticed a pattern of exchange among the commune members. If someone accepted a bowl, they would give something in return, like a piece of fruit. This was not a simple act of gratitude. It felt ritualistic, almost... transactional.

A gentle chime filled the air, silencing the communal chatter. All heads turned toward a raised platform at the far end of the lawn. There stood Hopeful in his white robe, his long hair cascading down his back, strong hands resting calmly on a wooden pulpit. His eyes gleamed with a charisma that was difficult to ignore. An anticipatory hush fell over the commune as he began to speak.

"Good morning, my Embraced. We gather here to celebrate the dawn of another day—a day filled with promise, unity, and enlightenment. As the sun greets us anew, let us be reminded of our purpose here: to love and to be loved, to seek harmony within ourselves and among one another. Let us break our fast together, not just in body but in spirit."

His words washed over the crowd with the gentle power of a lullaby. Ellie found herself reluctantly captivated by his presence. He had a way of commanding attention that was both magnetic and unsettling. His gaze swept across the crowd until his eyes locked on Ellie.

Her heart stuttered as Hopeful stared at her for what felt like an eternity. Cal's hand tightened around hers.

Hopeful finally shifted his gaze away, and she exhaled a relieved breath.

"We encourage sharing our thoughts, joys, and fears amongst ourselves," Hopeful continued softly. "Open your hearts to each other. Let the bonds of trust and unity strengthen us."

Her breath hitched at his words. She glanced at Cal, who was scrutinizing Hopeful with narrowed eyes. He gave her hand a reassuring squeeze, but she could tell he was equally unsettled.

Serenity stepped onto the raised platform, her robe swaying gently in the morning breeze. Her eyes shone with a mixture of pride and anticipation as she glanced over the crowd. Ellie noticed that when she looked at Hopeful, her gaze was full of reverence.

"Thank you," Serenity began, her soft voice carrying across the lawn. "Today, I want to share a joy that's warmed my heart."

As she spoke about the joy of being a part of the

commune, Cal leaned in closer to Ellie. "How long do you think this sharing session is going to last?"

Ellie shrugged lightly. She had no idea.

The breakfast continued in silence as people went up to the podium and shared their joys. Then Hopeful returned and preached some more about love, unity, and collective consciousness, interspersed with cryptic analogies that didn't make sense to Ellie's mind, but the members absorbed it all like gospel.

After breakfast, they were shuffled from one workshop to another, each more bizarre than the last. They learned about the healing properties of crystals, the commune's interpretation of astral projection, and what Ellie could only describe as an attempt at mind reading. She didn't see what any of this had to do with healing a failing relationship, but the other couples seemed to be enthralled by it all. Of course, Marla and Jeff were already indoctrinated by all of the visits—their robes were green— but now Tyler and Nico had drunk the Kool-Aid, eyes gleaming with the zeal of the converted.

As they sat cross-legged on a woven mat during an "aura harmonizing" session, the leader of the workshop—an old woman named Starlight with piercing blue eyes—began to chant a mantra softly. The other couples joined in, their voices building to fill the tent.

This was crazy.

They had to know this was all crazy, right?

She slid a glance toward Cal. He looked just as bemused and raised his brows in a silent, *"Can you believe this shit?"*

"Are we in an episode of The Twilight Zone?" she whispered.

He snorted, clamping his hand over his mouth to suppress his laughter. Starlight scolded them, and they both dipped their heads in mock contrition until she stopped glaring at them and returned to chanting.

Cal leaned in, his lips close to her ear. "Wanna make a break for it?"

They managed to sneak out of the tent while everyone was deep in meditative chanting. Once they were safely outside, they burst into laughter.

"Oh my God," Ellie gasped, swiping at the tears streaming from her eyes. "Did you see Marla's face during that crystal healing workshop? She looked like she was having an orgasm."

Cal cracked up all over again and doubled over, propping his hands on his thighs. "And that astral projection lecture? Jeff looked like he was about to ascend to a higher plane of existence right then and there."

"It's all so... ridiculous. They don't actually believe this stuff, do they?"

"Seems like." He straightened and sucked in a breath. "But, so far, this is all harmless New Age self-help crap. These people are weird, but I haven't seen any overt signs of danger."

"Are we wrong about this place?" She thought back to Hopeful's gaze on her during breakfast and shivered, rubbing at the goosebumps suddenly covering her arms.

No, they weren't wrong. Every instinct she had screamed that something was off about the commune. The rituals, the strange workshops, the weird hierarchy of robe colors—all of it was too orchestrated and too manipulative to be dismissed as benign self-help practices.

Plus, the girl had wanted to leave. Was she just a teenager rebelling against her unconventional upbringing? Or was there something more sinister at play here? And where was she now?

"Cal, we need to find out what happens when people decide they want to leave."

"I have a feeling nothing good." He made a face. "We should start by talking to some of the other brown robes if we can separate them from the flock. If they're not fully initiated, they might still be harboring doubts about this place."

"There you are!" Serenity chimed in her saccharine, sing-song voice. "You can't wander away like that! This mountain can be dangerous. We were worried."

Except she had been in the workshop, so how did she know they'd left? They'd only been gone a few minutes.

"Sorry about that," Cal said easily. "The incense was starting to give me a headache. I get migraines, and strong scents can set them off, so Ellie thought it best to get me out of there."

Ellie narrowed her eyes at him. Did he actually suffer from migraines? She hadn't known that, but it had the ring of truth to it.

"I apologize," Serenity said with genuine sympathy. "I used to get them, too, but Remedy cured me. We'll make time for you to see her later. She really is a miracle worker."

"That'd be great."

A chime sounded distantly, and Serenity paused to listen to it, then nodded. "It's time for the next session. Come."

She led them into a cabin that was set up much like theirs—a mishmash of bohemian aesthetics and modern comfort. Instead of a bed, pillows in vibrant colors were thrown haphazardly on the floor, and large tapestries covered the walls. For the first time all day, they were the only ones in the workshop.

Ellie's alarm bells started ringing, and she stopped just inside the door. "What is this session about?"

chapter
fifteen

SERENITY SMILED BACK AT HER. "We're going to dig into your specific problems as a couple."

"Oh. Um... I really don't think this is necessary." She tried to back away but found Cal directly behind her, blocking her escape. He closed his hand over her shoulder and gave it a gentle warning squeeze.

"This is why we're here, honey," he reminded.

Right. Shit. She had to play along, but it had been much easier to do so when the workshops were all about astral projection and crystals.

Serenity's smile never wavered. She seemed the embodiment of her chosen name. "It's nothing to be ashamed of, Ellie. All couples need a little help sometimes, and the best place to start is by simply acknowledging and accepting that. This retreat is about relinquishing our instinctive defenses and opening ourselves up to all the love that your partner and the universe has to offer."

Ellie considered herself an open-minded person. She believed in karma and ghosts and didn't think reincarnation was out of the realm of possibility. But these people, with their relentless optimism and mystic mumbo-jumbo, were fraying her nerves.

She glanced at Cal, but he wasn't going to be any help. His eyes sparkled with a hint of challenge, silently daring her to take the plunge. The bastard was enjoying this.

She turned back to Serenity. "Fine. Let's do it."

"Wonderful." Serenity moved to the center of the room and gestured for them to follow.

Cal took her hand, the touch igniting that stubborn flame low in her belly. Would she always feel like this when he touched her? Ten years, twenty years down the road, would she still get that flash of heat, that rabble of butterflies?

Not that she planned to be with him in twenty years.

"We need to do this," he whispered close to her ear.

Of course, she knew that. The longer they were here, the more convinced she became that these people knew something about her sister's whereabouts. The only way they were going to find Hope was to win the community's trust.

But that didn't mean she had to like it.

She drew a fortifying breath and followed Serenity's lead without another word.

"Sit," Serenity instructed, pointing to two pillows on the floor. "Get comfortable, then close your eyes and take a few deep breaths. We must prepare ourselves for our journey inward."

With a last look at Cal, Ellie descended to the floor, perching on a pillow decorated with fantastical bird designs and geometric patterns. Cal took a seat opposite her, legs crossed, hands floating uncertainly before settling on his thighs.

Across from her, Cal's face looked almost serene in the warm glow of the room's fairy lights. His eyes were closed, and the tension in his face had eased somewhat. It was as if he was genuinely trying to embrace this strange experience. Ellie wrangled her thoughts to focus, her eyes fluttering shut.

"Now," Serenity said softly. "Envision an energy field, wrapping your bodies in radiant warmth. The universe's love for you has no bounds."

Ellie couldn't help but snort at that one, earning a gentle reprimand from Serenity.

"Acceptance is key here, Ellie."

She clenched her teeth. Acceptance. The word echoed in her mind like the stupid gong. She'd accepted a lot of things in her life, but this? This was pushing her limits. Sitting across from Cal, pretending to be married when every fiber of her being wanted to keep him at arm's length, pretending she was interested in all of this esoteric mumbo-jumbo when all she wanted was answers—it was maddening.

"Once you let down your walls and take things whole-heartedly, you'll find peace. Are you ready to take that step with Cal?"

Was she?

No.

She could play a part, sure, but accepting Cal back into her life? That wasn't going to happen.

"Ellie?" Serenity prodded gently. "Let down your walls. You'll see the world much more clearly."

Ellie held back another snort. She could already see the world clearly, thank you very much. She didn't need some cult member to tell her what she was missing. Still, she closed her eyes again and tried to play along.

"Okay. I'm ready now."

"Good," Serenity said, and a gong rang through the room. Ellie cracked open an eye and caught Cal's smothered laugh, which he hid behind a cough.

"I know you think I'm crazy," Serenity said without malice as she set the gong's mallet back on the floor. "Believe me.

When my husband and I first came here, I thought the same thing. But give it a chance. Keep an open mind, and you might be surprised. This saved our marriage, and it can save your relationship. Can you promise me that you'll keep an open mind?"

Ellie glanced at Cal, who was watching her with an unreadable expression. The intensity of his eyes left her feeling exposed and bare. She swallowed hard and turned back to Serenity.

"I promise." It wasn't necessarily a lie. She was keeping an open mind, just not about Serenity's advice.

"That's all I ask," Serenity said with a gracious smile. "Now close your eyes and imagine a thread of connection between you and Cal," Serenity continued. "Does it glow bright with love, or do hurt and misunderstanding dim it?"

A thread? Ha. More like a steel cable. Their connection had always been unnaturally strong, even when they loathed each other—or, she supposed, it was more accurate to say when she loathed him. He'd never hated her, but oh, how she'd hated him at one time.

Did she still?

No, even as much as she wanted to.

Her cheeks warmed at the thought, and she was grateful for the cover of her closed eyes.

"I don't know about Ellie, but mine's glowing like a Christmas tree." Cal's sincerity was disarming. The note of raw honesty in them rattled her.

"Funny, I was going to say mine's glowing like a dumpster fire."

Cal laughed. Even with her eyes closed, she could picture that damned irresistible grin of his clearly. That grin and his sense of humor were some of the things that had initially attracted her to him.

"Conflict isn't necessarily a bad thing," Serenity said

before Cal could reply. "It can help illuminate the areas where we need growth and compromise."

Compromise? With Cal? It seemed as likely as the sun rising in the west. Still, she held her peace—no point in arguing with Serenity's boundless optimism.

"Just... let me know when we get to the part where we rid ourselves of all conflict and live happily ever after," Ellie grumbled, shifting on her cushion.

Cal let out another soft chuckle. "You always did like skipping to the end. No patience for the journey, but that's the fun part."

She scowled. "There's nothing wrong with wanting to know the ending first. If I had known our ending, I never would've..."

"What?" Cal's voice was filled with quiet regret, which left an ache throbbing in her chest. "If you'd known we'd end up like this, would you have wished for us never to have happened?"

Her eyes fluttered open. He looked genuinely hurt, and she wished she could take back her words. She didn't want a relationship with him, but that didn't mean she wanted to hurt him.

"I..." She started but found herself unable to finish, the words sticking in her throat like glue. The truth was, she wasn't sure if she would choose to fall for him again, knowing the hurt it would cause them both. "We can't turn back time. We can't change what happened. We are where we are now."

Serenity let out a hum of thoughtfulness before she spoke, her gaze bouncing between the two of them. "Sometimes, it takes a little time and distance to realize what we've always had. You're both here now, taking this step together. That tells me there's still hope."

Cal laughed, but it was hollow. "Hope," he echoed, his gaze boring into Ellie's. "I'm always holding onto hope."

Her heart clenched at the subtle double entendre— Hope, her missing sister, and hope, the emotion, the feeling of expectation, anticipation, even... of want. She had to swallow past the lump in her throat.

Serenity nodded. "Hope is a powerful thing, Cal. Never let it go."

Silence settled over the room, heavy and intense, charged like a summer storm. There were so many unspoken words and buried feelings. She didn't know how they could heal from it all.

"I think that's enough for today," Serenity said gently, breaking the spell. "Take some time to reflect on what we've talked about. We'll meet again tomorrow."

Ellie managed a curt nod before exiting the room as quickly as decorum allowed her. She needed to breathe, to clear her head of all thoughts about Cal and his damned hold on her emotions.

But he was right on her heels. "Ellie—"

She whirled on him. "This isn't real. You and me? We're done. We're not a couple anymore."

"I know."

"Do you?" she hissed, aware that they were drawing stares from other commune members in the nearby garden. "Because in there—"

He caught her hand as she gestured wildly toward the tent and lowered his voice to match her. "I'm playing my part, Elle. That's all."

"Your part? We are not a couple, Cal. We are not in love. And we never will be again."

His eyes flashed with a mix of emotions—hurt, surprise, regret. "I didn't say—"

"Save it," she cut him off, her heart pounding against her ribcage. "You're good at playing roles, aren't you? The perfect defense attorney who can make anyone believe anything."

Tears stung at the corners of her eyes, but she stubbornly blinked them back. She stalked back to their cabin and shut the door. But, of course, there wasn't a lock. They didn't believe in locks here, and Cal was able to walk right in.

He ran a hand through his blond hair and let out a frustrated sigh. "Ellie, I know I hurt you before. I'm sorry for that. But right now, we're stuck here, and we need to stick together. For Hope."

At the mention of her sister's name, her breath caught in her throat, and she wrapped her arms around herself. "And I suppose you're going to defend them too once we find proof that they're responsible for her disappearance? Are you just here to rack up more clients?"

Cal flinched as if physically stung by her words. "You know that's not true."

"Do I?" A harsh laugh tore out of her, brittle and broken, scraping the inside of her throat raw. "Your job is your life, Cal. You already chose it over me once. How do I know you're not doing it again?"

He reached out, but she stepped back, keeping a distance between them that was more than just physical. His face softened into a sad understanding that settled like a weight in the pit of her stomach.

"Ellie," he began again, softer this time, almost like a plea. "Please, just give me a chance to explain—"

"What's there to explain? That you did your job by getting Jaxon Throne a lighter sentence in a minimum-security prison?"

"Yes. Because he isn't a killer."

"He tried to kill Alexis. He wanted to kill Shane."

"And he's paying for that with ten years of his life, but he's doing it in a place where he can get the help he desperately needs for his drug addiction and PTSD. You really think he should've been thrown in a maximum-security prison to rot?"

"No." Exhausted, she dropped into a chair and shoved her hands into her curls. "No. But you didn't know the extenuating circumstances when you chose to defend him, and you were willing to do it anyway."

Cal paused. Moments passed as the tension in the room grew thicker with every deafening tick of the clock on the wall.

"Yeah, I was," he admitted finally.

The honesty in his words struck her in a place she didn't expect— it hurt, but it also relieved her somehow. "I can't give my heart to a man who defends monsters."

Cal's eyes darkened, his shoulders hunched forward as if he'd taken a physical blow. "You think what I do... you think that makes me a monster, too?"

Her heart clenched in her chest, compressing her lungs and stealing her breath. The silence between them stretched thin, taut, filling the room with a palpable tension that prickled against her skin like static electricity.

"No," she said finally. "I don't think you're a monster. I think you're a good man... too good. You believe in people's potential for redemption so much that you chose it over us. And that's why I can't love you again. "

chapter
sixteen

THAT'S *why I can't love you...*

If she'd taken a knife and carved his heart out of his chest, it would've hurt less.

That was it, wasn't it? The crux of the matter. It wasn't who he had defended or even what Jax had done. It was that he had chosen his belief in redemption over her. He had chosen ethics over love.

And that was a choice he would go on to regret for years and years to come.

For a few moments, he just stood there, letting the words wash over him, slowly removing the veneer of hope he had clung so desperately to. He wanted to say something, anything, but what could he possibly say that would make a difference? What could he say that would change the irrefutable truth?

He took a step toward her—a move born out of instinct more than rationale. But she held up a hand, her eyes hard yet glistening with unshed tears. "Don't."

His heart broke again at the sight of her pain, the pain he had caused. His knees threatened to buckle underneath him, and without a word, he turned and left the room.

The outdoors did little to provide him any solace. The trees were too tall, too big. Claustrophobic. The gardens appeared dull and lifeless, every vibrant color seemingly stripped away. He walked with no destination in mind and found himself in front of Vigil's cabin.

Yes. This he could handle. Focus on the problem of the girl.

He went to the door and knocked. No answer, but that wasn't really a surprise. Vigil was probably at the workshops like everyone else or patrolling the commune's grounds or—

A soft thump sounded from inside.

"Vigil?"

He raised his hand to knock again when the door creaked open an inch, then more, revealing the man himself. Behind him stood Sincere and a woman with short, sleek brown hair, high cheekbones, and dark eyes that seemed to miss nothing.

There was a pause, an awkward beat that went on longer than it should have.

"Sorry to interrupt," Cal said, already backing away. "I'll come back later."

"No, no need," Vigil said, stepping forward to hold the door wide open, his expression unreadable. "We were just wrapping up some business and could use a fresh perspective. Join us?"

The woman's eyes bugged. "Is this a good idea?"

Vigil glanced back at her and lowered his voice. "He knows about the girl."

She shook her head and paced away, rubbing her hands over her face. "Shit. This is bad. If newcomers already know—"

"He's here because of her." He met Cal's gaze. "Aren't you?"

This meeting was not like the structured workshops, and these people didn't radiate the practiced tranquility of the commune's other members. Suspicion and fear lurked in the corners of the cabin, slithering underfoot, hanging heavy in the air.

Curious, Cal stepped in, shutting the door firmly behind him. "Yes, I am."

The interior of Vigil's cabin was simple and utilitarian. There was a single bed, a chest of drawers, and no other adornments. The room was lit only by a small window, and dust particles twinkled in the beam of sunlight streaming through it.

"You already know Sincere," Vigil said, then nodded toward the woman. "That's Clarity. She teaches our children."

"More like indoctrinates them," Clarity muttered. "And I really wish you'd stop calling me by my Embraced name. My name is Evelyn."

"It's too dangerous to get out of the habit." Vigil shook his head and faced Cal. "True called you when she escaped, didn't she?"

True.

He finally had a name for the girl. It was somehow both a relief and an added weight. She wasn't just a voice on his phone or the girl on the video anymore. She had a name, an identity. It made her real.

"I think you already know the answer to that."

Evelyn—Clarity—bit her lip, casting a wary glance at Cal before turning to face Vigil. "This is insane. You can't just bring an outsider into this! How do we know we can trust him?"

Vigil ignored her protests. "You're here to help her." A statement, not a question.

After a day filled with vagueness, Cal respected his straightforwardness and returned it in kind. "Yes, I am."

Clarity flapped her arms in annoyance. "Vig—"

"He's a lawyer," Vigil snapped. "He might be able to help us legally."

"I'm a defense attorney, but, yeah, I may be able to help depending on what you need." Cal studied the group. "What is this? A coup?"

"More like a prison break," Clarity said. "We want out."

Sincere nodded. "Serenity, my wife, won't leave. She's too loyal to Hopeful. Truthfully, I think she's in love with him."

"So you want a divorce?"

"If that's what it takes. We have two boys—an eight-year-old and a three-year-old—and I want our kids as far away from here as possible."

"Are the kids in danger here?"

The trio exchanged a glance filled with unspoken words.

Finally, Clarity nodded. "Hopeful had me close down the school. He said—" Her voice caught, and she exhaled hard before starting again. "He said we don't need it anymore because our kids will be granted the gift of eternal youth. They'll never grow up, so they never need to learn." Tears spilled from her eyes. "I have a two-year-old daughter. I moved here with her because the school here really was doing amazing things for the kids. They're all smarter. They test higher than the state average. I liked the communal living and thought she'd be safer here than in a public school."

"But it's gotten weird," Sincere said. "This place isn't what it started as."

Cal glanced at Vigil. "And what about you?"

He shook his head. "I don't have kids."

"Then what's your stake in this?"

A muscle in his jaw ticked. "I just don't like where it's headed."

Yeah, the guy still wasn't telling the full truth. Cal didn't know how he knew it because Vigil had the poker face to beat all poker faces, but he did. "So why not just leave?"

"People who leave..." Clarity trailed off like she didn't know how to end that sentence. She looked at Sincere for help.

"Disappear," he finished. "We had a couple stay after last year's retreat, but a few weeks ago, they started voicing doubts. Within days, their cabin was cleaned out. It's the one you're in now."

That was not a comforting thought.

And he'd left Ellie there alone?

Fuck.

"I've looked for them," Vigil added. "They're gone. No trace. They either went into witness protection or never made it off this mountain. And I have enough contacts in security circles that I'd know if they got swept up by WITSEC."

Cal eyed the man. He'd spent enough time around the former soldiers of Redwood Coast Rescue to spot one. They all carried themselves a certain way and spoke with a kind of authority that civilians lacked. "You were military."

Vigil didn't confirm or deny.

Well, shit. That could only mean one thing—he hadn't just been regular military. He'd been in spec ops. He could prove to be a powerful ally... or a dangerous enemy.

"What were their names? The couple that disappeared?" He'd give the information to Pierce to check out.

"Benjamin and Olivia Harrington," Vigil said.

Cal's heart dropped. "Who?"

Again, the trio exchanged a glance.

"You know them?" Clarity asked.

"Ben Harrington was a client. He was arrested last year for DUI. It was his third, and he was facing jail time because he hit a pedestrian. I got him released on bond, and he skipped town."

"So maybe they're just hiding?" Clarity said, turning to Vigil. "Maybe they disappeared of their own volition. Maybe someone found out they were wanted, and that's why they left."

Vigil's lips thinned into a hard line. He shook his head. "That doesn't explain why they left all of their possessions behind. They had a stash of money in their cabin. You need money to live in the outside world, and they didn't take it."

"But why would Hopeful kill them?" Clarity's voice trembled, her face pale. "He preaches peace and love."

Sincere snorted. "Hopeful preaches whatever suits him best."

"What about the girl?" Cal asked. "She tried to leave. What happened to her?"

Clarity anxiously twisted her hand in the flowing belt of her light blue robe, then released it, then wound it up around her palm again. Judging by the belt's frayed end, it was an ongoing nervous tic of hers. "We haven't seen her since she was brought back."

That was what Cal was afraid of. If the girl were dead, it would crush Ellie. And, honestly, him, too. He'd forever wonder if he could've done something differently to help her in time.

He drew a fortifying breath, steeling himself against the answer to his next question. "Did Hopeful kill her?"

"No," Sincere said. "She's his daughter, and he's always held her up as some kind of prophet. He won't kill her, but he's almost certainly holding her captive somewhere and punishing her for trying to leave."

Cal decided to take a chance. Maybe it was foolish, but if he could get the answers he needed now, he could take Ellie away from here before she was in any real danger. "What about the girl's mother? Hope?"

Clarity covered a sharp gasp with her hand. "How do you know about Hope?"

"I have my sources." Cal knew he had crossed a line, and

going back wasn't an option. Each revelation was another step toward the precipice of danger. He couldn't put the brakes on now – not when Ellie was involved, not when innocent lives were at stake.

Sincere broke the tense silence that followed. "Hope... is gone."

"Did she escape?"

"No," Clarity said so softly that Cal had to strain to hear her. "Hope... she's dead." She looked down, her fingers worrying at the robe's belt again.

Dead.

Cal felt his heart stop for a beat.

Hope was dead.

This news was going to crush Ellie.

"When?"

Clarity twisted the belt of her robe around her hand again. "Just... right before you got here."

And wasn't that convenient for Hopeful? Every alarm bell Cal possessed was ringing off the hook. "How did she die?"

"I asked Serenity about it, and she said it was natural causes," Sincere answered. "The rest of the Blues all backed up that story, but..." He glanced over at Clarity, the only Blue in the room.

She shrugged helplessly. "I never saw her body. Usually, when one of us dies, the body is placed on an altar, and there's a large celebration of life so we can all say goodbye before burial, but not this time."

"Why not?"

"Hopeful claimed it was too hard on True to see her mother like that," Clarity explained. "He said he took care of the burial himself, and afterward, he built a shrine to her and started calling her Mother God. We have to pray to her every morning."

Cal squinted at them in disbelief. "And you all just accepted that?"

Vigil shrugged, his face impassive. "At the time, we had no reason not to."

"Honestly, I just thought it was his way of grieving," Clarity added. "I liked the idea that Hope was watching over us. She was my friend, and praying to her felt no different than talking to her like I always did when she was alive. But then, True disappeared..."

Sincere picked up the thread of the conversation. "We believe True found out what really happened to her mother, and that's why she ran away and contacted you."

Except True hadn't said her mother was dead. She'd said Hope was missing. And what about that other pale, thin woman who had appeared on the camera hours before True? He hadn't seen anyone among the commune members who looked like her. Could that have been Hope?

Cal ran a hand over his face. "Listen, I have to get back to Ellie." He'd already been gone far longer than he'd intended. "But before I go, do you have any idea where True might be hidden?"

They exchanged glances, a silent message passing between them. Clarity shrugged helplessly. "We've been searching since she disappeared. But Hopeful controls everything and everyone here. If he doesn't want her to be found, she won't be."

part two
truth

If you shut up truth, and bury it underground, it will but grow.

-Emile Zola

chapter
seventeen

IF HOPEFUL HAD LOCKED his daughter away somewhere, then it couldn't have been her he'd seen hiding in the woods during the bonfire. He'd been so sure it was the girl from the video, but now he wasn't certain of anything.

Cal left Vigil's place with his head spinning and hurried back to his cabin. The twang of unease he'd felt earlier at leaving Ellie alone prickled at him again, and he picked up his pace. He shouldn't have left her.

His heart hammered in his chest as he approached the cabin, the sense of foreboding seeping into his veins like poison. The door hung slightly ajar, and a cold dread seized him. He burst in, ready for a fight, but instead was greeted by a sight he hadn't expected: Ellie standing calmly in the middle of the room, Hopeful, lounging comfortably on the worn-out couch.

At first, he felt relief, grateful that she was unharmed. But then...

What the fuck?

Why was Hopeful here, smiling that weird, enigmatic smile?

"Ah. Cal. There you are," Hopeful said cheerfully. "I was just wondering if I should send out a search team."

Ellie rushed to his side and gripped his arm, her nails biting into his skin in warning. "I told him about the fight we had. He decided to keep me company until you returned."

Her gaze held his, and the fear he saw in it broke his heart. He promised himself he'd never leave her alone again and covered her hand with his. "I'm so sorry for everything." He hoped she knew he meant that and wasn't just putting on a show for Hopeful. "I shouldn't have lost my temper and left you here by yourself."

"Oh, it's all right," Ellie said a little too brightly. "We all say things we don't mean when we're upset."

Hopeful studied the two of them like they were fascinating specimens under a microscope. His thin lips curled into an even wider smile, his amusement palpable as he lounged on the couch like he owned the place.

"That's true," he said, his voice deceptively casual, his eyes glinting. "Emotions can cloud our judgments and actions. It's important always to keep a clear mind and open heart." He held Cal's gaze for a moment before pushing up from the couch. "I'm glad to see you two have mended your bond. A house divided cannot stand, especially not in these troubled times."

Was that a threat?

Cal's skin prickled, and he tightened his grip on Ellie, pulling her protectively to his side. "Thank you for your concern, but we're okay now."

Hopeful dipped his head slightly in acknowledgment and glided toward the door. He paused next to Ellie and gave her an almost fond smile. "Ellie, next time your husband gets the urge to storm off, remind him that this mountain is a dangerous place." He reached out to gently touch her shoulder, and she flinched. "You don't want anything happening to him out there."

With that, Hopeful swept from the room, his departure leaving a vacuum that seemed to suck the very air from the room. It was a moment before Cal remembered how to fill his lungs, his heart pounding a rapid tattoo against his ribs as he looked down at Ellie.

"Oh, God," she breathed. "Was that a threat? Did he just threaten you?"

"It's fine. He's just playing with us. Are you okay?" he murmured, brushing a stray curl from her face. His hand lingered on her cheek—he couldn't seem to drop it. "He didn't hurt you?"

"I'm okay." The slight tremble in her voice and the way she leaned into his touch betrayed her lie. "He just sat there and talked about love and the universe and something about renewal... I don't even know. I tuned him out. He likes to hear himself talk."

"I'm so sorry I left." He couldn't help himself—he pulled her in for a hug. She was trembling, and a simmering rage replaced his relief. It was not just about the vague threats Hopeful had thrown around. It was the way he had dared to touch Ellie, to invade her personal space, that incensed him.

He fought to keep his anger in check. Now was not the time or place to lose his cool.

After a moment, Ellie stepped back and wrapped her arms around herself. "Where did you go?"

He looked at the closed door and didn't fully trust that Hopeful wasn't still standing on the other side, waiting to eavesdrop. He took Ellie by the hand and led her into the small bathroom. It was tight enough that they almost had to stand nose-to-nose. He turned on the shower and hoped the water would provide enough white noise to cover their words.

She stared up at him with a bewildered expression, her eyes

looking impossibly huge behind her glasses. His heart clenched. She was so goddamn beautiful.

"I went to see Vigil," he said, gently lifting her glasses from her face as they began to steam up. She blinked up at him, her eyes a little unfocused but still rife with worry. "Why?"

"I don't know. I needed air, and that's where I ended up. I guess I wanted answers."

"Did you get any?"

"Some, but they only led to more questions." The shower steam enveloped them, offering a thin veil of privacy as he quickly rehashed his conversation with Vigil, Sincere, and Clarity, except he left out the part about Hope's supposed death. He had too many doubts about the story and didn't want to hurt her until he knew for sure.

When he told her about the girl, she exhaled in a rush. "Hope's daughter... my niece... her name is True?"

"Yes. And according to Sincere, she's also Hopeful's daughter."

"My sister had a child with that... that man?" Disgust dripped from every word.

"It appears so."

"Does Sincere or Vigil know where they are? Hope and True? They have to be here somewhere, right?"

He winced internally. He should tell her about her sister, but when he opened his mouth, the words wouldn't form.

"I don't know," he said instead. "I don't believe Vigil was being completely honest with me, and I need more information before I can make any assumptions."

Ellie sensed his hesitation, her eyes widening in alarm. "Cal... what aren't you telling me?"

He took a deep breath and tore his gaze away from her, staring at the tiny droplets of water that danced on the shower wall before evaporating into steam. The silence was deafening.

"Oh." She tried to back away from him, but there wasn't

any space for it. "Oh, God. It's about Hope, isn't it? She's dead."

"Ellie." Her caught her before she could fully retreat, his arms wrapping around her trembling figure.

"I don't know," he repeated, burying his face in her curls. "The story Vigil and Sincere told is... conflicting. I can't say for certain what happened."

Her breath hitched. "But you believe she's dead. That's why you didn't want to tell me."

"I don't know what to believe. There are a lot of inconsistencies, and I don't trust what I've been told. Not yet." He hooked a finger under her chin and lifted until her gaze met his again. The steam had caused her springy curls to go limp, and her eyes and nose were red from her tears, but she was still the most breathtaking woman he'd ever known.

Unable to resist, he pressed a soft kiss to her forehead. "I don't have the answers right now, but I promise you, I'm going to do everything in my power to find out the truth. And if Hope is alive, I will bring her home to you."

She relaxed against him and wrapped her arms around his waist. There was so much trust in the gesture that his heart damn near cracked open. Ellie was too sweet for this world. She wasn't made for lies and manipulations. She belonged off this mountain. She belonged with her dog and her friends, and it took every fiber of control in his body not to scoop her up and run away from this place with her.

A chime sounded in the distance. Even in their short time here, he'd started to recognize the different chimes the commune lived their lives by. That one was the dinner bell.

Ellie groaned and drew away from him. He missed the contact instantly but covered his disappointment by shutting off the shower.

"Yay," she said without any enthusiasm whatsoever. "More oatmeal."

"What, you don't think they're going to offer us a big, juicy steak?"

"Sorry, but I can almost guarantee it's more oatmeal or something like it. Cult leaders often withhold protein from their followers because it makes people more susceptible to other brainwashing techniques."

Despite everything, he grinned at her. He loved the way that brain of hers worked. "Leave it to you to turn a dinner conversation into an impromptu lesson on mind manipulation."

She rolled her eyes, but there was a small grin playing at the corner of her lips. "That's me, always learning. You should try it sometime."

"Sassy, Summers. Keep that up, and I may have to show you what happens when you mouth off to a lawyer."

"Oh, really?" She raised an eyebrow at him. "You going to hold me in contempt?"

Damn. When she said it like that, it sounded so dirty.

Never mind that lawyers weren't the ones that held people in contempt. He still appreciated her attempt at nerdy flirting.

"I guess you'll have to keep mouthing off so you can find out." His gaze dropped to her lips for a fraction of a second before he forced himself to pull away.

Fuck.

Now was not the time or the place.

Dinner was exactly what Ellie had predicted—a bland, oatmeal-like substance mixed with some kind of fruit. Everyone ate in silence, an eerie quietness that made his skin crawl.

Then, mid-meal, Merit murmured something in Hopeful's ear. He abruptly stood up and announced it was time for "reflection." Everyone was to return to their cabins for the night and meditate until morning. The commune members didn't find this the least bit strange and stood as one, leaving their meals half-finished.

But it was odd.

Hopeful stalked toward his cabin with Merit, Vigil, and Serenity on his heels.

Cal escorted Ellie back to their cabin, his hand protectively on her lower back. They didn't speak as they walked, and the silence felt heavy, charged with apprehension.

As soon as the door closed behind them, Ellie spun toward him. "Did you see Hopeful's face? Whatever happened, he was pissed."

He removed his robe and hung it on a hook by the door, then sat down on the bed to remove his boots. "Yeah, I noticed." He'd also noticed the way Merit glanced their way as if they were the threat.

"I wonder what spooked him." Ellie walked over to the window and peered out into the gathering darkness. "Do you think we've been discovered?"

He paused from unlacing his boots and considered it. If their cover was blown, they had to leave tonight. No fucking way they were sticking around if Ellie was in imminent danger...

But he didn't think so. His gut said that Hopeful's ire wasn't pointed their way.

Not yet, anyway.

Yes, there was danger, but he suspected that it was internal, something within the commune itself. Maybe Vigil, Sincere, and Clarity weren't the only ones uncomfortable with the way things were going around here.

Finally, he shook his head. "The way everyone reacted... it seemed routine for them. Nobody was startled except for us."

"And Nico and Tyler."

"Yeah, exactly. The outsiders. Everyone else acted like it was perfectly normal for Hopeful to cut dinner short, so maybe for them, it is."

She rubbed her arms as if to fend off a chill. "We need to find True and get out of here."

"We can't do it tonight. Not with Hopeful and the Blue Robes on high alert." He patted the bed beside him. "Come, sit."

Reluctantly, she moved away from the window and joined him on the bed. He could see fear in her eyes, bright and haunting. It woke something deep inside him, a protective instinct that roared to life. He wanted to reach out, pull her into his arms, and anchor her to him as if he could shield her from the world outside.

Instead, he settled for a reassuring squeeze of her hand. "The best thing we can do tonight is get some rest." His sleeplessness last night was catching up to him, and he felt sluggish, unbalanced. "I have a feeling we're going to need it."

She nodded. "You're right."

He cracked a smile. "Wow. You actually admitted I'm right about something? Are you feeling okay? Is this a sign of the apocalypse?"

She rolled her eyes but exhaled a soft laugh as she crawled into bed, which he counted as a win.

They lay in silence together for several minutes.

"Cal, can you just...?" She trailed off, but she didn't need to finish.

"Come here." He opened his arms and waited until she nuzzled closer before wrapping them both in the blanket. Having her in his arms felt right—it always had—and he didn't understand how she couldn't feel it, too.

As she nestled into him, he breathed in her familiar scent, the faintly floral aroma of her shampoo calming his frazzled nerves. He stroked her back in long, soothing motions, whispering comforting words into her hair.

"I hate this place," she murmured sleepily against his chest.

"Me, too."

She mumbled something incoherent in response, her breathing gradually slowing as she drifted off to sleep against him.

He wanted to follow her, and his eyes drifted closed before he forced them open again. He had one more thing to do first.

He climbed out of bed and stepped outside to meet Pierce...

But Pierce never showed.

chapter
eighteen

DAY THREE.

According to all of Ellie's research, it only took three days to indoctrinate someone into a new belief system. This was the turning point for most people—the moment they decided whether or not the cult was their cup of tea.

It definitely wasn't hers.

Or, thankfully, Cal's.

But Nico and Tyler? They were all in. At breakfast, they chattered about all the spiritual enlightenment they were experiencing and how they felt more connected than ever. They didn't seem to notice the weird shift in mood among the commune members. Everyone still had that air of manufactured tranquility and bright smiles, but they were all jumpier than usual.

The day wore on with a series of group activities—meditation, yoga, and lectures that Ellie could only describe as "spiritual peer pressure." All of it was designed to break down the walls they built around themselves. To make them belong.

Instead of lunch, they were ushered to yet another workshop on "spiritual enlightenment"—a term she had begun to associate with hours of monotonous chants and flowery language.

The members sat in pairs under the shade of a towering redwood grove. Ellie found herself with Serenity, while Cal was paired with a man called Equinox for a "heart-sharing" exercise.

Whatever that meant.

Serenity took Ellie's hands into hers and looked deeply into her eyes. "We are mirrors, reflecting each other's souls. I see kindness in you, Ellie. I see strength, too, but also so much fear and uncertainty."

Ellie nodded uncomfortably, unsure what she was supposed to say in return. Serenity seemed to be waiting for a response, but Hopeful's approach saved her from having to formulate one. He placed a hand on Equinox's shoulder, and the man instantly popped to his feet, making room for Hopeful to sit across from Cal. His gaze flickered to Ellie, and unease gnawed through her as he reached for Cal's hands.

"I see great courage in you, Cal," Hopeful began in a solemn tone, "and a relentless pursuit for justice. You seek to bring balance to an imbalanced world." His grip tightened enough to leave imprints on Cal's skin. "But you must take care and learn to pick your battles, or else your pursuit will end in disaster."

Cal's bland smile didn't falter, but Ellie could see the traces of worry in his eyes. And something else.

Fear.

Callum Holden was scared.

Hopeful released his hands and stood. Serenity and Equinox both bowed to him. He didn't bow back, and Serenity's smile slipped for a moment before she launched into a tangent about how their intentions shape their actions and how shared enlightenment could help them realize their true potential.

Ellie barely heard her words. Her attention was focused on Cal, who sat rigidly, his fingers flexing slowly. Hopeful's grip had left red marks on his hands, and he looked shaken, his usually steady gaze clouded with uncertainty.

At that moment, she wanted nothing more than to hug him.

The workshop continued with more intense eye-gazing and sharing of personal stories.

Ellie was on autopilot. Her responses were generic, her mind elsewhere. All the while, she kept stealing glances at Cal, whose face remained impassive. Occasionally, he would meet her gaze and force a smile that was a fraction of its usual wattage.

When it finally ended, Ellie was the first one up, practically bolting away from the grove. She waited anxiously outside until Cal emerged, his face a blank mask. Without a word, she reached for his hand and led him away from the gathering.

Only when they were far enough away did she turn to him. "You have to leave."

He scoffed. "I have to leave?"

"Yes. He knows who you are!"

Cal sucked in a sharp breath, then released it slowly before shaking his head. "No, he doesn't. He only knows what we told him—that Calvin Miller is a lawyer."

"He threatened you last night and again just now."

"He's trying to rattle me, but I think it has more to do with you than me. He's fascinated by you, Elle. He can't keep his eyes off you."

She had noticed that. Every time she turned around, she found him watching, his gaze tracking her every move. "He gives me the creeps."

"Which is why I have no fucking intention of leaving without you. I promised I'd help you find your sister and niece and I don't walk away from my promises."

The wind rustled through the trees around them, causing shadows to dance and flicker. It seemed nature itself held its breath, waiting for what would happen next.

He reached out and cupped her face, drawing her gaze back to his. "I won't leave you behind, Ellie. Not here. Not ever."

She looked at him, struck by the intensity in his voice. He was offering her his loyalty, his determination— himself, really. And yet she kept rejecting him, this sweet, protective, intelligent man.

Why did she keep doing it?

And why did he keep putting himself through it?

She stood on tiptoes and kissed him, an unexpected rush of emotion propelling her forward. His grip tightened on her face as he returned the kiss with fervor. It was a deep, lingering kiss that spoke volumes more than words could express.

A footstep crunched nearby, breaking the spell of the kiss, and they pulled apart. Vigil emerged from the trees and waved them over.

"Something you two need to see," he called, his face grim.

Ellie followed Cal toward him, her heart pounding in her chest. The kiss had been... It had felt so right. She glanced at Cal, catching his eye as they walked together. He gave her a small smile that made her stomach flutter.

Maybe kissing him had been a foolish move, but she couldn't bring herself to regret it.

Vigil led them deeper into the woods to a small clearing where an old shack stood. The place appeared decrepit and long abandoned, but what stood out front caught Ellie's attention—a black 1977 Trans Am with California plates.

Her heart leaped into her throat.

"This is where Hope and Hopeful lived when she first came here," Vigil said. "Back then, the commune was known as The Free People, and it was run by Shepherd—his father."

"Were you here back then?" Cal asked.

"No. None of us were, except for Remedy and Merit. They're his aunt and uncle."

Cal grunted. "A family affair. What did Merit say to Hopeful at dinner last night? It spooked him."

Vigil sighed. "I don't know. They kicked me out of the room. Hopeful doesn't trust me anymore, so I'm leaving tonight." He took a small ring of keys from his pants pocket. "But I wanted to give you these. They open every locked door in this place."

Ellie took the keys from Vigil and held them tight in her hand. They felt cold and heavy. "Thank you, Vigil."

Vigil gave her a slight nod. "My name's actually Trent."

She smiled back. "Thank you, Trent."

He turned to Cal. "I'll be at the bottom of the hill below the apple orchard at three a.m. I've got a ride waiting if you want to come."

"Thanks, but we have to find the girl first." Cal offered his hand, and the other man took it in a firm shake.

"I know, but the offer stands. If you find her, she's welcome to come, too. Good luck."

"We'll need it. Hey," Cal called as he started to turn away. When you get off the mountain, I'd appreciate one more favor. Could you contact Sheriff Ash Rawlings in Steam Valley and tell him what's going on up here?"

Vigil—Trent—gave a smile that bordered on mean. "With pleasure."

As he slipped away, Ellie's gaze returned to the Trans Am, and a cold dread seeped into her bones. She'd known her sister was here somewhere, but seeing the car in person made it all too real. The paint was faded and peeling. Leaves and a layer of dirt covered the hood from years of neglect. But it was undeniably the same car Hope had been last seen in.

Cal put his arm around her, pulling her close. "We're going to find her, Elle."

She nodded, her gaze fixed on the car's fading black paint. The past was coming back in a rush of dream-like images of Hope laughing and dancing.

Cal squeezed her shoulder gently. "Come on. Let's see what's inside."

The shack was small and musty. Decades worth of dust and cobwebs covered every surface, and the wooden floorboards creaked ominously under their weight.

In one corner stood an old, rusted stove, its door hanging unhinged. A battered couch occupied another side, its cushions sunken in from years of neglect. But it was the wall covered with old photos that drew Ellie's attention.

Cal picked a picture off the wall and studied it. She walked over and frowned at it. It was a group photo from years ago, the members of the commune all standing in front of the main building with broad smiles on their faces. But it wasn't the group that caught her attention. It was a figure at the center of the frame holding a baby. A young woman with wild, curly hair and a rebellious smile.

Hope.

There she was.

Alive.

Healthy.

Ellie reached out for the photo, needing to see it up close. Cal relinquished it without a word, but he watched her closely as she ran her fingers over the grainy image.

The tender way Hope held the baby contrasted starkly with the wild child she'd been back home. Was that what the commune offered her? A chance for peace? To start fresh and reinvent herself? But then, why had she never reached out and never let them know she was okay?

"This must be True." The baby, barely a year old and with

dark curls like her mom, reached out a chubby hand toward the camera.

The man beside them, with his arms around them both, was Hopeful.

They all looked so happy, and Ellie couldn't reconcile this joyful version of her sister with the troubled woman her mom had told her about.

Her hand trembled slightly as she put the photo back on the wall. She needed answers, but the shack offered more questions than solutions.

She glanced at Cal, finding the same confusion mirrored in his eyes. He reached out and took her hand, squeezing it lightly. It was a comforting gesture, one that kept her grounded amidst the disarray of emotions swirling inside her.

"Let's see what else we can find," he said. He began rifling through drawers while Ellie moved toward a small wooden desk tucked in the corner of the room.

She hesitated before opening the first drawer, torn between dread and anticipation. When she finally pulled it open, she found stacks of old letters and envelopes yellowed with age yet unopened. The return addresses varied—some from California, where they used to reside, and others from unfamiliar places across the country.

Unmailed letters?

Ellie dug deeper and pulled out a faded journal, its leather cover worn with age. Her heart pounding, she opened the front cover to reveal her sister's familiar scrawl. Her name— Hope Summers—was written on the inside cover, followed by a series of dates starting from the year she disappeared.

Ellie sat cross-legged on the floor and began to flip through the pages, her eyes skimming over mundane details about chores and meetings, slowly forming a picture of commune life. Cal joined her, but his attention focused on a box filled with old cassette tapes accompanied by a beat-up tape recorder.

"Elle," he said, holding up one of the tapes. He blew off the dust and squinted at the label. "This one says, 'Hope's Testimony'. Want to give it a listen?"

Ellie nodded, her heart racing as Cal inserted the cassette into the tape recorder and pressed play. The room filled with static before Hope's voice rang out, clear and strong.

She should know the voice by heart, she thought. Hope's voice should be as familiar to her as Alexis's, but instead, it belonged to a stranger.

The recording was hopelessly staticky and occasionally skipped entire words, but Hope sounded like a woman who had found her purpose.

"I used to believe that I was worthless... that my life meant nothing. But now... I understand my worth. I am important here. I am loved. I have a family."

Ellie's heart clenched as tears welled in her eyes. She already had a family. Maybe her relationship with Mom hadn't been great, but she had two sisters who adored her. Didn't they mean anything to her? How could she forget about them so easily?

Cal's hand found hers, his warm presence a beacon of comfort in the midst of their grim discovery. She clung to him as Hope's recording played on, her heart aching for the sister she hadn't known.

As the tapes continued, Hope's stories became more disjointed, veering wildly from recounting the mundane - meals they ate, jobs assigned—to the bizarre rituals and Hopeful's sermons that summoned both adoration and apprehension.

She spoke of True's birth, her voice taking on a tender note that made Ellie's heart ache.

"She's my salvation," Hope said softly. "My chance to do something right."

The tape ended, and Cal popped it out of the recorder. He then randomly chose another one from the stack and slid it into the slot.

Hope's voice filled the room again, muffled but full of fervor. "... he showed me the truth. Freedom isn't about doing whatever we want. It's about living in harmony with our purpose. He knows the way to eternal peace, and I'm the key."

Ellie stiffened. "The key? What the hell does that mean?"

"Wait. Listen." He rewound it a little before pressing play again.

Hope's words filled the room once more, her voice shaking now. "He's dangerous... he's not what he pretends to—"

The tape ended.

The silence in the room was deafening. Ellie stared at the tape recorder, her heart pounding in her chest.

He's dangerous...

What had happened to make her sister change her mind so abruptly?

Cal put a comforting hand on her shoulder. She didn't look at him, instead reaching out to eject the tape from the player.

A sudden noise had both of them jumping—a creaking sound, like someone stepping on old wood. Cal was on his feet in an instant, pulling Ellie up with him and dragging her into the old armoire. She held her breath as the door to the shack squeaked open, and a beam of sunlight spilled into the room.

A figure stepped in, blocking out the light as he moved further inside.

Hopeful.

His gaze swept over the room before settling on the tape recorder sitting on the floor in front of the couch. His brows furrowed, a look of confusion replacing the usual calmness on his face. Then realization dawned, turning into anger.

He strode toward the tape player, picking it up and inspecting it, his hands shaking slightly. With a swift motion, he yanked the tape out of the player, his eyes darting around the room as if looking for signs of an intruder.

Ellie's heart pounded so loudly in her ears that she was sure Hopeful would hear it. But he turned away from their hiding spot, and she exhaled silently in relief.

Suddenly, Hopeful's gaze shifted to the photo wall. He walked over to them, stopped in front of Hope's picture, and touched it tenderly. His expression softened into something unrecognizably gentle—almost affectionate—but it hardened into a steely determination.

He kissed the tips of his fingers and pressed them to the photo. "It's almost time, my love."

A cold shiver ran down Ellie's spine. She squeezed Cal's hand tightly. His grip on her tightened in response, offering silent comfort.

Hopeful crossed back to the desk and pulled a package out of one of the drawers. Then, after one last look around, he left.

They stayed frozen in the wardrobe a few minutes longer until Cal dared to crack open the door.

"Fuck," he said on a harsh exhale and helped her out of the wardrobe. "That was too close. Let's go."

"Wait." She grabbed Hope's journal and stuffed it into the pocket of her robe.

Cal gave her a nod of approval before grabbing the box of tapes and shoving as many as he could into his pockets. While he concealed the recorder against his chest, she headed for the door, poking her head out to ensure the coast was clear. Seeing no one, she slipped out, Cal hot on her heels.

chapter
nineteen

AS SOON AS they were safely back in their cabin, Ellie threw herself into Cal's arms. She didn't think about it—it was just a natural reaction, like drawing breath.

"Oh my God. I can't believe he didn't catch us."

"Hopeful's gonna shit bricks when he realizes we've got his dirty little secrets," Cal said with a grin.

She grinned back at him, and in an instant, something changed. The lingering charge between them sparked to life. Their lips met with an urgency that had nothing to do with the danger nipping at their heels and everything to do with the raw need coursing through them.

He pushed Ellie against the door, crushing her to him. His hands went to her waist, pulling her up on her tiptoes. Her fingers raked through his hair as her glasses skewed to the side, fogging up in the heat of their shared breath.

She could feel his cock hardening against her belly, and a thrill heated her blood.

Cal broke the kiss first. He kissed a trail down her throat, teeth grazing her skin. "We've gotta stop," he murmured, though he didn't sound convinced.

"No, we don't."

"You'll regret it—"

"Just shut up and fuck me, Holden."

Cal lifted her easily, bracing her against the rough-hewn door. Ellie wound her legs around his waist, pulling him closer. He fumbled for a moment before aligning himself with her entrance.

"Ellie," he murmured, half warning, half plea.

But she was past caring and tilted her hips. He slid into her like he was made just for her, stretching her, filling her until her body clenched around his, and she gasped out his name.

Cal held her there, lodged deep inside her as if he was afraid to move. His atypical stillness made her laugh.

"You're not going to break me."

"Fuck." The word came out on a rough exhale as she rolled her hips. "No, but I'm afraid I'm gonna break me."

She smirked and rolled her hips against his in response, causing him to groan and bury his face in her neck. He groaned in response, his lips finding hers again in a desperate kiss that sent a shockwave of pleasure through her. His fingers dug into her thighs, his grip almost bruising. She relished it—the raw, primal edge of him. He moved in short, rough strokes, scraping her bare back against the weathered wood.

"You feel so fucking good," Cal breathed into her ear, punctuating his words with a hard thrust that had her gasping. "I'll never get enough of you."

Every nerve ending seemed on fire as he plunged deeper and deeper. She arched into him, her teeth sinking into his shoulder to muffle the moan that tore from her throat. She tightened her legs around him, wanting him as close as possible.

Her world narrowed down to the sensation of being filled and claimed, the rasp of his labored breaths against her ear, the rough wood behind her digging into her skin. She was shaking, her body straining for that inevitable tumble over the edge.

And then his teeth sank into her shoulder, and she shattered. Her cry echoed in the empty cabin, her body spasming around him in waves of pleasure.

"That's it," he murmured, soothing the bite with his tongue before pressing open-mouthed kisses to her neck. "When you come, you light up like a goddamned supernova. It's so fucking beautiful to watch. Do it again."

And she did. Again and again, Cal drove her over the edge with a single-minded focus that was both thrilling and terrifying.

His fingers tightened on her thighs, his movements growing increasingly erratic. His breath hitched as he neared the precipice, and Ellie felt a burst of triumphant satisfaction. She gripped him tighter, her nails digging into the solid muscle of his back, and pressed her mouth to his ear.

"Come for me now, Cal. Let me feel you."

At her words, something wild flashed in his eyes, and he groaned, his head falling in the crook of her neck, his hot breath ghosting over her skin. His pace became erratic, and she knew he was close to breaking. "God, you're so…" He couldn't finish his sentence as his body stiffened. The sight of him undone—teeth gritted, muscles straining, forehead slick with sweat—sent her over the edge. A wave of pleasure washed over her, so intense it felt like she was being ripped apart and pieced back together all at once.

"Cal!" His name tore from her throat, muffled against his shoulder as her body convulsed around him, the pleasure so sharp and overwhelming it bordered on pain.

He pressed his forehead to hers, their heavy breaths mingling in the close space. His grip on her tightened as he thrust a few more times, riding out both their climaxes. Then, spent and shaking, he let out a long breath and rested his forehead against hers again.

"Fuck," Cal muttered at last. "Just—fuck." His voice was rough with spent desire and awe and something else she couldn't quite place. "What was that?"

She had no idea. "Um... Adrenaline high?"

He laughed, and it sent pleasant little shocks through where they were still joined. "Best damn high I've ever had."

"Can we..." She hesitated. If she took this step with him, there would be no going back. "Can we do it again?"

His grin was searingly bright in the dim light as he scooped her into his arms and strode toward the bed.

Cal had never seen anything more beautiful than Ellie naked, spread out on a bed, waiting for him to lose the rest of his clothes and join her.

He shucked the robe and tunic and kicked off the cotton pants. The entire time, Ellie's gaze devoured him. She dragged her lower lip between her teeth, her blue eyes wide and ravenous as they roamed over his body, lingering on his lengthening cock.

Damn, she was playing with fire, he thought as he climbed onto the bed. It wasn't fair how effortlessly she could bring him to his knees.

"C'mere," she breathed, reaching out to him, dragging him down for a kiss that ignited every nerve ending in his body. He situated himself between her thighs, cursing in a strangled whisper when he felt her slick heat against his already sensitive cock.

"Ellie," he groaned as he slid back into her into her. She

whimpered, arching her back off the mattress to grind against him, making his eyes roll back.

This time, it wasn't fear or adrenaline; it was pure desire — for Ellie and only Ellie. His hands traced down along the inside of her thighs, making her tremble.

"Cal... harder..." she panted, her nails digging into his biceps.

His world narrowed to her and her alone, to the feel of her beneath him, the sounds she made, the way she called his name. He increased his pace, driving deeper inside her with every thrust.

Ellie matched him stroke for stroke, urging him on with breathy moans and whispered words of encouragement. Her eyes were half-lidded, pupils blown wide with pleasure.

He pulled out to the tip, his fingers trailing along her thigh, hitching her legs higher over his hips before he entered her again with a slow, steady push. She rocked against him, moving with him like they'd been doing this dance for centuries — it was intimate and familiar and so goddamn intense.

Heat gathered at the small of his back.

"God, Ellie," he bit out, his rhythm faltering as he fought against the approaching climax. Her muscles clenched around him, sending him spiraling closer toward the edge.

He had to slow things down, or he wasn't going to last. He was too sensitive, too wired, every nerve ending singing with raw, unchecked desire for the woman beneath him. He rocked his hips slowly, his hands sliding up to cup her breasts, thumbing her hard nipples.

It wasn't enough.

"Cal... don't stop." Her fingers dug into the muscles of his ass, and she wrapped her legs tighter around him, grinding herself against him in a rhythm that made stars explode behind his eyelids.

He tried one last time to pull back, to regain control. But the feel of her around him, the way she was moving and pleading his name, it was too much.

"Just go," she urged desperately, her hands shooting up to claw at his back. "It's okay, just go."

He gripped her hips, lifting her slightly as he thrust harder and faster into her. The sound of their bodies colliding echoed in the dim room, mingling with Ellie's soft cries of pleasure.

She was a vision beneath him—flushed and disheveled, the blonde curls spread over the pillow, glasses askew on her nose. Her cries of pleasure were the sweetest music to his ears.

He gave one final thrust before he shattered completely, his climax ripping through him in blinding pulses.

"Fuck," he panted, easing himself out of her to lie beside her on the bed. "I need a moment."

Ellie propped herself up on her elbow, chuckling softly as she traced lazy circles over his chest. "Can't keep up with me, Holden?"

"Keep up with you? Ellie Summers, I can run circles around you," he teased back, rolling onto his side to face her. His gaze dropped to her parted lips and then lower still, lingering on her bare breasts. Her heart pounded visibly in her chest; he could see the rapid rise and fall.

Cal reached out and cupped one of the soft mounds in his hand, his thumb gently brushing her hard nipple. She gasped in surprise and pleasure, and he took that as an invitation. He leaned in, gently sucking on that sensitive peak. She tangibly shivered as his tongue swirled around it before giving it a gentle bite.

"Cal..." she moaned softly, threading her fingers through his hair to hold him close.

He shifted his attention to the neglected breast, lavishing it with equal affection before kissing and nibbling his way down her stomach. Ellie squirmed underneath him, anticipation causing her muscles to tense as he continued his journey lower.

It felt like ages before he finally reached the destination between her thighs. The scent of her arousal was intoxicating, and he breathed it in deep before giving a long lick right where she needed him the most.

The first touch of his tongue against her clit had her bucking off the bed, a strangled cry erupting from her throat. It was raw and animalistic and made the already hot blood coursing through Cal's veins turn molten.

It was so good - the taste of her, the scent of sex hanging heavy in the room - enough to make him lose himself completely. Every stroke of his tongue had her writhing beneath him. Her hands found their way back into his hair, twisting into messy locks as he moved his tongue in rhythmic circles.

Short licks and long ones, soft nips and firmer sucks. He tried everything until he found the perfect tempo, the rhythm that made Ellie whimper and gasp, her hips rising off the bed to meet his face.

Ellie's hips began to move in sync with him, grinding against his mouth. He could feel the tension coiling tighter within her, the occasional spasms that threatened to tip her over the edge. She was falling apart, and he was there to witness it - every whimper, every shiver, every ragged breath she took, all because of him.

Her thighs clamped around his head as she got closer, and he could feel the tell-tale tightening of her body. Her breath grew shallow and ragged.

"I'm... I'm going to..."

She couldn't finish her sentence as he worked a finger into her sex and sucked hard on her clit.

That was it.

Ellie's body bowed off the bed, her grip on his hair tightened convulsively as the dam broke. She screamed his name, her entire body convulsing as she came hard, all her pent-up tension releasing in an explosion of ecstasy.

It was fucking perfect as he rode out her climax with her, tasting her sweetness on his tongue.

Cal kept his mouth on her, lapping up her release until her grip on his hair eased, and she fell back against the mattress, panting like she'd just run a marathon. He gave one last lingering kiss to her sensitive flesh before crawling back up her body, leaving a trail of kisses in his wake.

He was so hard now that it was almost painful. He needed release, and he needed it now. Seeing her lying there, all flushed and sated and beautiful, was enough to make him lose his mind.

"Cal," she purred, a satisfied smile playing on her lips. Those same lips he was dying to feel around him.

"Ellie," he growled back, desire simmering in his eyes.

With a swift movement, she tugged him closer, her hand wrapping around the base of his erection.

His breath hitched as she began to stroke him slowly, agonizingly drawing out his pleasure. He couldn't help the low groan that slipped from him.

"Mmm, like that?" she teased, looking up at him with those wide blue eyes full of mischief and satisfaction. She traced her thumb over the tip of his cock, catching a drop of pre-cum and swirling it over his head.

In response, he bucked into her grip. His world narrowed down to the sensation of her hand on him.

"Just like that," he managed to gasp out, his voice hoarse with raw need. His hands found her hips, gripping them as if they were his anchor in the sea of overwhelming pleasure.

She tightened her grip on him, using her own slickness to make her strokes smoother. He could feel his pleasure mounting with each pass of her hand. Ellie shot him a wicked grin before leaning down and flicking her tongue against the head of his cock.

The sight of her mouth on him was nearly enough to send him over the edge. She took him in slowly, swirling her tongue around the sensitive head before sinking around his length. The sensation of her warm, wet mouth enveloping him was heaven and hell combined. It was more than he could handle, yet not enough.

She set a slow pace, taking him deep before pulling back, only to repeat the torturous rhythm. She fondled his balls gently, adding to the pleasure that was threatening to consume him. He watched her with hooded eyes, captivated by the sight of his slick cock disappearing into her mouth.

The feeling was too good, toe-curlingly good, and he couldn't stop the low growl that escaped his throat.

She pulled back, releasing him with a soft pop before tracing her tongue along the underside of his cock. She was teasing him, driving him closer to the edge, but not quite there yet. Cal could only groan, his head falling back against the pillow as she continued her sweet torture.

He gritted his teeth against the urge to release. He didn't know how he had any more cum inside him, but he was seconds away from spilling it all again.

"Ellie... Fuck..." His voice cracked on the last word when she sucked hard, sending waves of pleasure coursing through him. "Gonna..."

"Don't you dare," she breathed against his tip. "Not yet."

Cal's eyes shot open at her command. He was gasping for breath, his world shattering into a million points of light. Sweat trickled down his face as he bit down on his lower lip so hard he tasted blood. Ellie moved up to straddle him, her curls tumbling down around her and tickling his chest. A devilish smirk spread across her face, and he could only groan in response, already knowing he was putty in her hands.

She positioned herself above him, his cock pressing against her entrance. Ellie then slowly sank down on him, taking him deeper and deeper inside her. Every inch of him filled her, stretching her, making her gasp and arch her back. Her walls clamped around him, squeezing in a rhythm that had him bucking against her.

"Ellie..." His voice was a whisper, barely audible above the pounding of his heart in his ears.

The look in her eyes was mischievous, a spark of delight making them gleam. "Yes, Cal?" She paused at the base of his cock, fully sheathed within her.

"Jesus," he groaned out, rolling his hips up to seek more of the exquisite friction. Ellie laughed lightly, placing her hands on his chest for balance as she started to move.

A slow grind at first, circular motions that had Cal seeing stars as she contracted around him. He gripped her hips tighter, guiding her up and down on his shaft. Each downward slide had him groaning out loud, his head falling back onto the pillows as she leaned down to capture his lips in a fierce kiss. Their tongues matched the rhythm of their bodies.

The sight of her above him, flushed and wild-eyed as she rode him, was too much. He could feel the knot in his stomach growing tighter.

He gripped her hips hard, stopping her movements. Ellie let out a whimper of protest but stopped when she saw the wild look in his eyes. He flipped them over so she was underneath him once again—he liked having control.

With her underneath him, he set a punishing rhythm that had her crying out with every thrust. Her legs wrapped around his waist, pulling him even deeper within her with each stroke.

It was raw and animistic, their bodies crashing together. She arched her back off the mattress, meeting his thrusts halfway. Her hands roamed his back, fingers leaving trails of fire wherever they touched.

"Feels so good, Cal," she breathed out, her voice thick and heady with desire. Her eyes were wide and glassy, gazing up at him like he was her savior.

He could only grunt in response, too lost in the sensation of her body gripping him tight. His hands found her breasts, thumbing over her nipples until she was writhing beneath him. The sight of her falling apart was doing crazy things to his self-control.

"Cal," she cried out, her voice breaking as she succumbed to the pleasure coursing through her body. He could feel her walls contracting around him, the waves of her orgasm tipping him over the edge.

"Yeah... fuck... Ellie!" he gasped, his release hitting him like a freight train. His vision blurred at the edges, and all he could focus on was Ellie beneath him, her body shaking with the aftershocks of her climax.

Slowly, he came back to reality, the world outside their bubble starting to filter in. Their ragged breathing filled the room as they lay there entwined, neither willing to move.

Finally pulling himself together, he rolled onto his side and pulled Ellie against him, her back against his chest. He wrapped an arm around her waist and kissed her shoulder lightly, his nerve endings still buzzing from the multiple rounds of mind-blowing sex.

"Can't move. Don't want to," Ellie murmured into the quiet, her voice laced with smug satisfaction that only post-sex endorphins could bring.

Cal chuckled against the shell of her ear, his chest vibrating against her back. "Yeah, me neither," he agreed, nipping at her earlobe before letting his mouth drift lower, placing soft kisses across her shoulder and neck. But reality had a way of intruding, and his mind was already drifting back to the tapes and journal they'd found.

"Shit," he muttered under his breath.

"What is it?" Ellie asked, her voice drowsy.

"I hate to ruin this, but we can't stay in bed all night."

She groaned, but after a moment, she nodded against him. "Yeah, yeah, you're right. Just give me another minute... or ten."

He smiled down at her, caressing a stray strand of hair away from her face. Her glasses lay discarded on the makeshift nightstand nearby, revealing the freckles that dotted across the bridge of her nose.

Ellie Summers was stubborn as hell, smarter than anyone he knew, and beautiful in ways he didn't have words for. He was hopelessly wrapped around her finger, and he wouldn't have it any other way.

"Ten minutes," he murmured, his fingers tracing down her side. "Then we get back to work."

chapter
twenty

ELLIE DIDN'T THINK she could be more content than she was in that moment. Cal's warmth seeped into her, his strong heart beating a steady rhythm against her back. But she knew they couldn't stay like this forever. Hopeful was planning something, and based on Vigil's hurry to leave, she didn't think his plans were of the happy-sunshine variety.

"What do you think the package was?" she asked, tracing lazy circles on Cal's chest. "The one Hopeful took from the desk?"

He lifted a shoulder. "Something tells me it's probably not his stash of old porn magazines."

She pinched his nipple.

"Ow!"

"Oh, you liked it."

He gave that giddy, boyish grin that made her heart flutter. "I did."

She could tell by the way his cock jumped against her. The man was a boundless font of energy and marveled at the fact that he was already ready for another round.

"Oh my God, Cal. You're insatiable."

He growled in response, his hand tangling into her curls as

he pulled her back to meet his lips. "Guilty as charged," he breathed against her mouth before capturing it in a deep, passionate kiss.

"You said only ten minutes."

"We can do a lot in ten minutes." He rolled, tucking her underneath him, and she gasped at the feel of him nudging at her entrance. She opened her legs wider and accepted him in. There was no urgency in it. It was slow, lazy, not as raw as before. She ached, and every slide of him was delicious torture. His fingers curled into her hair, and he held her trapped under him, his gaze holding hers.

He didn't say the words again, the ones that scared her so much, but he didn't have to. They were right there in his eyes.

And for the first time, she let herself wonder what it would be like if she accepted that love and let herself fall for Callum Holden. The life they could have together would be beautiful and never boring.

Somewhere in the distance, a dog's bark ripped through the night air, followed by shouts and then an eerie silence.

Cal stilled on top of her. "Fuck. Razzy!" He was off her in an instant, and by the time she sat up, he already had on his pants and was digging through the tangle of their clothes on the floor for his shirt.

She jumped out of bed and caught her dress as he threw it in her direction. "How could that be Raszta?"

"Pierce followed us up here. Or, more accurately, followed you. I think he has a thing for you."

Her head spun at the double whammy of information. Pierce followed them? He had a crush on her?

"Wait, what?" She shook his head. It wasn't computing. "Are you serious?"

"He was going to camp nearby and pull you out if things got too dangerous."

"And you're just sharing this now?" Ellie yanked the dress over her head, the cool cotton settling on her still-flushed skin.

Cal tugged his shirt over his head. "I'm sorry, but I thought it better not to tell you. I didn't want to put you in a position where you might have to lie. You're a horrible liar. I was afraid you'd inadvertently put him in danger."

She growled, but, dammit, he was right. She was an awful liar. "It sounds like he's in danger now."

"Yeah. Fuck," Cal said softly and caught her by the shoulders as she started for the door. He stared down into her eyes for a handful of heartbeats. "I want you to get to the car."

"But—"

He stopped her protest with a hard kiss. "I'm going to find Pierce and Raszta, and we'll need a quick getaway."

And he wanted to keep her as far away from trouble as possible. She wasn't sure she liked that, but she understood. "What about the girl?"

His expression was grim. "We can't help her if we're dead."

Holy shit. That thought honestly had crossed her mind. Sure, the commune was a weird place, but they all preached love, harmony, and peace. They didn't seem the type to kill. "Do you really think Hopeful would kill us?"

"I believe he has before—the couple that went missing right before we got here. Ben and Olivia Harrington. They didn't just leave all of their shit and money behind. They're dead, and if he's done it once, he won't have any qualms about doing it again."

A sudden realization struck. "You think he killed Hope, too."

"Unfortunately, yes. I'm starting to think he killed her and hid it from everyone, including his daughter. That's why True just said her mother was missing when she called me. She didn't know." Cal picked up the boxes of tapes and placed them in her arms. "We'll take everything we have to the police. There has to be something in here to incriminate Hopeful."

God. She was in so far over her head with this. But he was right—the best thing she could do right now was to keep the car running.

He held out the car keys and held them for a moment too long when she reached to take them.

"If I don't come out in a half hour, you don't wait. Go tell Ash everything."

"Cal—"

"I mean it. Leave without me."

She swallowed hard, her fingers tightening around the keys. "You better come out, Cal Holden."

"But if I don't, promise me you'll get yourself to safety."

She looked at him, her blue eyes wide behind her glasses, her heart pounding with fear for him and for her niece. But she nodded, accepting the keys. His hand lingered on hers for a moment longer before he pulled away.

"I love you," he said softly.

He didn't wait for her to respond and walked out of the cabin.

She followed him, but he was already running toward the commune's center. She threw one last look over her shoulder as he jogged in the opposite direction of their freedom, and her throat closed up.

She should've said it back.

Why couldn't she say it to him?

She turned and ran toward the front gate. Razzy's barking ricocheted behind her, staccato, almost gunshot-like, and she flinched at the undertone of fear and anger in it.

She hoped she'd have another chance to tell him.

Cal raced toward the barking, his senses on high alert. Raszta's barking was a frantic warning. If the dog could talk, he'd be screaming, "Back the fuck up!"

None of the fairy lights strung around the commune were lit, and the darkness was disorienting. Shadows seemed to flit and flee at the edges of his vision.

Suddenly, Raszta yipped, and silence fell.

No.

He pushed himself harder. Ahead, two shadows wrestled on the mat used as the community dining table while the rest of the commune enclosed them in a circle, watching the fight in eerie silence. Nearby, a small shadow lay on the ground, unmoving.

Raszta.

Gritting his teeth, Cal charged into the circle, breaking the onlookers apart, and he got his first clear look at the two men fighting. One was Pierce, his face a grim mask of pain and determination. The other was a Blue Robe, but his back was to Cal, and he couldn't see his face.

Out of the corner of his eye, he saw Raszta start to stir and rushed over. The dog was dazed and had but seemed okay otherwise. Cal let out a breath and refocused on the fight.

Blue Robe threw a punch that collided with Pierce's jaw. He retaliated with a swift kick to the man's side. The Blue folded in half with an *umph*, but it didn't stop him. He rounded on Pierce, a knife glinting ominously in his hand.

Cal didn't waste another second. He picked up a broom someone had dropped nearby. It wasn't a weapon, but it was better than nothing. He rushed into the fight just as Pierce was tackled from behind by another Blue Robe who'd materialized from the crowd.

"Hey, assholes!" He swung the broomstick and hit one of them square in the back. The man grunted and staggered away from Pierce, freeing him to deal with the other guy.

"Enough."

The command wasn't shouted, but it carried over the noise with an authority that sent chills down Cal's spine. Hopeful emerged from the crowd, his long hair falling around his shoulders. He wore a white robe with the hood pulled back, his pale face lit by the moon. His eyes, deep and dark, bore into Cal.

The fighting stopped instantly. Everyone turned to look at their savior and guide.

Cal straightened, broom still clutched in his hand like a lifeline as he met Hopeful's cold gaze.

Pierce scrambled to his feet. Sweat and blood trailed down his face in messy rivulets. His fists were clenched at his sides. He watched Hopeful with barely contained rage, then his gaze shifted to his dog, and his relief at seeing Razzy up was palpable.

Raszta lumbered to his side and glared at Hopeful, a low rumble coming from his chest. Even so, he wasn't exactly intimidating—a thirty-pound mop dog with his dreads pulled up into a now-lopsided ponytail. A Rottweiler would've been more helpful in this situation.

"Are you hurt?" Cal asked.

Pierce shook his head and swiped at the blood streaming from his nose. The guy was seething.

Cal turned back to Hopeful, broom still in hand. "What happened to all that shit you preach about love and harmony?"

"This is love." His smile was thin, brittle, a shard of ice in the moonlight. "Love is achieved through discipline, through obedience."

"That's not love. That's fear."

Hopeful sighed. "And here I thought we were finally starting to see eye to eye." He nodded to the Blue Robe that Pierce had been fighting with, and the man moved forward to stand beside Hopeful.

Sincere. He wiped his split lip on the sleeve of his robe, leaving a streak of red, and gave a smile that was all white teeth and arrogance.

That lying fucker. He'd said he wasn't in the inner circle. Had Vigil known? What about Clarity? She was a Blue, too. Were they spies, too, or had they meant what they said about wanting out?

Cal took his eyes off the men long enough to scan the crowd. He didn't see either of them among the faces, but he did spot Jeff and Marla, who both looked shell-shocked. Tyler and Nico were also there. Tyler looked sick. Nico supported most of his partner's weight and just looked scared.

Hopeful turned toward the crowd and held out his arms as if to embrace them. "I have learned tonight that we have traitors among us."

Gasps filtered through the crowd as everyone eyed their neighbors suspiciously.

Hopeful patted the air in a calming gesture. "We have found them, and they have been properly punished for their betrayal." His gaze shifted back to Cal and Pierce. "However, these outsiders pose a far greater threat. They represent every-thing we swore to leave behind. The corruption, the greed, the lies!"

A murmur of assent rippled through the crowd.

"They want to tear us apart. To dismantle this sanctuary we have created. To steal away our Mother God. Will we let them?"

"No!" The response was immediate and vehement.

"Will we protect Her?"

"Yes!"

"What should their punishment be for threatening Her?"

"Re-education!" The crowd chanted, several members raising their fists in the air. "Re-education! Re-education!"

From both sides of the crowd, two men stepped forward. Pierce made a hand signal to his dog, and Raszta bolted away.

"Let it go," Hopeful called as several people tried to catch Razzy. "The animal can't harm us."

Pierce smirked, and that small, knowing smile seemed to unsettle Hopeful more than anything else that had happened. His expression hardened. "Take them to the Re-Education Chamber."

Where were they?

Ellie stared at the entrance of the commune, her heart in her throat, choking her with fear.

Come on, Cal. Come on. Come on.

The SUV's engine rumbled softly behind her, and she bounced on the balls of her feet. She felt exposed waiting out here.

Something was wrong.

The feeling prickled at the back of her neck, a creeping chill that wouldn't budge no matter how hard she tried to shake it off.

Suddenly, there was a rustling in the underbrush nearby, and she whirled around, her heart pounding in her chest. Raszta burst out of the thicket, his dreadlocks flying out behind him as he galloped toward her.

"Razzy!" Ellie dropped to her knees, throwing her arms wide open. The dog skidded to a halt in front of her, his pink tongue lolling out from the side of his mouth. His dark eyes were wide with terror, and he was panting heavily.

"Oh, Razzy," Ellie murmured, pulling the dog into a tight hug. She could feel his heart hammering against his ribs, matching the frantic beat of her own. She pulled back slightly and looked at him, then at the entrance. "Where are they?"

But Raszta only whined and squirmed in her arms, his claws scratching against the earth as he tried to push himself back into a standing position.

She let him go. "Razzy, where are they?"

Before she could try to interpret his doggy distress signals, several figures ran out from the commune's entrance. Raszta bolted into the trees.

"Wait!"

He didn't stop and disappeared into the dark.

"Shit." She spun back to the figures, but it wasn't Cal and Pierce.

Marla and Jeff.

Had they been sent to find her?

She stiffened and groped around in the car for the tire iron she'd found while stowing the box of tapes in the trunk. She'd left it on the seat in case she needed a weapon and closed her hand around it.

But then Nico and Tyler followed hot on their heels. Tyler was pale and wide-eyed. Halfway to the car, his knees gave out. Nico almost dropped him, and Jeff ran back to help.

"Thank God you have a car," Marla said.

"Where are yours?"

"We don't own one," Jeff said, grunting under Tyler's slight weight.

"Ours is in town," Nico said. "Sincere picked us up in the commune's van."

Ellie studied them, trying to gauge whether they were telling the truth, and her gaze finally landed on Tyler. He really didn't look good. There was no way he could be faking that pallor to his skin.

Ellie made the split-second decision to trust them and released her grip on the tire iron. She rushed to open the SUV's back door. "What's wrong?"

"They took his insulin and convinced us he no longer needed it. Jesus." Nico shook his head in stunned horror. "How did they convince me of that? I'm a fucking doctor!"

"Dentist," Tyler said, his voice slurred. "You're a dentist, Nic."

"But I knew better, and I still let them brainwash—"

"Don't beat yourself up," Ellie said. "Brainwashing is powerful and happens faster than you think. We are all susceptible."

As the men loaded Tyler into the backseat, she looked over at Marla. "Where is Cal?"

"Hopeful has him and your other friend."

No.

She swung back to the gate, but Marla grabbed her arm, stopping her.

"You can't go back in there alone. You won't be able to help them. You'll only get caught, too."

She wanted to deny it. She wanted to run into the commune like a badass action heroine, swinging that tire iron and rescuing her boys. But she knew Marla was right. She was out of her depth here.

Promise me you'll get yourself to safety and take these bastards down...

She slid into the SUV's driver's seat.

"Get in," she ordered, her voice surprisingly steady. "We're getting the hell out of here and bringing back the cavalry."

chapter
twenty-one

SAWYER MURPHY KNEW THAT BARK.

He paused mid-throw, much to Zelda's annoyance. She huffed her displeasure at having her game of fetch disrupted.

"Hang on," he told her and tilted his head, waiting for the bark to sound again.

There.

Yeah, that was definitely Raszta. There was no mistaking that weirdly raspy bark. Razzy always sounded like he indulged in three packs a day.

"Hey, Pierce. Where have you been?"

No answer.

Okay, that was weird. Pierce usually whistled in two short bursts when he was in the vicinity, so he didn't startle Sawyer.

"Pierce?"

Nothing.

A cold nose bumped against his hand. Not Zelda. The nose was much smaller. He rubbed a hand over the dog's head and found Raszta's ponytail knocked askew. He looked down and tried to focus, but Razzy was standing too still. Without movement, he couldn't see anything but the blurry impression of a dog.

"Hey, buddy. Why are you out here alone? Where's your person?"

Raszta gave an anxious whine and gently nipped at Sawyer's fingers.

Something was wrong.

His stomach knotting with dread, he straightened and grabbed his cell phone from his pocket. "Call Ash," he told it.

The line rang twice before Ash picked up with a curt, "Yeah?"

"Raszta just showed up from the woods without Pierce."

"Fuck," Ash muttered. "Cal and Ellie are missing, too."

That knot in his stomach twisted ever tighter. He called Zelda to his side and strapped her back into her harness. "I'll round up the team. Or at least what's left of it." With Pierce missing, Shane on his honeymoon, and Connelly away on a book tour, there wasn't much of a team right now to round up.

"Yeah, you do that," Ash said. "I'll be there in ten."

Zelda led the way and Raszta trailed at his side as he hurried back to the rescue. He'd just reached the back door when he heard tires screech to a halt out front.

No way that was Ash arriving already.

He changed directions and headed toward the parking lot. There he found a flurry of movement that his wonky eye-brain connection struggled to translate. People were spilling out of a vehicle that had the same shape as Pierce's hulking SUV.

"Sawyer!" Ellie's voice. She rushed toward him, and he had the impression of blond curls and big, terrified eyes before she stopped moving and faded into blurriness again. "Call Ash. We need an ambulance."

"Who's hurt?" he demanded.

"Tyler."

Who the fuck was Tyler?

Still, he grabbed his phone again and told it to call Ash. As he waited for the sheriff to pick up again, he asked, "Where are Cal and Pierce?"

Ellie's voice came out strained. "In danger."

chapter
twenty-two

THE RE-EDUCATION CHAMBER was a rusted shipping container plunked down in the middle of the commune's gardens. The damn thing looked innocuous like its only crime would be messing up someone's Instagram shot of the grapevines. But inside, it was a whole other game.

It was hot and smelled of piss and sweat. There was a single chair bolted to the floor with leather straps on the armrests and legs. A rolling cart held an ominous contraption that looked suspiciously like an old electric shock therapy machine.

Fuck.

"Put the mute one in the chair," Sincere ordered from behind them.

The men shoved Cal down in the corner and chained him to the wall by his hands while Pierce was forced into the chair. Pierce's eyes were flat, and his jaw set as the leather straps cinched around his wrists and ankles.

"Comfortable?" Sincere approached Pierce with a serpentine grin. He caressed the old machine like a lover and flicked a switch. A weird static humming filled the air.

The sound was like fingernails on a chalkboard to Cal's

ears. His gaze met Pierce's across the room. The former soldier didn't say anything—couldn't say anything with his hands strapped down—but his gaze burned with silent hatred.

For Sincere?

Or for Cal?

He couldn't tell.

Sincere lifted two gleaming electrodes and walked back to Pierce. He placed them on either side of his captive's temples.

"You can stop this," Sincere said casually. "Just tell me where Ellie went."

Cal gritted his teeth. He'd chew his damn tongue off before he gave them anything.

"No?" Sincere started flipping the switches on the old-fashioned machine. The damn thing whirred like a dying animal, and Cal could see the fear flicker in Pierce's eyes for just a split second before they turned back to granite. He shook his head, silently telling Cal not to say anything.

Seeing Pierce there, strapped to that chair, stoic as a stone — it made him wish he could just take his place.

"No," he snarled finally. "We're not telling you a fucking thing."

Sincere chuckled, a dark sound that echoed in the confines of the chamber. "Let's see how long that resolve lasts."

With that, he cranked a dial on the machine, and Pierce went rigid in the chair, every muscle in his body straining against the leather straps. His eyes met Cal's, a silent plea for him to stay strong. Funny how he was the one being tortured but was still worried about Ellie. He didn't make a sound, but his dark eyes shot wide in pain, the muscles in his neck taut under the strain.

"I don't know where Ellie is," Cal said.

The goddamn machine whirred to life once more. Sweat poured off Pierce like rain down a windshield. Blood trickled from where he'd bitten into his lip. His veins stood out on

And still, he didn't make a sound.

Sincere cranked the knob further, and Pierce's body convulsed violently, his mouth falling open in a hoarse whisper of a scream that was the first sound Cal had ever heard the man make.

"Stop! You'll kill him. I swear I don't know where she is or what she's doing." Cal fought against his restraints, his heart pounding mercilessly against his chest. He met Pierce's gaze once more—those eyes were still stoic but now bloodshot and streaming tears. It was a sight he knew would be seared into his memory forever.

Then Pierce's gaze shifted to Sincere, and in a barely-there rasp of a voice that sounded painful, he whispered, "Fuck. You."

Sincere simply smiled, an expression that was all teeth and no warmth.

It went on like that for minutes— hours— an eternity until finally, someone knocked on the container's door. Sincere stepped back, panting with excitement or exhaustion. Cal couldn't tell which one. Probably both.

Hopeful stepped in and scanned the scene without a flicker of emotion. "Anything?"

"He's strong. I'll give him that," Sincere chuckled, wiping off sweat from his forehead as if he'd just finished a satisfying workout. But his eyes were wild, manic with a sense of power that made Cal's stomach roll with disgust.

Pierce was no longer convulsing. He was barely conscious, sagging against the restraints like a puppet with its strings cut. His breaths came out in ragged gasps, sweat coating his face and matting his dark hair into inky spikes. Blood dribbled from the corner of his mouth.

"So you've gotten nothing useful?" Hopeful stared with those icy gray eyes. "Time is running out. Your Mother God needs answers before The Great Renewal arrives."

"Then perhaps we should change our focus," Sincere replied, moving toward Cal.

Fear wrapped icy fingers around Cal's spine, but he held his ground. "I don't know where Ellie is," he repeated for the hundredth time, the words forming a cold, hard knot in his throat.

God, he hoped she was safe.

Hopeful studied him for a long, cold minute before finally turning his attention back to Sincere. "Leave him," he said finally. "It doesn't matter where the woman went. She won't stop us, and we have other priorities now. We need to prepare."

As Sincere moved back to shut down the machine, a fever-bright, fanatical gleam appeared in his eyes. Why hadn't he seen that before? It was impossible to miss.

Despite himself, Cal exhaled in relief when the humming stopped. He watched as Hopeful turned to leave the chamber, his robe billowing behind him like some goddamn messiah in a B-rated movie. Sincere was right on his heels like the obedient dog he was.

Cal waited a few minutes to ensure they were gone before climbing to his feet and walking as close to Pierce as his chains would allow.

"Pierce? Jesus. I'm so sorry. Talk to me." The moment the words were out of his mouth, he realized how stupid they were. Pierce couldn't talk. "Give me some kind of sign you're okay."

Pierce's eyes flicked open. "Not... your... fault," he mouthed, each word a struggle.

His voice was like glass-spiked shards of gravel and sounded so painful that Cal winced in symphony. "Don't talk, man."

Pierce's eyes narrowed in silent defiance before the lids

drooped, the effort visibly draining him. A moment later, he slumped forward against his restraints, unconscious.

"Fuck!" Cal pulled on his chains, but it was useless. He couldn't get closer to Pierce, couldn't help him. Frustration and helplessness strangled him, and he vented it with a furious yank on the chain. The shackles bit into his wrists, but he relished the pain. Anything was better than the icy fear twisting his gut.

He'd always believed that everyone deserved a fair chance, a chance to be heard, to tell their side of the story. He'd whole-heartedly thought everyone deserved to have someone on their side.

But now?

Fuck that.

Hopeful and Sincere and all the rest of those deranged lunatics playing god didn't deserve a damn thing. Except maybe a first-class ticket straight to hell.

Minutes passed like hours. Or maybe it was actually hours? Time had lost all meaning, and Pierce hadn't so much as twitched.

The silence was oppressive, a tomb-like stillness that soaked into Cal's bones and messed with his head. He tried to fight the sleepiness creeping in, but it was a losing battle.

Finally, the door creaked open again, startling him awake. His heart lodged in his throat as he prepared for another round of Sincere's twisted games, but instead of the psychopath, it was a girl in a white robe, her silhouette outlined in gold by the rising sun.

Like an angel.

Cal blinked, not entirely sure he could trust what he was seeing. "Hello?" His voice was hoarse.

The girl tilted her head and stared at him with an intensity that had him shifting uncomfortably. She was a small thing.

Young, with pale blue-green eyes too old for her age. Her dark hair curled around her heart-shaped face.

She moved forward, and Cal tensed, expecting more pain. But instead, she passed him and moved toward Pierce.

She reached out with pale hands to touch Pierce's face, her fingers tracing his sweat-dampened skin with surprising gentleness.

And the pieces finally clicked into place in his sluggish brain. "You're True, aren't you? You called me for help."

She glanced over her shoulder at him and nodded once before returning her attention to Pierce, wiping the blood from his mouth with the sleeve of her pristine robe. "I was scared, but I shouldn't have involved you."

"You didn't 'involve' anyone. You asked for help when you needed it, and that's okay."

She stroked a hand over Pierce's head in an almost motherly way. "You're suffering because of me."

Cal forced a smile. "Pierce and I are tough cookies. We'll be okay. We're here because we want to help you."

She shook her head. "It's too late."

"Too late for what?"

She didn't answer, just continued silently wiping away the blood and sweat from Pierce's face.

Okay. Maybe she'd be more responsive if he tried another tactic. "True, I know your aunts, Ellie and Alexis."

Her gaze snapped to his. "The woman that was here with you is my aunt?"

"Yes. She's been looking for you and your mom for a long time. So has Alexis."

She finally settled Pierce back so he wasn't straining against the leather straps, then turned to face Cal. "I was told I don't have any family left except—" she broke off and didn't seem inclined to finish the thought.

"Except these nutjobs?" Cal finished for her, glancing around the grimy container. "They lied."

True blinked, her pale eyes round in the dim light and so much like Ellie's.

"They always lie," she said with a sad kind of resignation. "But it doesn't matter. It's too late."

"I don't understand. Why is it too late?"

The morning chime sounded in the distance, and she inhaled sharply, hurrying back toward the door.

"True, wait!"

She paused but didn't look back. "Don't eat or drink what they give you today."

And then she was gone.

chapter
twenty-three

"OF ALL THE CRAZY, fucked up things this group has done, you and Cal joining a fucking cult takes the cake," Ash fumed as he paced the command center at Redwood Coast Rescue. On a good day, his personality was like a storm cloud, but now he'd exploded into a thunderhead.

Ellie couldn't blame him for his anger. What they'd done had been stupid and reckless, and it may cost Cal and Pierce their lives.

Cal.

Her throat closed up, and tears she couldn't control spilled down her cheeks. She ripped her glasses off and pressed her hands to her eyes. She hated that she was crying. She wanted to be strong and capable like Alexis.

God, she wished her sister were here, but Alexis and Shane were off the grid for their honeymoon and wouldn't return for a few more days. And even if Ellie could get a hold of them, she wouldn't. After everything they'd been through, they deserved to enjoy their time together without more drama.

"Ash, enough." Anna's tone was reprimanding. She scowled at her brother as she finished brewing a mug of tea, then crossed the room to hand it to Ellie. "You're not helping the situation."

He rounded on her. "I told them to stay away from it and let me handle it."

"Well, maybe you should've explained why you wanted them to stay away rather than just ordering them to do it," Rose said lightly. She was lounging on one of the couches along the wall, stroking a hand over the big black German Shepherd beside her. Dante was so very much like Ash. He watched the action play out between the humans with intense, narrowed eyes as if deciding who he needed to bite next.

Ash pointed at his wife. "You stay out of this. I'm still pissed you told them about the commune."

If Rose was bothered by his anger, she didn't show it. "Honey, you're always pissed about something. And they were going to find out one way or another. The fact there's a cult on the mountain isn't exactly a secret around here."

"I didn't know about them," Sawyer chimed in from his seat in front of the computer.

Zak straightened from his lazy sprawl behind his desk, the boot of his prosthetic leg hitting the floor with a hard thunk that made all the dogs in the room perk up. "Yeah, well, no offense, buddy, but you spend most of your time in this room listening to the computer babble at you."

A faint furrow appeared on Sawyer's forehead. He turned back to the computer. "You'd all be lost without me at this computer."

Zak held up his hands. "Hey, I'm not denying it. We need you there. Have you found out anything useful about this Hopeful guy yet?"

"Still digging," Sawyer muttered and slid his headphones on.

As the conversation raged around her, Ellie wrapped her hands around the mug of tea and inhaled the steam. It was earthy and sweet, reminding her of the tea Remedy had given her on their first day at the commune.

The thought turned her stomach, and she set the mug down untouched. Puzzle curled close to her side and rested his head in her lap, staring up at her with worried brown eyes. She ran her fingers through his fluffy reddish-gold fur, pausing to adjust the red bowtie on his collar. She'd bought it for him in the perfect shade of red to match her glasses after seeing Veronica's Papillon, Alfie, wearing one and thinking it was the cutest thing in the world.

The sudden warmth of a hand on her shoulder jolted her back to reality.

"Ellie." Anna's voice was gentle, her eyes kind. "This isn't your fault."

Dammit. She was crying again, wasn't she? She impatiently wiped at her eyes. "I left him there. Left them both, and who knows what Hopeful is doing to them."

"You did what you had to do." Zak's firm voice broke through the swirl of her self-reproach.

"But I should've chosen Cal over—"

He shook his head and held up a hand, cutting her off. "Sometimes there are no right choices. Sometimes there are only shitty ones, and all you can do is choose the least shitty option." His expression was grim. He was speaking from experience. "You got out, you got four other people out, and got Tyler Erickson medical help. If you had made any other decision than the one you did, he would've died before reaching a hospital. That's not nothing. So, no more guilt. We'll work out how to get Cal and Pierce out."

"Got something," Sawyer said suddenly and pulled off his headphones. A picture of Hopeful—younger, with short hair, but definitely him—appeared on the room's large main screen. "Lance Shepherd, a.k.a. Hopeful. His father was Mark Allen Shepherd, who just went by his last name and started the commune in the mid-70s. It was called The Free People back then. It was your run-of-the-mill free love-type commune and appears to have been widely accepted as a legitimate community by everyone around here. But then Shepherd died about twenty years ago, and something happened up there."

"Hope disappeared twenty years ago," Ellie said, and the picture on screen shifted to a digital scan of a now-defunct local newspaper. The headline read:

"Leader of Local Commune Dead in Apparent Suicide."

The article went on to detail Shepherd's death from an overdose of hemlock and his son Lance taking over.

"When Hopeful took control, there was a mass exodus of members," Sawyer continued. "They changed their name and locked down tight for several years. They stopped coming into town, and rumors of weird ceremonies and cult-like behavior started floating around—all based on information from the people who left the commune around that time."

"Like my parents," Rose said. "Dad said they left because things started getting weird."

Right around the time Hope had appeared at the commune. Ellie's stomach twisted with a dread she didn't want to examine too closely.

"And Hopeful has been running this show ever since?" Anna asked.

"Seems like it." Sawyer had resumed his search, fingers dancing over the keys as the computer read off items so fast it sounded like it was speaking another language. "They started recruiting again about seven years ago by hosting various retreats throughout the years. They also began selling teas and home remedies online. They've got a pretty extensive website."

Anna stood, crossing to stand behind Sawyer's chair. She read the screen over his shoulder, a faint frown of confusion on her face. "Why would anyone want to join this cult?"

Ellie thought about Marla and Jeff. About Nico and Tyler.

And all the others she'd met at the commune. Some were vulnerable, some lost... all seeking something they thought they'd find with Hopeful.

"Because they're looking for something," she said quietly. "And Hopeful convinced them he could help them find it."

Sawyer turned around in his chair. His pale blue eyes were unfocused, looking past her shoulder.

"Okay," Zak said finally, breaking the silence. "So we know more about Hopeful and his freaky cult. How do we get in and find Cal and Pierce without stirring up a hornet's nest? We—" He broke off, and a thoughtful expression crossed his face.

"I don't like that look," Ash said warily.

"What look?" Zak asked, all innocence.

"The one you get when you're about to suggest we do something stupid or reckless or both."

"It's not stupid."

"So it's reckless."

"Just hear me out. With the way you've been pruning all of the bad apples from your department, you don't have the manpower to storm the commune. And I don't have enough guys available to fill in the blanks."

"I know where you're going with this, but no. I'll just have to call in the state police or the FBI." He pulled his phone from his belt by his badge, but Zak snatched it away.

"Do you want another Waco here?"

"He's got a point," Sawyer said. "We don't know what their weapon situation is up there."

Silence fell over the room for several heartbeats.

Rose finally broke the silence. "Waco?"

Ash groaned softly. "Sometimes I forget how much younger you are than me."

She grinned at him. "You may be an old man, but you're my old man. So, what's the Waco?"

Ellie looked over at Rose. At twenty-seven, they were the same age, born nearly five years after the siege. The only reason Ellie knew about it was because true crime was her whole life.

"A cult in Waco, Texas, was accused of weapons violations," she explained. "When the FBI and ATF tried to execute a search warrant, it ended up in a shootout. Four officers died, six more were injured, and the compound was under siege for fifty-one days. It finally ended in a fire, and over seventy people died."

"Whoa," Rose said, her blue eyes wide. She turned to her husband. "Yeah, we definitely don't want that. I vote we don't call the FBI and go with Zak's idea instead."

"This isn't a democracy," Ash muttered, but he was ignored.

"I vote for Zak's idea, too," Anna said.

"Okay, but I can't be involved with this. The legality of it is too gray." Ash shook his head and picked up the box of Hope's recordings, which Ellie had brought in with her. "I'll take these back to the station and start going through them."

They all watched him go.

Ellie thought she should be worried because they were crossing a line that Ash, as sheriff, couldn't cross.

But she wasn't.

She just wanted Cal back.

She shifted her gaze over to Zak. "So, what exactly is your idea?"

He grinned, and there was more than a little glint of mean in it. "We go ahead and stir up that hornet's nest."

chapter
twenty-four

ZAK HADN'T ELABORATED on what he meant by stirring up the hornet's nest but instead excused himself to make some calls.

When he came back, he nodded. "We lucked out. They were in Nevada on a training mission. They're on their way. ETA ninety minutes."

Everything kicked into high gear then, and within an hour, the team was loading up the dogs to head up the mountain for the rescue mission.

Ellie grabbed Puzzle's harness and buckled him into it. She was just strapping on her boots when Zak stepped up next to her, blocking her path. "You're not going."

Outrage burned through her. "Like hell I'm not."

His gaze flicked down to Puzzle. "He's not certified."

"That excuse is so flimsy it's transparent." She crossed her arms over her chest. "We've been on missions before."

"Not ones like this. He's not a war dog, and we haven't desensitized him to gunfire."

She lost some of her defiance at that and glanced down at Puzzle. His tail wagged at the possibility of heading out on an adventure, knocking someone's half-empty mug off the nearby coffee table. The dark liquid splattered across the floor like an oil spill.

She looked up, meeting Zak's gaze again. "Are you expecting a war?"

His smile was grim. "That's why I called in the big guns."

"Who?"

He didn't answer and instead pointed at her. "Stay."

At her side, Puzzle obediently sat, but his tail still wagged, spreading the coffee mess around with each swish.

"I'm not a dog!" she called as Zak and the rest of the guys marched out. "I'm not just going to sit and stay on command."

"Welcome to my world," Sawyer muttered from in front of his computer. "I don't get to do anything fun anymore, either."

She whirled on him. "Who did he call?"

Sawyer's fingers stopped tapping at the keyboard, and he looked in her direction with his unfocused eyes. "Ghost-busters?"

"I'm serious."

He hesitated for a heartbeat, then sighed and dragged a hand over his face. "He called in the team that rescued him from Afghanistan."

"Oh shit." She'd never heard the full story of Zak's time as a POW or how he lost his leg, but she had heard the rumors of his rescue by some kind of badass black ops team. "He thinks it's that dangerous?"

"Well, he hasn't really talked to them since his rescue... if that gives you any indication."

Ellie glanced back at Puzzle. The fur on his back was standing up, and the light in his eyes dimmed. He could sense her worry. She held out her hand, and he pressed his head against her palm. "So those guys... they're... what? Mercenaries?"

"I think they prefer to be called private contractors. They specialize in hostage rescue and do dirty work that government agencies can't touch due to legal entanglement."

The words hit Ellie like a sucker punch. She sank into the nearest chair, staring with wide eyes at Sawyer. Puzzle whined and nudged her knee with his snout, but she barely noticed. Her mind was whirling, too full of what-ifs and worst-case scenarios.

"Are they... are they any good?" she asked, although she wasn't sure she wanted to hear the answer.

Sawyer snorted, a sound somewhere between amusement and disdain. "They're the best. They don't always obey the rules, but they get the job done."

Fear curdled in her, bitter and cold, choking out any semblance of rational thought. She thought about Cal, strong, stubborn Cal, wrapped up in something so dangerous that Zak had to call in a team of mercenaries.

All because of her.

Infiltrating the commune had been her idea.

And then she'd left Cal there...

She popped to her feet. "I am not sitting this one out."

Sawyer whipped around in his chair. "Ellie—"

But she was already out the door with Puzzle at her side.

By the time she got to the parking lot, the team had just finished loading their gear in Redwood Coast Rescue's new K9 unit trucks. She slipped alongside one of the vehicles—the one farthest from Zak's—and crawled into the backseat, keeping low. She bribed Puzzle to lie down in the footwell with a treat.

His tail thunked on the floor as he gobbled up the piece of freeze-dried chicken. To her ears, it sounded like a drum, and she winced.

"Shh. We have to be quiet."

The driver's side door opened, and a border collie

launched into the cab, followed by Donovan Scott sliding into the driver's seat.

The big, heavily tattooed former Marine met her gaze in the rearview mirror, then his mouth tipped up in a smile. "Zak will not be happy."

She straightened up in the seat. "That's too bad because I'm going. I know the compound. You guys don't, and neither do those mercenaries Zak hired. No matter how good they are, they'll appreciate not going in blind."

Donovan shrugged and started the engine. "Hey, I'm fine with it. You probably have a better understanding of cults than any of us, and I'd prefer not to go in blind myself. I want to get home to my wife and kid tonight."

Ellie nodded, relief washing over her. A tiny sliver of guilt pricked at her for roping Donovan into her plan, but she pushed it away. It was Cal's life on the line, and dammit, she'd do whatever it took to bring him back, even if it meant facing Zak's wrath later.

They pulled out onto the road, and neither spoke for several minutes. She felt Donovan's eyes on her in the rearview mirror. "You scared?"

She took a deep breath. "Terrified."

"Nah, you'll be fine." He gave his border collie, Spirit, an ear scratch, then returned his attention to the road. "What's it like up there at the commune? There's been rumors about it as long as I can remember. In school, kids used to say they did twisted shit up there, like animal sacrifices and kinky blood magic sex rituals."

She exhaled the breath caught in her throat on a short laugh. "If they do any of that, I didn't see it." But she wouldn't put the sex rituals past Hopeful. "Honestly, it was all very tame at first. Lots of meditation and yoga and group therapy sessions where everyone talks about their feelings until you want to puke rainbows. But then they started talking about crystals and auras, and it just got... weird."

"So, basically, it's a New Age RWCR." He made a face. "Rylan has us all doing yoga during our group therapy sessions now."

All of the members of Redwood Coast Rescue had their demons. They had all faced war and came back in pieces, but they had found healing in each other and their dogs. Their weekly group therapy sessions played a huge role in that healing process. She'd seen first-hand what it had done for Shane. Her new brother-in-law was an entirely different man now than when they first met.

"Yoga isn't so bad," she said.

Donovan grumbled. Then, after a beat, he muttered, "No. It's not."

By the time they reached the outskirts of the commune, dawn was beginning to paint the sky a deep, rich blue. Ellie peered out of the window, her heart pounding like a drum as she looked at the familiar landscape. She squeezed Puzzle's collar in her hands, drawing comfort from his warm presence.

Donovan pulled onto a narrow track off the main road. He turned off the engine and took out his radio.

"Spirit in position," he said in a low voice. Whenever they communicated on a mission, they used their dog's name like a callsign— something Ellie hadn't gotten used to yet and often messed up during training exercises.

There was a brief silence before Zak's voice crackled over the speaker. "Copy that. HORNET entering into enemy territory via airborne insertion. ETA: fifteen minutes. Stand by."

Donovan set the radio down and settled back in his seat.

"Wait, we're just going to sit here?" She stared at the radio, then at him.

Donovan shot her a side glance, amusement in his eyes. "Ellie, we're not knights storming a castle. We're a K9 unit. We go in later, not first, so the best thing we can do for Cal and Pierce right now is give HORNET the space they need to do their thing."

He was right.

She clenched her fists in her lap and scowled out the window at the pale yellow light brightening the horizon behind the mountains. Puzzle nudged her hand with his snout, and she absently scratched his ears.

Of course she knew Donovan was right, but it didn't make waiting any easier when Cal was just right there up the road in that godforsaken commune with a man who was likely, certifiably, a lunatic.

She settled back into her seat, trying to ignore the quiet hum of nerves below her skin. She took slow breaths, counting them out in her head, attempting to calm her racing heart. "I've never been very good at waiting."

"Yeah, me either."

"This sucks." She'd never been good at waiting.

Donovan chuckled softly. "When I was in Afghanistan, we had this saying—'Embrace the suck.' It meant that some situations were just going to be hard as hell, but resisting it, fighting against it, only made it suck more. So we just... embraced it."

She glanced over, a frown creasing her brow as she considered his words. "So you're saying I should embrace the fact that this... waiting sucks?"

He shrugged. "Pretty much, yeah."

Embrace the suck.

It sounded ridiculous, yet there was a weird sort of wisdom to it.

She squinted into the growing brightness outside and strained her ears, hoping to hear... something. Anything. She desperately wanted to know what was happening beyond those trees.

She heard nothing. Saw nothing. She didn't know whether that was a good or bad sign.

Embrace the suck.

With a sigh, she leaned back in the seat and forced herself to loosen her death grip on Puzzle's harness. The dog woofed softly and rested his head on her lap, all but melting into her.

Embrace the suck.

It felt like an eternity before Zak's voice finally crackled over the radio again. "HORNET secured perimeter. Spirit, you're clear to move in."

"Copy that," Donovan replied and fired up the engine.

The commune appeared out of the foggy dawn like a specter— eerie and ghostly quiet. Several men stood under the Hope's Embrace archway in camouflage gear with large guns in their hands. None of them seemed to be in much of a hurry, which could only mean one thing...

There was nobody left to save.

Oh, God.

Ellie surged out of the truck before Donovan had it completely stopped. The men swung toward her, raising their weapons as one, and she skidded to a halt, holding up her hands.

"Shit," Zak said and pushed to the front of the group. "Fuck. Stand down. She's one of mine." He strode toward her, his face a carefully blank mask.

"Zak." Her voice cracked on his name, and she swallowed hard against the knot of tears in her throat. "Where's Cal?"

Without answering her question, he glared at Donovan, who had just jogged up to join them. "What the hell is she doing here?"

Donovan shrugged, unabashed. "She's stubborn. I like that about her."

Zak swore under his breath before turning back to her. His gaze softened slightly around the edges. "Ellie..."

"Tell me." The words came out as a command more than a request. Her heart was pounding so hard she was sure it was going to burst.

There was a long pause before Zak finally spoke. "Ellie, listen. They're all dead, but—"

The world dropped out from underneath her.

"Whoa." One of the mercenaries darted forward and caught her before she collapsed. "Easy now, darlin'. Take a breath. C'mon. Breathe. There you go."

As he lowered her to sit on a nearby stump, she stared at him, uncomprehending the words he was saying. But he had a kind face under the camouflage paint, with blue eyes the color of worn denim. His accent called to mind dusty plains and cowboys astride horses herding cattle.

"Hi... Ellie, is it? I'm Jesse. Here." He pulled a canteen off his pack and handed it to her. "Take a sip."

"Shit, Hendricks," someone else from the group said, and his accent was from deep in the Louisiana bayou. "Maybe you coulda dropped that bomb with a little more tact?"

"She didn't let me finish," Zak muttered and crouched down in front of her. He took the canteen from her shaking hands and handed it back to Jesse. "Cal and Pierce aren't among the bodies. It's just the commune members."

"They mostly committed suicide," Jesse added.

"Mostly?" Wow, was that her voice? Why was it so faint, so far away?

Jesse's eyes brimmed with sorrow. "Some appear to have been forced. Especially—" His voice broke, and he cleared his throat. "Especially the kids."

"Oh my God."

Another mercenary crossed to stand beside Jesse. Not a man, but a woman with gorgeous brown skin and braids pulled back into a bun at her nape. "Hi, Ellie. I'm Lanie. You okay?"

She couldn't answer. Not really. The world was spinning, her vision narrowing in a way that made her feel both hot and cold.

Mostly committed suicide.

Some appear to have been forced...

Especially the kids...

Those words replayed through her mind on a loop.

Ellie shook her head furiously. "What about True? My niece. Dark curly hair, light blue-green eyes. Just a teenager. Is she...?"

Lanie frowned and glanced back at the rest of her team. They all shook their heads, and she turned back, gentling her voice. "We didn't see her."

Then she was out there somewhere, too. Maybe she was even with Cal. That was the best-case scenario because he'd protect her with his life. The worst case...

She was dead, and HORNET just missed her during their sweep of the compound.

Ellie popped to her feet and swayed a little before catching herself. "I... I want to see. I need to see."

"Ellie..." Zak began, a note of warning in his voice.

"I need to," she insisted. And if they left on foot, Puzzle could track them. "You said he's good at trailing—one of the best you've seen. He *can* find them."

Zak exchanged glances with Lanie, who nodded. "It's not a bad idea. Our K9 team is..." She hesitated. "Unavailable right now."

One of her teammates scoffed at that.

Lanie ignored them. "So we could use the help."

"Then Ranger will do it," Zak said, setting a hand on his dog's head. Ranger's radar dish ears twitched, and his yellow eyes watched the humans with startling intensity.

"Ranger's only trained on cadavers for the last few years," Donovan reminded him. "With all of those bodies in there, he won't be able to help. And Spirit's a bomb-sniffer. Shane and Clue aren't here. Pierce and Raszta..." He let the thought trail off without finishing it. "We're shorthanded. It'd be stupid not to use her and the pup."

Zak let out a breath. "All right." He held up his hands in defeat. "It's not ideal, but let's see what Puzzle can do."

"Thank you," Ellie said.

Zak just shook his head and turned toward the entrance. "I still don't like it."

If she was honest, neither did she. Puzzle was so young, still a puppy in many ways. Was he ready for this?

The knot of dread in her stomach twisted tighter with each step they took toward the commune, but she forced herself to keep moving forward, one step at a time.

She had to know. Had to see for herself that Cal was not among the victims and make sure True wasn't there.

The smell hit her first—a strong, musty odor like old socks. She'd smelled it before when she and Cal first arrived, but now it was a thousand times worse, mixed with the scent of death.

The first body they came to was Remedy, still in her garden. She lay among the flowers and vegetables with her arms spread wide as though embracing the earth. She looked asleep, a half-smile frozen on her blue lips that was both heart-breaking and terrifying.

Jesse carefully stepped around the body and bent to examine a nearby plant. After a moment, he straightened and backed away. "That's hemlock. Knew I recognized the smell."

"Fuck," the Cajun guy muttered. Ellie still didn't know his name. "That's a hell of a way to go."

Zak looked back at Ellie, his gaze worried. "You sure you wanna keep going?"

"Yes," she replied, her voice firm. "Puzzle needs Cal's scent to track him."

They moved further into the commune, passing bodies strewn about like grotesque dolls. Each one caused a fresh stab of fear to pierce Ellie's heart, but none were Cal or Pierce or True.

She paused the group by the cottage she and Cal had stayed in and started to go inside, but the Cajun guy stopped her.

"Me first, cher."

She didn't argue and stepped back, letting him sweep through the door with his weapon aimed.

"Clear," he called back after a moment, and she followed him in.

It was weird being back. The bed was still rumpled from sex, just as she and Cal had left it. The clothes they'd both worn into the commune were still folded up in the dresser. She pulled open the drawer and lifted out Cal's shirt, pressing it to her face and inhaling deeply. She could only faintly smell him in the fabric, but Puzzle would be able to pick up the scent.

"We'll find him," Cajun said.

She started. She'd forgotten she wasn't alone. "Thank you..." She turned toward him. "I'm sorry. I don't know your name. I've just been calling you 'Cajun' in my head."

"Actually, that's what most people call me. Other than my wife. She usually calls me 'pain in the ass,' but for some reason she still loves me." He grinned and shifted his weapon to hold out his hand. "Jean-Luc Cavalier."

Ellie accepted the shake and was charmed when he lightly kissed her hand.

"Cajun!" Lanie called from outside. "Stop flirting and get your ass back out here, or I'll tell your wife you're misbehaving again."

Jean-Luc's grin only widened, his eyes sparkling with mischief in his grease-painted face. "Promise?" he called back as he headed toward the door. "Claire loves it when I misbehave."

Ellie managed a shaky laugh as she followed him back outside. She hadn't known she could laugh in a situation like this, but she felt lighter for it. Later, much later, she'd realize Jean-Luc had done it on purpose, turning on the charm to help her relax.

"Puzzle, here." She bent down to press Cal's shirt to her dog's nose. "Find Cal. You love this game. Let's go find Cal." He sniffed intently, then gave a low murmur before pressing his nose to the ground.

It didn't take him long to find the scent.

He bounded a few steps toward the woods—all big puppy paws and clumsy legs he hadn't quite grown into yet—but then he stopped and looked back at her. There was happy excitement in his eyes that reminded her so much of Cal.

"Yes, Puzzle. Let's go." Her throat closed up, and she could barely form the words. "Go find Cal."

chapter
twenty-five

PUZZLE CHARGED FORWARD, weaving enthusiastically through the trees as Ellie and the others followed. His tail wagged high and proud, an enthusiastic flag leading them deeper into the woods.

The trees stood like guards, their ancient trunks lined with moss, and the sun filtered through the canopy, splashing the foliage with hues of gold and green. The forest was alive with whispers - the rustle of branches swaying in the wind, distant bird calls, their own breaths coming out in quick bursts.

It was beautiful in a haunting sort of way.

"You got a good dog here," Jean-Luc said. He didn't even sound winded, while she was panting trying to keep up with Puzzle's break-neck speed. "Reminds me of the pup I grew up with. Beauregard. Now he was a loyal dog, but he couldn't sniff out a squirrel in a nut factory. Your boy there's got a good nose and the drive to use it."

Her boy.

She smiled at the dog as he crossed back and forth over the path, looking for the scent. He was a good boy. The best.

Suddenly, Puzzle stopped in his tracks, tail standing still.

His ears perked up, nose twitching in the cool morning air. Then he suddenly darted into a dense cluster of ferns.

"Find something, buddy?" Ellie called, brushing past a low-hanging branch to catch up.

She found him sitting at the thick base of a redwood. His head drooped and he gave a low, distressed whine.

Ellie's heart pounded as she approached him. There, at his feet, propped up against the tree, was a body.

"Cal." His name was a choked gasp as she dropped to her knees next to him...

Except it wasn't Cal.

Hopeful.

His long hair spilled around his shoulders in a sweaty mess, his mouth ajar in an O of surprise. One hand rested limply on his chest under the blossom of blood on his white robe. His body was cold and rigid. He'd been dead for a while.

Puzzle whined again, butting his head against her leg.

"Good boy," she muttered, running her fingers through his fur. She sat back on her heels as relief and horror warred inside her. "This doesn't make sense."

Zak crouched down beside her and studied the body. "No, it doesn't. Who shot him?"

Suddenly Puzzle bounded off into the underbrush, disappearing from their sight. Ellie scrambled to her feet and took off after him, branches slapping at her face and arms. Puzzle barked like crazy, his voice echoing off the trees, sending up a flock of birds. He had Cal's scent.

Finally, the underbrush opened up to a small clearing where Puzzle danced around in front of a house she recognized—the old house from the group picture she'd found online while looking for True. It looked like someone had renovated it since that photo. Now it boasted fresh gold paint and bright white trim. Flowers bloomed in the neatly kept yard.

Something about the place tugged at a long-forgotten memory...

A children's book with a pretty yellow house on the cover...

And an older sister who used to read that book over and over to her...

"I'm gonna have a house like this someday, Elle. A pretty little yellow cottage in the woods."

"Will it be magic like in the book?"

"I think it will be."

"Can I come visit?"

"You'd better," Hope had said as she lovingly twirled one of Ellie's ringlets around her finger. *"You're always welcome in my house."*

The memory crashed into Ellie like a wave, stealing the breath from her lungs. Before she knew what she was doing, she moved toward the house.

"Wait!"

She ignored Zak's warning and walked up the steps, tracing her hand along the railing. The door opened before she got to it and there stood Hope.

Her hair was just as wild and dark as Ellie remembered, her eyes the same piercing light blue, but that was where the similarities ended. Her skin was sallow, her body thin from years of malnourishment or drug use or both.

"Hope," she breathed. "You're alive."

The suspicion in Hope's eyes softened slightly. "Ellie?"

Her voice was more hoarse, more broken than Ellie remembered, but it held the familiar lilt of their shared childhood. She looked at Ellie with a gaze that held many long, harrowing years of pain and survival.

Ellie nodded, feeling a lump in her throat. "Yeah, Hope. It's me."

Hope's lips twitched in something like a smile. "Elle... you're all grown up."

Tears welled in Ellie's blue eyes, stinging and hot. "And you're... you're..." She swallowed hard against the lump that had lodged itself in her throat.

"I'm alive," Hope finished for her, stepping back and opening the door wider, inviting her in.

Ellie launched herself at Hope, arms wrapping tightly her waist. Hope stood stock-still for an instant in shock before she slowly raised her arms to pat Ellie's back awkwardly.

Puzzle barreled past them, his tail wagging furiously as he pranced around a teenage girl with dark curly hair and light blue-green eyes.

True.

A brief expression of panic flitted over her features, and she stared at Hope like she expected and explosion. When none came, she relaxed slightly and turned toward Ellie. Her eyes seemed to scream, "Help!"

True looked so much like Hope, it was almost eerie. The same soft curls, the same striking eyes. Except there was something different about her, something more innocent, less tarnished. Maybe it was just wishful thinking, but she wanted to believe that this girl still had a chance to escape the life her mother had chosen.

She turned back to her sister. "Where's Cal?"

"He's around," she replied nonchalantly, as if they were asking about a misplaced pen and not a missing person. "He needed some time for... soul searching."

Ellie swallowed down her fear. She wasn't sure she wanted the answer to her next question, but she had to ask it. "Is he alive?"

"For now." Hope's gaze slid toward the mercenaries standing in her yard with their guns raised. She smiled. "But it doesn't matter. None of us will be for much longer. The Great

Renewal has started and if you're smart, you'll save yourself the horror to come like my family did."

"I'm your family."

Hope laughed at that, a bitter, pained sound. "No, Ellie. Not anymore. We haven't been family since your mother kicked me out." She looked at her daughter. "The woman who birthed me is selfish and evil. She will rot in hell when the end times come."

Terror lanced through her. The look in Hope's eyes… it was fanatic, unhinged.

"Mom's not evil," she protested. "Yes, she can be selfish sometimes, but she loves us and she's only human. She's not meant to be perfect. None of us are."

"True is. She's the embodiment of purity and light. She's here to lead us to salvation."

The conviction in those words made Ellie's blood run cold. Then realization struck her like a thunderbolt. "You're Mother God, aren't you?"

"No." She nodded toward her daughter. "She is. I am merely her harbinger. The bringer of her destiny."

Ellie's gaze flicked to True. The girl was trembling, tears silently trailing down her cheeks. "You ordered those people to kill themselves. It wasn't Hopeful."

Hope gave a serene smile. "Before something better can begin, everything else has to end."

"Did you kill Hopeful, too?"

"I set him free. I set them all free."

This was not the fun, careful sister she remembered, the sister who had promised her a magical yellow cottage in the woods. This was a woman twisted and broken by beliefs that were hurting everyone around her.

A noise from the edge of the clearing caught Ellie's attention. Zak, Donovan, and the mercenaries were inching closer, their guns pointed at Hope. But Hope seemed blissfully unaware, or maybe she just didn't care. She continued speaking, this time addressing True.

"And you, my angel... you will lead them into the new age."

True was shaking her head, tears streaming down her face. "No... I don't want to. Mom, this is wrong. I can't..."

"This is your destiny," Hope snapped.

"No, it isn't!" True's voice was like a sharp snap of a twig. "You're wrong. This isn't normal, Mom. This isn't how things are supposed to be." With that, she bolted past her mother, past Ellie, out into the yard. She held her hands high over her head. "Don't shoot. I want to leave!"

Zak and the team moved in and surrounded her, tucking her away to safety behind the shield of their bodies.

"No!" Hope wailed. "No, she's my salvation! You can't take her from me!" She lunged out the door, but the mercenaries were faster. They closed in on her, their guns raised.

"Hands on your head," one of the mercenaries ordered. Followed by another shouting, "Face down on the ground! Now!"

Hope didn't move for a solid five seconds, and the tension was a palpable thing, thrumming through the air like an electrical charge. Puzzle whined beside Ellie, his tail tucked between his legs, and she reached down to pat his side reassuringly, even as her own hands trembled.

"Hope, please," she called, her voice breaking. "Please, just... stop. You've lost control. You've lost yourself. You need help."

Hope glanced over her shoulder, smiling that deranged smile. "You're wrong. I've found myself."

In that moment, Ellie saw it— the mania, the delusion. Hope was submerged in her own reality, her judgment drowned in the flood of conviction, and no amount of talking was going to change her mind.

Then, she launched at the nearest mercenary. He didn't blink, didn't hesitate, and pulled the trigger.

The gunshot echoed like a thunderclap, bouncing off the trees and seeming to shake the very ground itself. Puzzle howled, a terrible, mournful sound that sent spikes of ice through Ellie's chest. She was frozen in horror as Hope crumbled to the ground, a bloom of dark red spreading across her stomach.

"Hope!" She darted toward her sister even as one of the mercenaries moved to intercept her. But she was too quick, too desperate. She slid on her knees through the damp grass until she was at Hope's side, pressing her hands over the wound to stop the blood.

Hope's eyes fluttered up to meet hers. "Elle..." she gasped, her breath hitching in pain. Her fingers clawed weakly at Ellie's arm. "They'll... they'll all be saved..."

"Mom!" True screamed, breaking free from Zak's protective grasp and rushing toward her mother.

"Someone hold her," Lanie shouted as Jesse landed hard on his knees at Hope's side. He pulled his pack off his back and dug through it for a roll of gauze.

"Ellie," he said gently. "I'm a medic. Let me see the wound."

Numb, she sat back and watched Jesse apply pressure to the wound, efficiently working to stem the blood flow.

Hope gasped in pain, her hand reaching out blindly. Ellie grasped it tightly, squeezing to let her know she wasn't alone.

True was beside them now, sobbing as she clung to Hope's free hand. "Mom... please don't leave me. This isn't what I meant to happen. I just wanted out. I just wanted to be normal."

Hope's eyes fluttered open. "My angel," she wheezed. Her teeth were stained with blood. "Don't... listen to them. You know... your destiny."

"Mom, please…"

Hope's eyes glazed over, and she exhaled one last time, a rattle deep in her throat.

Jesse swore softly under his breath and attempted CPR. Somewhere in the distance, she heard Zak's voice calling for a medivac.

Minutes passed.

Finally, he sat back and looked at Ellie for a regret-filled heartbeat, then at True. "I'm sorry. She's gone."

For a moment, everything went still. The world seemed to halt in its tracks, the air turned brittle, shattering at the mere thought of breathing. Cold dread filled Ellie's veins.

"No." True's shattered whisper cut through the deadly silence. "No! You're lying!"

She lunged at Jesse, but Zak stepped in, catching her mid-air. She fought wildly, her fists pounding on his chest. But Zak held onto her, wrapping his arms around her and murmuring soft comforts until the fight drained away and she went limp.

Ellie couldn't tear her eyes off Hope's lifeless face. The deranged smile was gone now, replaced by a vacant tranquility. It was the same expression on all of the cult members' faces.

A hand landed on her shoulder. Donovan stood behind her, his eyes haunted. "I'm sorry, Ellie," he muttered, his voice choked with emotion. "I had to."

Only then did she realize that it had not been one of the mercenaries who had taken the shot but him.

"It's okay, Van. This is what she wanted. She didn't give you a choice." Her voice sounded hollow even to her own ears, and she shook her head, slowly climbing to her feet. "We need to find Cal."

True inhaled sharply and gazed up with a tear-stained face. "I know where he is."

The temperature in the shipping container was becoming stifling, the air thick, stalling in Cal's lungs with every breath. He was dripping sweat and thirsty, and his head felt like it was splitting open. There was a metallic taste in his mouth—blood or fear, either one fit. Cal eyed the tray of food on the floor beside him. There was a cup of tea on it. He could drink that and—

No. True had said not to eat or drink anything.

He kicked out, knocking the tray out of his reach and removing the temptation. The clatter of it skidding across the floor seemed as loud as a gunshot, and he jumped in surprise.

Or... was that actually a gunshot?

He strained his ears but heard nothing but the thud-thud-thud of his heart pounding. He glanced over at Pierce, still slumped unconscious in that chair, and grimaced. The guy's face was ashen, his lips tinged with blue.

With a grunt, Cal pushed himself up to a sitting position. Everything spun for a moment before settling back into place.

"Pierce," he rasped, voice hoarse from disuse and dehydration. "Pierce, come on, man. Wake up."

No response.

Just like all the other times he'd tried.

That was the worst part—the brutal silence broken only by Pierce's uneven breathing, which seemed to grow shallower with each passing minute.

Cal closed his eyes, leaning his head back against the metal wall, trying to keep the panic at bay. He took one steadying breath, then another.

There had to be a way to get out of this.

Suddenly, there was a noise. Distant at first but growing louder. It sounded like... barking?

He held his breath and listened, praying it wasn't just desperation playing tricks on his senses.

There it was again.

A distinct bark, followed by the sound of voices.

The container doors creaked open, daylight streaming in like a knife through the oppressive darkness.

"Cal!"

The relief that hit him was immediate, the tears that followed unexpected. Ellie stood illuminated in the doorway, her blond curls an untamed halo around her head. She had never been a more welcome sight.

"Elle," he croaked, his throat raw.

She hurried to his side, her gaze flickering briefly to Pierce's motionless form. "We need help in here," she called to someone over her shoulder.

More figures moved into the tight space—men he didn't recognize dressed in camo and face paint. They freed Pierce from the chair and gently carried him out.

"Who...?" He couldn't finish the question—his mouth was too dry—but she understood anyway.

"They're Zak's friends. He called them in to help find you."

As if conjured by his name, Zak appeared in the doorway with a pair of bolt cutters. "Hey, Cal. How are you doing?"

"Been... better."

"Yeah, we're getting you out of here." As he positioned the cutter on the chain, he added, "Medivac is five minutes out."

Cal winced as the chain fell off.

"Thanks," Cal managed, rubbing the raw skin around his wrists. He was helped to his feet by Zak and Ellie, a wave of dizziness hitting him as he stood.

Ellie was at his side instantly, her arm sliding around his waist to hold him steady. "Cal, are you okay?"

He wasn't. He felt like shit. He was overheated, hungry, thirsty, and the world around him kept spinning in a dizzying dance of light and shadow. But he looked into those clear blue eyes behind her smudged glasses, and, somehow, he felt better. "I am now."

There was a moment between them, a brief flicker of something that was over too quickly, shattered by Zak's gruff voice. "All right, lovebirds, stop making googly eyes at each other. We need to get moving."

"What about Pierce?"

Zak grimaced and slung the bolt cutters up onto his shoulder. "The medic's working on him."

"Is he any good?"

"The best in the business." Something dark moved through Zak's eyes. "These guys saved me, brought me home from Afghanistan. If anyone can save Pierce, it's them."

twenty-six

CAL WAS ADMITTED to the hospital for two nights for severe dehydration, but he was ready to get out of there after the first few hours. By the first morning, she was about as successful at keeping him still and quiet as she was at keeping Puzzle from eating all of her socks. Which was to say, not successful at all.

"Cal, you need to rest. Don't make me tie you to this bed."

"While that sounds fun..." He stood up and wobbled a little, grabbing the overbed table to steady himself. "I want to see Pierce."

She rolled her eyes, but instead of arguing with him, she just got a wheelchair from the hallway.

He eyed it with suspicion as she wheeled it in. "Thanks, but I can walk."

"You can barely stand, and you have an IV. It's either this or you sit your gorgeous ass back down on that bed and relax like the doctor ordered."

Cal smirked. "You're kinda hot when you're bossy."

Ellie's face flushed as she gave him a playful shove back into the bed. "Not helping your case, Holden. You're staying put."

He caught her hand before she pulled away, and for once, his expression was serious. "Elle, I need to see him. They hurt him because of me. Please."

She held his gaze for a beat, saw the worry and guilt eating away at him, and sighed. "Okay. But let me see if he's up for a visit first."

Cal grumbled but settled back into the bed. "Ellie," he called when she got to the door. "Tell him I'm sorry."

Her heart clenched. It was wrong for Cal to look so... sad. "I will. Please try to rest. I'll be back in a few minutes."

The hallway outside was bustling with nurses and doctors, their movements quick and urgent. The smell of antiseptic hung in the air like a heavy blanket, and Ellie quickened her pace to escape it.

Pierce had been upgraded from critical to stable yesterday and moved into a regular room down the hall from Cal's. She found him propped up in bed, his dark eyes glued to a silent TV, but he didn't appear actually to be watching the news segment. He looked miles away.

She tapped on the door. "Pierce?"

He glanced up as she entered, and his gaze softened.

"Hey." She walked in and perched on the chair beside his bed. She'd visited him every day, but now that she knew he had a thing for her, there was an awkwardness between them that hadn't been there before. She liked him—she'd always liked him, but only as a friend. She wished she'd known about his feelings before... but even if she had, it wouldn't have made a difference. There was only one man who had ever sparked her interest, and he was currently battling his guilt a few doors down the hallway.

But Pierce needed a friend now, and she hoped he would still consider her one.

She studied his bruised and battered face. "How are you doing?"

He simply shrugged in response and avoided her gaze.

"Cal wants to visit if you're up for it."

His lips thinned, and he shook his bandaged head, wincing.

"No?"

Pierce just shrugged again, his gaze distant. He was always quiet, but it used to be a calm kind of quiet like he'd made peace with himself. Now, the air around him was charged with anger and other emotions she couldn't put a name to.

She hated seeing him in so much pain.

"Dude," Ellie said, cracking a half-smile, trying to lighten the mood. "He's been driving me up the wall. I swear I'm about ready to smack him with a bedpan."

It worked. The corner of Pierce's mouth twitched in what might have been a reluctant smile.

"He blames himself," she said softly.

Pierce's brow furrowed, his gaze flicking back to her face.

"Anyway," she said, shifting uncomfortably in her seat. "He asked me to tell you he's sorry."

Pierce just looked at her. His expression remained closed off, making Ellie feel like she was talking to a wall.

"Okay," she finally said, standing up. "I'll let him know you're not ready yet."

He didn't try to stop her as she left the room. Out in the hall, she took a breath to ease the tightness in her throat.

Physically, he'd heal from the torture inflicted on him, but mentally? She wasn't so sure.

That evening, when Ellie left the hospital to shower and change her clothes, Zak called to warn her that Alexis and

Shane were on their way home. Since they were off the grid and unreachable by phone, he'd radioed them to let them know what happened, and they'd decided to cut their honeymoon short by a day.

Ellie was not looking forward to this conversation and decided to wait on her porch, throwing a stick for Puzzle until they arrived.

To Ellie's surprise, only Alexis stepped out of the car. Clue, the scruffy mutt Alexis had found in an alleyway in Chicago, hopped out behind her.

Puzzle gave a delighted *woof* at seeing his cousin and bounced off the porch. He tripped over his own big feet and skidded across the grass on his face for a moment before righting himself.

"That dog doesn't know how to dog properly," Alexis said with faint amusement.

"I know. He's a dummy, but I love him."

They both watched in silence as the dogs circled, sniffing each other wildly.

Ellie hated to break the tentative peace, but she figured she might as well get the lecture over with. "Where's Shane?"

Alexis's lips thinned. "He went to the hospital to see Pierce. And Cal. Though, Cal annoys him, so mostly Pierce."

"Good. Maybe he'll get more of a response from him than I did. He's... shut down."

"What the hell, Ellie?" Alexis's green eyes flashed with fury as she stalked up the sidewalk. "You *infiltrated* a *cult*?"

"Yes."

"I... just..." She turned away and shoved her hands into her hair, muttering something about not being able to leave Ellie for even a week. Then she swung back. "My God, Ellie! What were you thinking? You could've been killed."

"I found Hope."

Alexis stumbled to a halt. "I'm sorry. You... what?"

"She was there. She kind of started the cult. Or, I guess, took it over."

Alexis blinked in disbelief. "She's alive?"

"No. Not anymore. But she has a daughter."

"Holy shit. I need to sit down." Alexis sank onto the front step of Ellie's porch and put her head in her hands. "This is... this is a lot. Holy shit. A daughter?"

"Her name is True. She has Hope's eyes," Ellie whispered, her voice choked with emotion. "She's been through hell, but she's very strong and brave. You'll like her."

"Of course I will. She's our niece." Alexis sighed, rubbing her temples. "I can't believe it. Hope had a daughter."

"She needs us, Lexi. She watched her mom die in front of her. We're all she has left."

Silence fell between them, broken only by the sound of Puzzle and Clue grumbling happily as they rolled around in the grass together.

"I need to see her," Alexis finally said. "But first..." She slid a considering gaze in Ellie's direction. "I've been dying to ask, what the hell is going on with you and Cal?"

Ah, there it was. She should've expected it. "Nothing."

"Bullshit. Something happened between you two at the wedding."

Ellie looked down at her lap, picking at the frayed edge of her jeans. She thought about lying, but her sister would see through it. "Yes. Something happened."

"I knew it! And...?"

"And what?"

"Was it good?"

"Oh my God."

"I'll take that as a yes."

"I have nothing more to say about it."

"Well, I do."

Ellie sighed. "Lexi—"

"No." She held up a hand, stopping further protest. "I need to say my peace. You can't keep holding my trauma over Cal's head."

"I'm not—"

"Yeah, you are. You're blaming him for what happened to me when he had nothing to do with it. It's time to stop running and deal with it."

"*I* need to stop?" Outrage burst through Ellie. "What about *you*? You always just charge on ahead. You focused on Shane's problems and then Connelly and Veronica's, but you never once took a moment to stop and process anything that happened to you."

"That's not true," Alexis said softly. "I am dealing with it. In therapy. And in the middle of the night, with Shane holding me through the nightmares. The difference is I don't want to dwell on it like you do. I don't want it to define my entire life. I want to be known as more than just the only surviving victim of the Shadow Stalkers. I'm more than what they did to me. The fuckers. May they rot in hell." Tears flooded her eyes, but she didn't let them fall. She touched the thin scar on her throat where Jaxon Thorne's knife had sliced open her neck. "And I'm more than what Jax did to me. He's a very damaged man who was consumed by rage and drugs. I've forgiven him for it. Shane has forgiven him. Why can't you?"

Ellie's throat closed up. "He tried to kill you after you already went through the unthinkable. The Stalkers failed—"

"Not for a lack of trying," Alexis muttered.

"No, you survived them because you were smarter and stronger, and they underestimated you. They were never going to break you. But Jax... almost succeeded, all because he wanted to hurt Shane. He cut open your throat! You only survived by a fluke of luck."

"Oh, Ellie." Alexis pulled her in for a hug. "I'm still here, and I'm the happiest I've ever been." She drew back and wiped away the tears Ellie couldn't control. "You want to know what I think?"

Ellie gave a watery laugh and swiped at her running nose. "No, but you're going to tell me anyway."

"Yes, I am, and you're not going to like it. I think you've been using what Jax did—and the fact that Cal took him on as a client—as an excuse so you don't have to risk your heart. Because your heart is at risk with Cal. He's so incredibly in love with you. Absolutely wild about you. And you love him, too."

"I don't—"

"Stop," Alexis said firmly. "You do. You have from the moment you met him."

Ellie's face flushed hot. She opened and closed her mouth a few times, searching for a counterargument but finding none.

"Come on," Alexis prompted, bumping her shoulder. "Just admit it already."

"No."

"Ellie Mae, don't you lie to me."

"Ugh, don't use my middle name." She exhaled a long, slow breath and scrubbed her hands over her face in defeat. "Okay, yes. Happy now? Yes, I love him."

"There, don't you feel better?" Alexis asked, her smile all smug satisfaction.

"Maybe," she muttered, just because she couldn't bring herself to admit that she did feel better—lighter, somehow. "But it's... complicated."

"Love is always complicated. But that doesn't mean it isn't worth it. Take the chance on Cal. I promise you won't regret it." Alexis squeezed her hand. "Now, let's go meet this niece of ours."

chapter
twenty-seven

TRUE SAT in Zak and Anna's living room, small and pale in a Lost County Sheriff's Department sweatshirt. The shirt was too big for her, coming almost to her knees and swallowing her arms. Her hair was clean and brushed back into a braid, making her eyes look even bigger in her thin face. She flipped through the TV channels, staring at the screen with astonished eyes. Anna's sweet Golden Retriever, Winston, sat beside her, his head resting on her lap, his eyes closed as she stroked her free hand over his head. Ranger, the Dutch shepherd with intense yellow eyes, lay on the floor nearby, watching over his charge like a mama bear watched her cubs.

"My God," Alexis breathed after peeking into the room. "How old is she? She's so tiny."

Ash pulled the parlor's double glass doors shut and led the way back to the kitchen, where Zak and Anna waited. "Best guess is fourteen. Maybe fifteen. She doesn't know, and there are no records of her birth, so there's really no way to know for sure."

"What's going to happen to her?"

Ash sighed. "Both her parents are dead, so she'll have to go into the system."

"No," Alexis and Ellie said at the same time.

"We're foster parents," Anna said. "We can request to take her so she doesn't end up with strangers."

Ash frowned at his twin sister. "I thought you guys were trying to adopt a baby. Will you be able to do both?"

"It can wait." Anna shrugged, though her feigned nonchalance didn't quite show on her face. The thought of waiting for their much-wanted baby obviously hurt her, but she'd put it aside for True. She was just that kind of person. "True needs a place to live, and we have the room for her. Besides, it might be good for her to meet Bella. They have a lot in common."

"No, don't put your adoption on hold," Alexis said and looked at Shane, who winced before schooling his face back into a blank mask. Ellie could plainly see the internal battle he fought. He had only just learned how to live among people again, and despite his new friends and wife, he was still very much a loner. But he was also a hero at heart, and heroes don't let kids suffer needlessly.

Finally, Shane nodded. "She's family. She's not going into foster care on my watch."

Alexis's face glowed, and she turned back to Ash. "We'll take her home with us," she said.

They were well-meaning, but every instinct Ellie had screamed that it was the wrong move. She laid a hand on her sister's shoulder. "She doesn't know you or Shane. Let me take her." The girl didn't really know Ellie either, but at least she wasn't a complete stranger like Alexis and Shane were.

Alexis's eyes widened. "Really? Are you sure?"

No, she wasn't. But Alexis and Shane were newlyweds trying to navigate a world that hadn't been kind to either of them, and they didn't need the stress of a damaged kid on top of that. Ellie had the space in her house and the time to do whatever was needed to help True heal. The more she thought about it, the more convinced she became that it was the right call.

"Yes. I'm sure."

Alexis studied her face for a long moment, then gave a slow nod. "If you ever need anything, we're here to help."

"Day or night," Shane added. "You call, and I'll be there."

God, she loved them. She wanted to hug them both, but she settled for just wrapping her arms around her sister. "I know. And I'll definitely take you up on that so often you'll regret offering."

A smile ghosted over Shane's hard mouth. "Never."

"Can we talk to her?" Alexis asked. "I have so many questions."

Ash waved a hand toward the front parlor. "If she's willing."

True looked up, startled, when Ellie, Alexis, and Shane walked into the parlor. She studied them all with eyes far too world-weary for such a young girl, then set the TV remote aside and uncurled from the couch. "You're my aunts, aren't you?"

Alexis nodded and moved slowly into the room, lowering herself to the cushion on the other end of the couch. "We are. I'm Alexis. And this..." She held out a hand to Shane, and he stepped forward, lacing his fingers through hers. "Is my husband, Shane."

True stared at their clasped hands for a beat before lifting her gaze again. "Mom talked about you sometimes."

"Oh? What did she say?"

"That my grandma brainwashed you, and I couldn't trust either of you. She talked about kidnapping you to the compound to help you see the truth."

Alexis blinked in shock. "What truth is that?"

True shook her head hard, and tears brimmed in her eyes. "I don't really know. The truth never stayed true for long with

Mom. I... I don't think she was well, like, mentally. Clarity snuck me a psychology textbook once, and I read about something called bipolar disorder. It sounded a lot like Mom. I thought she needed help."

A lump rose into Ellie's throat, choking her. "Is that why you called Cal?"

True looked at her. "Is that your husband?"

"We aren't married. We just said we were to get into the retreat."

"Oh." True frowned. "Then what are you?"

Good question.

One Ellie didn't have an answer for, so she settled for the easiest explanation: "We're friends."

She didn't look convinced by that. Judging by Alexis's knowing smirk and Shane's sudden interest in the ceiling, neither were they.

"Is he okay?" True asked suddenly. "And your other friend?"

"Yes, they're in the hospital, but they'll both be okay. Thanks to you. Cal said you told him not to eat or drink anything offered to him."

True twisted her hands in her lap. "I was so afraid he wouldn't listen."

"You knew they were all going to poison themselves?"

"Yes. As long as I can remember, it's all they ever talked about. Mom and Dad convinced everyone it was the only way to survive The Great Renewal."

Alexis leaned forward. "What was that supposed to be?"

"I don't know exactly. Mom talked about some kind of big, prophesied disaster—it changed often, but most recently, she claimed it would be an earthquake that would swallow the West Coast, and everyone would die during it except for the Embraced. But then it became everyone had to die, but the Embraced would rise again when it was over. It was always something that would happen in the future, but suddenly, a few weeks ago, things changed. I got scared." She met Ellie's gaze. "That's why I called Cal. I found his card stuck between the pages of the textbook, and I researched him when Clarity gave me time on her computer. I saw he was looking for Mom and thought he could help, so I told him Mom was missing."

"Why did everyone at the commune already think Hope was dead?" Ellie asked.

"Mom decided it was better that way because prophets are always more revered after they die, so she had Dad tell everyone she was dead. But she controlled everything from the background. Nothing happened at the commune without her say-so."

"I'm so sorry," Alexis whispered. "I know it couldn't have been easy living with her."

"It wasn't." True hunched in on herself. "But she was my mom. She wasn't all bad."

"Of course not. You're allowed to miss her." Alexis slid closer and covered True's tightly knotted hands with hers. "I miss her, too. She was a great big sister before she left, and I loved her so much."

"We both did," Ellie spoke up. "But I'm also so angry with her for everything she did to Cal. And to you. It's okay to feel conflicted about her right now."

After a long moment, True nodded and blinked back the tears that she never let spill. "So what happens to me now?"

Alexis looked at Ellie, passing her the conversational ball.

Ellie moved to sit on True's other side. "We were just talking about that. You can come live with me if you like."

"Or us," Alexis added. "But no hard feelings if you'd prefer to stay with Ellie. We get it. We just want you to be happy and feel safe."

True looked back and forth from one sister to the other. "I think... I want to go with Ellie."

chapter
twenty-eight

ELLIE DIDN'T COME.

Cal frowned down at his phone as he left the hospital. He'd fully expected her to be here when they released him.

Why wasn't she here?

Panic tried to rear its ugly head, but he squashed it down. There had to be a perfectly reasonable explanation. He dialed her number and got dumped straight into her voicemail.

Was she avoiding him again?

Jesus, he hoped not. He didn't think his heart could handle it.

He thought they were past all that. He thought they were something more now. What kind of something more? He didn't know. Something real, something good, something that lasted forever.

He shoved his phone back into his pocket and strode toward the parking lot. Zak and Donovan had brought his car over for him last night, and he found it easily enough among all the sedate sedans. He slid behind the wheel and powered up the engine, a low growl echoing in the early morning hush. As he pulled out of the hospital's grey concrete parking lot, his thoughts were as turbulent as the rolling waves crashing onto the Northern California coastline.

All right, it was time to hammer out their relationship once and for all. He was all in. He needed to know if she was, too.

He drove to Ellie's bungalow, a charming little piece of property nestled between towering redwoods and the salty Pacific. He parked outside, and just as he was about to knock, he realized he could hear music—cheesy 80s pop music, to be precise.

He paused with his hand poised to knock, his anxiety softening into bemusement.

Well, this was unexpected.

His fingers rapped gently against the worn wooden door, though she probably wouldn't be able to hear over Cyndi Lauper's strident insistence that girls just wanted to have fun.

No answer.

He tried the knob and found it unlocked.

Pushing the door open, he walked into a scene so wildly unexpected that his brain took a moment to register it.

Ellie was dancing.

No, not just dancing.

She twirled, bounced, and shimmied with the kind of abandon that only comes when you think you're alone. She held a hairbrush like a microphone and sang into it. Puzzle pranced around her legs, his tail knocking into everything, as he gleefully joined the dance party, leaping and bounding with unbridled joy.

And there was the girl.

True sat on the couch, watching Ellie with something close to wonder on her face.

Ellie twirled and spotted him and fumbled the hairbrush. "Oh. Cal!" Then her eyes widened. "Oh, no. They released you already? I'm so sorry I wasn't there. The nurse told me they weren't going to until this evening."

"I got an early release for good behavior." He moved farther into the room and sat down in a chair. "Please, don't stop on my account."

Color infused her cheeks, making her freckles stand out. "I was just teaching True about the art of dancing to 80s music. And, you know, how to properly use a hairbrush as a microphone."

"All very important life skills," he said gravely.

Ellie pointed the brush at him. "Exactly. I knew you'd get it."

As the song changed to Bon Jovi's "Livin' on a Prayer," he pushed out of his seat and took the brush from her. "You also need to know how to play a proper air guitar." He bounced around to the music, banging his head and strumming on the brush. Ellie joined in until all three of them—him, her, and the dog—were howling out the lyrics.

True giggled.

The sound sent his heart soaring. He grinned and held out the brush to her. "You try now."

True blinked at him, her light blue-green eyes wide and startled. "Oh, I can't... I mean..."

"Nonsense," Ellie interrupted, sweeping over to the couch and hauling True to her feet. "You're a Summers. Dancing like a fool is in your blood."

True's face flushed a lovely shade of rose, but she took the hairbrush-mic with a shaky hand and started bobbing awkwardly to the music. A few bars in, she relaxed, a tiny smile teasing the corners of her lips. Soon enough, she was twirling around the room, her dark curls bouncing with each step.

Cal watched, his heart feeling like it might burst with affection for them both. Ellie met his gaze and beamed with pride before joining True in a wildly uncoordinated dance-off that had Puzzle barking in delight.

The three of them danced and sang until they were all breathless. Ellie laughed so hard she doubled over, clutching her stomach while True collapsed onto the couch, giggling uncontrollably. Puzzle flopped down at Ellie's feet, tongue lolling out, tail thumping against the floor in exhausted delight.

Eventually, they all ended up on the couch, with Cal sandwiched between Ellie and True, more content than he'd ever felt in his life. He glanced over at Ellie to find her watching him, an unreadable expression in her bright blue eyes.

He knew then that he wanted this. He wanted them—this family. Ellie and True, and even Puzzle. He wanted the chaos and the laughter and the unexpected dance parties. He wanted the raw, real moments that came with being part of a family. Being part of this family.

"We're gonna teach you how to break it down 90s style next," Ellie said, her voice soft and warm, her blue eyes twinkling with joy.

"Absolutely," Cal agreed. "Just wait until you see me do the Macarena. It's a sight to behold."

"I just bet," Ellie said dryly.

True blinked at him, surprise etching across her young face. "What's a Macarena?"

Cal glanced at Ellie, and they both burst out laughing. "Oh, you're in for a treat."

And that's how they spent the rest of the day— dancing and singing and laughing until their stomachs hurt. When night fell, they ate pizza at the coffee table and introduced True to Ellie's favorite movie, *The Princess Bride*.

Puzzle tried at various points to steal pizza from the box when they weren't looking. He finally gave up, but only because he found a stray sock to steal.

Ellie quoted lines from the movie, making True laugh with her impressions until True eventually drifted to sleep. Not wanting to disturb her, they shut off the TV and covered her with a blanket before Ellie took his hand and pulled him toward the bedroom.

Neither of them spoke.

Neither of them had to.

They just moved, coming together in a clash of bodies and lips.

It was primal, passionate, and yet somehow tender—the rush of their breaths mixing in the quiet room, hands exploring familiar paths of soft skin and hardened muscle.

Cal pressed kisses up the side of her neck to her jaw until he found her lips again. His name tumbled from her like a prayer—one he'd happily answer a thousand times over, one he wanted to hear every night for the rest of his life. He loved how she felt in his arms. Loved that he could make her feel this way.

His hand slid up her shirt, fingers tracing paths of fire along her ribs. She arched against him, a soft mewl of desire spilling from her lips. And Cal... He could only think about how much he wanted more. More of her, more with her, more everything.

Finally, he pulled back, breath ragged as he looked down at Ellie. Her blue eyes were dark with desire, glasses perched precariously on the tip of her nose, and he found himself laughing softly. She was so awkwardly adorable. He loved that about her, too.

"Ellie," he said softly, cupping her face with both hands. "I need you to understand something."

"What's that?" she whispered.

"I have never, never before wanted someone the way I want you. You're it for me. And it's not just physical," he added, pressing a kiss to her jaw. "Though that's pretty great, too. It's... it's in the way you laugh, the way you tilt your head when you're thinking, the way your glasses slide off your nose..." He gently took her glasses off and set them on the bedside table, replacing them with a kiss on the tip of her nose. "It's the way your freckles cluster like constellations. The way you blush when you lie, or when you get drunk, or when you come... it's every look, every gesture, every detail about you, Ellie. It's... it's everything. You have completely, irrevocably enthralled me."

Ellie felt a heat spread across her cheeks. She watched as a flicker of vulnerability flashed through his eyes.

God.

Nobody had ever said anything like that to her before, and the way he was looking at her... it was magnetic, pulling her in like gravity.

She reached up, brushing a thumb against his stubbled jaw, her heart pounding in her chest like a drum.

"Cal," she whispered, her voice choked with emotion. "I..."

He caught her hand and pressed a kiss to her palm. "You don't have to say anything right now. I know it freaks you out. I know that's why you keep pushing me away, and that's fine. Just know I love you. I've loved you from the moment you walked into me at the rescue. And I'm not going anywhere."

With that, he pressed his lips to hers. It wasn't the searing kiss of passion they'd exchanged earlier. This was intimate, slow, and timeless. It was as if Cal wanted to memorize her.

Ellie's heart fluttered at his touch, a slow burn of desire building from her very core. His confession, so raw and sincere, had shattered any defenses she had left. Her arms found their way around his neck, bringing him even closer until there was no space left between them.

With a gentle moan, she kissed him back with everything she was feeling, her hands tangling in his hair as their tongues danced, teasing and exploring. The taste of wine and desire lingered on his lips, making her mouth water for more.

The stubble on his jaw scratched lightly against her skin as he nibbled on her bottom lip before trailing more kisses down her neck. His hands glided softly over her back, tracing the contours of her waist until they found the hem of her shirt. With a sudden movement, he lifted it over her head, revealing her lacy bra.

The air was chilly against her heated skin, but it wasn't enough to cool the fire that burned inside her as he took one of her breasts in his hand, gently squeezing it through the fabric. She arched into his touch, yearning for him to remove the barrier between them.

His lips trailed back up to hers again, and she nipped at his lower lip, demanding entrance. He obliged with a groan, reconnecting their mouths as he slid the cup of her bra down. He released her mouth, and his warm breath fanned across her sensitive nipple before he captured it between his lips and sucked gently.

Ellie gasped in surprise as a shockwave of pleasure shot through her body. This was so different from their previous encounters— tender and caring instead of rough and desperate. It felt right in a way that she couldn't explain. Her head spun as he moved to the other breast, paying equal attention to both before pulling away to look at her once more. His eyes were full of lust and adoration like she was some kind of goddess who'd graced him with her presence. No other man had ever looked at her like that.

"Cal." His name was the only word she could form as her

whole body throbbed with need. She was utterly lost in him—in the electricity of his touch, in the intimacy of their locked gazes.

"I love you, Ellie," he whispered, pressing a gentle kiss on her bare shoulder. It was a soft admission but uttered with so much conviction that it coursed through Ellie like a surge of electricity.

Love is always complicated. But that doesn't mean it isn't worth it.

Her stomach fluttered as her sister's words floated through her mind.

Take the chance on Cal.

Nobody else was ever going to make her feel like this. Nobody else was going to look at her with such worshipful intensity. No one else could touch her soul like he did. Nobody else was ever going to love her like Cal did.

Yes. She would take the chance.

As the decision settled over her, a bubble of joy expanded to fill her entire body, and she wrapped her arms around him, pulling him close and burying her face in his neck. "I'm so sorry I kept pushing you away. I was just.. scared. You're it for me, too. It's you. I knew it since I walked into you that day at the Rescue. You caught me and kept me from falling, and nobody's ever done that for me before. I've always had to rely on myself and my sister, and the thought of letting someone else in was terrifying. But I'm ready now. I love you too, Callum Holden."

Cal froze for a moment before his arms wound around her more tightly. His body vibrated with barely repressed emotion, tremors wracking him as he pulled her in impossibly closer. Their heartbeats pounded in sync, a throbbing echo that filled the silence of the room.

"Say it again," he murmured into her hair, his voice rough.

Ellie laughed softly, butterflies dancing in her stomach as

she pulled back to look at him. His brown eyes were bright with joy, crinkling at the corners as his lips curved into a grin.

"I love you, Cal." Finally admitting it out loud felt powerful and right on her tongue. "I love you so much."

"You have no idea how long I've been waiting to hear those words from you." He threaded his fingers into her curls and showered kisses over her lips, nose, and eyelids. "Will you let me marry you and love you for the rest of our lives?"

"I'm a packaged deal now," she warned. "True is staying with me."

"Then I'll love her, too, like she's my own daughter. She deserves parents who actually care about her and put her needs above their own." His hand splayed over her belly. "And when we're ready, I want to add to our family—a couple of girls with my eyes and your curls."

"And a boy with your perpetually messy hair and crooked smile." She could picture it all so clearly, and a strange mixture of fear and exhilaration surged through her. It was as though she were standing on a precipice, teetering on the edge of a magnificent canyon with nothing but a vast expanse of open sky before her. Taking the leap, embracing the fear, and letting go of the doubt...

It was the most terrifying thing she'd ever done.

But with Cal, she knew she'd survive the fall into the unknown, into the thrill of what might be.

"Yes," she answered finally. "Please love me for the rest of our lives."

epilogue

"HAS ANYONE SEEN PIERCE?"

Sawyer turned toward Zak's voice. "I haven't seen anyone in a long time, man."

"I'm serious. Have you talked to him?"

The note of concern raised the little hairs on Sawyer's neck. "Not since..." He trailed off. Pierce hadn't been right since they rescued him from the Hope's Embrace compound. He'd always been a silent, intense presence in the room, but the intensity had felt ramped up, his silence screaming louder than any words.

"Not since he picked up Raszta after he was discharged from the hospital," Sawyer finally finished.

"Shit," Zak muttered. Sawyer heard the scrape of a chair and the thump of Zak's prosthetic on the hardwood as he stood. "I'm gonna go talk to Rylan."

But if Pierce had confided in their resident shrink, Rylan wouldn't be able to discuss it with Zak or anyone else.

Sawyer came to a decision then. Call it a hunch, call it instincts honed from years in combat, but something told him that Pierce was in hiding, licking his wounds... and he had a good idea where he might find him. The last thing Pierce needed was isolation. He needed support from people who truly understood war scars and how they could rear their ugly heads even when you thought they'd fully healed. He needed his teammates. His friends. His family-by-choice.

"Come on, Zelda." Sawyer patted his thigh, and she sprang up, bumping her head against his hand as if to say, *I'm here.*

"Up for a walk?"

Her tail wagged. He felt it swish against his leg and saw the blur of it shifting through his hazy field of vision.

There was nothing better than watching her tail wag.

He strapped her into her harness and packed a backpack with water, protein bars, dog food, and treats—then he doubled up on everything. He also threw in a First Aid kit just in case. Then at the last moment, added extra bear spray and a gun. He didn't plan to be gone long—he was just going to hike up to Pierce's usual camping spot—but in his mind, you could never be too prepared when you were a blind man hiking alone in the rugged Northern California mountains.

The sun was high in the sky by the time they reached the base of the mountain, and in the heat of the afternoon, sweat was sweeping into his clothes.

Shit, it was hot.

He muttered a curse under his breath but told Zelda to walk. She knew the trail intimately and easily guided him around obstacles. It was only about three miles of moderately difficult terrain up to Pierce's favorite camping spot, but by the time he got there, he was drenched in sweat.

"Pierce," he called.

Silence.

No answering whistle.

No raspy hello bark from Raszta.

He took a step, and his foot hit something soft. Heart in his throat, he bent down and groped around until he found soft nylon—a sleeping bag. He felt around some more and found a backpack, its contents spilling across the ground.

"Pierce!"

Still nothing.

Only the rustle of the hot breeze through the trees and the crunch of rocks under his own feet.

Or... no.

He strained, listening for the sound that had caught his attention.

Someone nearby was talking.

So, not Pierce.

Probably other hikers, but maybe they had seen where Pierce had gone.

He straightened and ordered Zelda to follow the sound. "Hello?"

The talking stopped.

"Hey, sorry to bother you. Have you seen a guy with a dog up here?"

No answer.

"Hello?"

The hairs stood straight up on Sawyer's arms as an eerie silence fell. The birds had stopped singing. Even the rustling leaves and whispering wind seemed to have stilled. It was as if the forest was holding its breath with him.

"Hello?" he repeated.

Zelda growled at something right before her barks echoed through the hollow silence. Sawyer stiffened, his hand going to the bear spray.

"Who's there?" he challenged, angling himself in the direction Zelda was facing. He heard a gasp like someone who had been holding their breath for too long had finally let it out.

"Whoa! Easy, guy," a male voice finally responded, sounding shocked and a bit wary. "Just out here hiking."

Sawyer didn't let his guard down. "Have you seen a man with a dog?"

"Other than you?" someone else said. There were two of them.

"Dog... you mean that black mop on legs?" the first guy said. "Yeah, we passed them on the trail yesterday."

"Which direction were they headed?"

"Oh, that way."

The guy had to be pointing in the right direction.

Sawyer reigned in his frustration. "Can you please tell me in words?"

"Wait, are... are you blind?" the second guy asked. He sounded younger, maybe a teenager, which was the only reason Sawyer didn't snap at him.

"Holy shit," the first guy said. "He is. What the hell are you doing up here by yourself? Ranger Harper!" he called, his voice fading as he turned away. "There's a blind man up here. I think he's lost."

"I'm not—" Sawyer started, but then a female voice floated up the mountain on the wind and every cell in his being sparked to uncomfortable life.

"Mr. Grassley, I told you to stay—" She broke off and gasped. "Sawyer?"

Lucy Harper.

The strong, feisty park ranger he'd helped rescue from a serial killer last year and hadn't been able to stop thinking about ever since. It was completely inappropriate given the way they'd met, and he'd never act on his attraction, but knowing that didn't stop her from dominating his fantasies for the last year.

"Lucy." Jesus, why was his voice so strangled? He cleared his throat and tried again. "Uh, hi."

"Sawyer." Lucy sounded just as surprised to see him as he was to hear her. "What are you doing here? Are you hiking alone?"

"Uh, yeah. Just Zelda and me. We're looking for my friend Pierce. I don't think you ever met him, but he's... quiet and intense. Can stare an oil stain off a driveway. Uses sign language. He travels with a little black dog with dreadlocks."

"We saw him," the older man—Mr. Grassley—said. "Yesterday, going down the trail when we were coming up."

"He looked pissed," the younger man added.

"Joel, language," Mr. Grassley snapped.

"Sorry, Dad."

More voices floated up from further down the mountain, and Lucy said, "Over here."

Two more people joined them—a woman and a man. The woman's voice was low and gravelly, the kind of voice that could carry over a crowd without straining. The man, on the other hand, talked in hushed whispers like he thought he was on an undercover mission.

"Ranger Harper, we heard shouting," the woman said.

"It's okay," Lucy replied. "This is Sawyer. He's part of Redwood Coast Rescue."

There was a pause. Then: "Holy shit," the man said. "The blind Marine? I read an article about you."

Sawyer winced. It wasn't exactly how he loved being introduced. There was more to him than his blindness, but ever since that article about him in a popular wilderness magazine got picked up by mainstream media, it was all anyone ever wanted to talk about.

Resigned, he nodded and waved vaguely in the direction of the voices. "That's me."

"Wow. I'm Theodore, and this is my wife, Bea. It's so nice to meet you. You're an inspiration, man. If I lost my sight, I wouldn't be as brave as you."

Mr. Grassley scoffed. "You mean to tell me that you're part of a rescue team? Are you honestly trying to find someone out here?"

Sawyer worked his jaw hard enough that it popped. "Yes," he bit out.

Zelda whined, pressing against his leg. Sweet girl that she was, she never liked tension or conflict.

"Can we help?" Theodore asked, enthusiasm bounding in his voice like an eager puppy.

Grassley grunted. "We didn't pay for this tour to look for a lost man."

"Actually," Lucy said and seemed to relish correcting him. "If there's a lost hiker, it's everyone's duty on the trail to keep an eye out for him."

"We'll be glad to help," Bea said gruffly, barreling over Grassley's next protest.

Just as Sawyer opened his mouth to thank them, the world seemed to lurch beneath his feet. Zelda yelped and slammed into his side, causing him to stumble.

"What the—"

The ground heaved violently beneath them.

Earthquake.

The stench of unsettled earth and the high, shrill cries of frightened birds filled the air. Zelda howled with terror, her nails scrabbling on the loose dirt as she fought to keep her balance.

Rocks calved off the mountainside, tumbling down around them and exploding on impact, sending shrapnel flying. For a moment, he was back in a warzone with mortars raining down and enemy fire coming from every direction.

Nowhere was safe.

"Get down!" Lucy shouted. She sounded calm and in control. "Protect your heads!"

Sawyer crouched, pulling Zelda close and protecting her as

best he could while rocks skittered and rolled around them. Dust filled his nostrils, grit stinging his eyes. His ears rang.

The shaking seemed to go on forever like the mountain was rebelling against the world itself. Beads of sweat trickled down his neck as he clenched his jaw tight against the fear threatening to crawl out his throat. He'd survived war zones, injuries, and the sniper's bullet that had claimed his sight, but this... this was something entirely different.

Then— silence. It came on just as suddenly and shockingly as the earthquake itself. Only the sounds of their heavy, ragged breaths and distant echoes of tumbling stones filled the air.

He raised his head and coughed to clear the dirt from his mouth. His eyes felt gritty. "Lucy?"

"I'm here," she gasped from his left. "I'm okay. Everyone?"

"We're okay," Bea croaked.

"Oh my God," Joel said, his voice cracking. "Dad!"

There was a lot of scrambling around him then—voices talking over each other, Joel crying. He saw lots of movement, flashes of faces and hands, and—

A branch snapped like a gunshot, breaking off a nearby tree. He saw it falling through the air with startling clarity. He also saw the vague outline of a person standing directly underneath it and dove toward them. "Look out!"

His hands connected with the person's back, shoving them out of the way. But he wasn't fast enough. The branch landed on him, and it was like getting hit by a concrete block. His knees crumbled, and pain exploded through his head...

And then there was nothing but blackness.

The Redwood Coast Rescue adventure continues with Sawyer Murphy's story, Searching Blind.

And if you want to see more of the men and women of HORNET, check out Seal of Honor.

also by tonya burrows

Redwood Coast Rescue

Searching for Rescue

Searching for Risk

Searching for Justice

Searching for Redemption

Searching for Shadows

Northern Rescue

Northern Escape

Northern Deception

Northern Salvation

HORNET

SEAL of Honor

Honor Reclaimed

Broken Honor

Code of Honor

Reckless Honor

Honor Avenged

HORNET: Class Alpha

Fragmented Loyalty

Wilde Security

Wilde Nights in Paradise

Wilde for Her

Wilde at Heart

Running Wilde

Too Wilde to Tame